PRAISE FOR DYLANN CRUSH

"Get a crush on Crush!"

—*New York Times* bestselling author Lori Wilde

"This is for certain, I say 'I do' to reading Dylann Crush! What a rollicking fun ride as Bodie and Lacey team up to save their town and pretend their way to their own real happily ever after."

—Debbie Burns, author of *A New Leash on Love*

"Crush (*Hot Fudge & a Heartthrob*) sparkles in this small-town, friends-to-lovers contemporary, the first in her Tying the Knot in Texas series. . . . Crush's skillfully crafted romance is both sexy and sweet."   —*Publishers Weekly*

"This first in Crush's Tying the Knot in Texas series has southern charm, sizzling chemistry, and an adorable rescue dog."   —*Booklist*

"Filled with romance, a couple of plot twists, a meddling but well-meaning family, a mayor determined to win, and some humor, *Crazy About a Cowboy* is small-town romance with a lot of heart."   —Harlequin Junkie

"An entertaining story that made me laugh, smile, and fall in love with the characters and town of Ido."

—A Novel Glimpse

"I enjoyed this charming small-town romance that totally gave me Hallmark-movie vibes!"

—Readaholic Book Reviews

Kiss Me Now,
COWBOY

Dylann Crush

JOVE
New York

A JOVE BOOK
Published by Berkley
An imprint of Penguin Random House LLC
penguinrandomhouse.com

Copyright © 2022 by Dylann Crush
Excerpt from *The Cowboy Says I Do* copyright © 2020 by Dylann Crush

ISBN: 9780593438732

First Edition: August 2022

Printed in the United States of America
1 3 5 7 9 10 8 6 4 2

Book design by Alison Cnockaert

To Christina Hovland and Kenny Chesney,
who were equally responsible in different ways
for Cowboys in Paradise coming to life.

1

⌒∾♡∾⌒

Justin

"Forzas aren't quitters."

Justin Forza took in a deep breath through his nose and met his dad's hard glare with a softer version of his own. "I know, Dad. You've drilled that into me my entire life. I'm not saying I want to quit. I just need a little more time for my shoulder to heal."

Grabbing hold of his right shoulder with his left hand, Justin rolled it forward. Pain radiated through the socket, but he didn't flinch.

His dad picked up a saddle from the tack room, and Justin followed him to the last stall in the barn. They didn't have time for this conversation. Not again, and especially not now. He was supposed to be on his way to pick up his best friend, Em. If they didn't hit the road soon, they'd never get to Dallas in time for the concert tonight.

"I've got to go get Emmeline. Can we table this for now?" Justin sighed, not looking forward to the inevitable continuation of the same conversation. Whether his dad picked it up again tomorrow or the next day, it was bound to happen. Monty Forza had never been accused of letting a sleeping dog lie, not even when it appeared to be as dead as the arguments the two of them had been flinging back and forth for weeks.

"The two of you going to that concert in Dallas tonight?" Monty's mood lightened at the mention of Emmeline's name. She had that effect on people. Em had a way of bringing out the best in folks, even someone as hardheaded and coldhearted as his father.

"Yes, sir. Knox is playing, and Decker invited us to watch from his dad's suite." Justin had been friends with Knox and Decker since the three of them could ride a horse. Seeing as how they'd learned how to ride before they could even walk, Justin couldn't remember a time in his life without them.

"I can't believe a good woman like Emmeline's still available." Monty's eyes narrowed. "Won't be long before some good-looking, smart-talking cowboy scoops her up."

Justin gritted his teeth. He and Emmeline were friends. Had been since second grade when she'd shown up at school with two long braids and a smile as wide and open as the Great Plains of Texas. She'd fit right in with the tight trio of him, Knox, and Decker. Over the years, the four of them had done just about everything together.

Then Emmeline started changing, and Justin couldn't help but take notice. Her lanky limbs gave way to curves that wouldn't quit. The hair she used to pull up and out of the way fell in soft waves around her shoulders. Green eyes, the color of the fields surrounding his family's ranch in the springtime, took on a new shine.

He wouldn't admit it to anyone, especially Emmeline Porter, but he'd fallen hard for her their junior year at Blewit High and had been pining for her ever since. Knox and

Decker had figured it out, but his secret had been safe from Emmeline for the past twelve years.

"You need anything else before I head out?" Justin fingered the key to his heavy-duty F-350—the one luxury he'd allowed himself to indulge in with the winnings he'd earned over the years as a pro bull rider. The rest had gone into savings, waiting for a time when he could retire from the circuit and invest in a place of his own.

"Nah. Y'all have a good time tonight. We'll pick this conversation up again tomorrow. Just remember, the longer you wait to get back in the game, the harder it's going to be, son." Monty tossed the saddle over the back of his favorite ranch horse.

"I know." Justin let out a long exhale. He didn't want to sit out from the bull-riding circuit any longer than necessary. Securing the world championship was the only thing standing in the way of what he really wanted out of life . . . Emmeline.

This year should have been his. He'd started off the year in the top ten and, after winning a few events in February and March, had earned enough points to put him in the top five. Once he secured the title and the cash prize that went with it, he'd planned on announcing his retirement on the spot and finally telling Emmeline how he felt.

But things never seemed to go as planned. Instead of being the one to catch, he'd been bucked off a ranker bull on the last night of a three-day event in Nashville with half a second to go. He'd healed from his surgery and a severe concussion, but his shoulder still wasn't quite where he needed it to be.

His dad was right, though. If he didn't commit to an upcoming event, he'd lose out on the entire year and have to start over again in January. That would mean waiting at least another eighteen months to come clean with Emmeline. He had no idea if she felt the same, but he knew one thing . . . it wasn't worth the breath he'd waste telling her how he felt about her if he still planned on riding bulls.

She'd made one thing perfectly clear over the years . . . she'd never date a rodeo cowboy.

The sooner he got back to riding, the sooner he could snag the title his dad expected, and the sooner he could finally admit his feelings.

He just hoped it wouldn't be too late.

Emmeline

"Here you go, Daddy." Emmeline held the fork out to her father. It had clattered to the table when one of his tremors started.

"Dammit." He closed his fingers around it. "Pretty soon I won't even be able to feed my damn self."

Emmeline swallowed hard. She hated seeing him struggle. "Some days are just more difficult than others."

He glanced at her across the solid oak table—the one he'd built with his own hands before he got injured—and frowned. "I don't know how y'all put up with me."

"It's because you're so lovable." She got up from her chair to kiss his cheek. "I've got to get ready to go. Justin's going to be here soon. You need anything else?"

A spasm ran through her dad, making his hand twitch again. "Nah. I'll be fine. Your mama will be home soon, anyway."

Emmeline put a hand on her dad's shoulder and squeezed. She'd volunteered to come sit with him while he ate dinner tonight since her mom had a garden club meeting. It's not that he couldn't be left alone, but dinnertime always proved to be extra frustrating, and sometimes his temper got the best of him.

"You want me to cut that up smaller for you?"

"I'm fine, baby girl. You go have a good time. Tell the boys I said hello and to come around and visit once in a while when they're in town, will you?"

"Will do." Wouldn't do any good to remind her dad "the boys" weren't boys anymore. That's how he'd always referred to them, ever since Em started hanging out with the trio of troublemakers in second grade. They were grown-ass men now, at least on the outside. Even though she hadn't seen Knox in a couple of years, and didn't spend much one-on-one time with Decker, she couldn't help but notice how much Justin had changed the last few times she'd seen him.

Em picked up her purse and slung the strap over her shoulder messenger bag–style. Before she had a chance to peek through the front window, the door leading to the garage opened, and Justin walked in.

"Speak of the devil." Her dad pushed back from the table.

"Don't get up on my account." Justin reached out to shake her dad's hand. "I didn't mean to interrupt your meal."

Emmeline's breath caught at the sight of him. He'd been gone more than he'd been home over the past several years, traveling from one rodeo to the next, and fitting in other events along the way. Justin had what her mama liked to call "presence" and he always seemed to fill a room with it, whether it was her mama and daddy's eat-in kitchen or a venue the size of Madison Square Garden. It wasn't something he did on purpose. Either a man had it or he didn't.

And Justin Forza had it in spades.

"You want to join me for a quick bite?" her dad offered.

"Homemade chicken-fried steak, mashed potatoes, zucchini bread, and creamed corn. We can fix you up a plate right quick."

Justin rubbed a hand over his washboard abs. "That sounds wonderful, but we'd better get a move on if we're going to make it in time."

"Y'all have fun tonight." Her dad picked up his fork again. Emmeline held her breath, hoping he wouldn't drop it in front of Justin. Her daddy didn't like to appear weak, even though he had no control over the brain injury that had saddled him with challenges he'd face for the rest of his life.

"You ready, Em?" Justin turned toward her, the full force of his bright blue gaze hitting her smack-dab in the center of her chest.

"Yeah. You want a water bottle for the road?" It would take them about an hour and a half to make the drive from their tiny hometown of Blewit about ninety miles southeast of Dallas into the city—just a hop, skip, and a jump away when considering a place as big as Texas.

"Got one in the truck already. Mr. Porter, it was nice to see you, sir."

"Don't forget that bag of zucchini your mom set aside for him." Her dad nodded toward a plastic grocery bag of summer squash her mom had picked that afternoon.

Em handed the bag to Justin. "Don't even think about trying to leave it here."

His grin widened so much the dimple on his left cheek popped.

"Come back when you have more time, son. I want to hear all about how you're recovering. That was a wild ride you took back in March." Her dad lived for stories of Justin's time on the road, though Emmeline could do without them.

There was something crazy about a man who'd risk life

and limb to seat himself on the back of a two-thousand-pound animal whose sole purpose in life was to buck him off as quickly as possible. She'd known enough bull riders in her life to reach that conclusion. Seeing how her dad's love for the sport had ruined his life, she'd never understand why a man would do that to himself once, let alone hundreds of times over the course of a career.

"Shoulder's doing okay and my concussion's better. I just need a little more time to heal, and I'll get back out there again." Justin shifted the bag from one hand to the other, and Em bit her tongue.

The last ride he'd taken almost killed him. If he were ever going to stop putting his life on the line, he would have done it then. She'd hoped the last concussion would change his mind about pursuing such a dangerous career. Their friend Decker had even mentioned the possibility of getting Justin a job with his dad's oil business.

But Justin wasn't a suit-and-tie kind of guy. He'd lived his whole life in jeans and a pair of well-worn cowboy boots. No matter how much Emmeline wished things would change, he'd never give up his chase for a world championship. How could he when his dad and brother reminded him of his failure to do just that about twenty times a day?

"See you later this week, Daddy." Emmeline pressed a kiss to her dad's temple. If Justin wanted to see what the future had in store for him, he ought to take a good, long, hard look at her father. His dogged pursuit of the perfect ride had almost ruined his marriage and nearly taken his life.

Justin held the door for her, and she brushed past him. He must have just showered, because she caught a whiff of the fresh, clean scent of that bar soap he loved. Some guys she knew dabbed on enough cologne or aftershave, it smelled like they'd gone swimming in it. Not Justin. He always smelled like soap, leather, and the great outdoors.

The late afternoon sun beat down on her as soon as they stepped outside, and she was grateful he'd left his truck running. He pulled open the passenger side door before she reached it. As she climbed into his truck, the blast of the air conditioner chased the heat away.

"You don't have to race around opening doors for me," she teased.

"And risk word getting back to my mom that I've lost my manners?" He shook his head, the smirk stretching across his lips telling her he wasn't taking her seriously. "No, thank you."

If his mama would give him a tongue-lashing for not opening a woman's door, no telling what she'd do if she found out about some of the stunts he, Decker, and Knox had pulled over the years. It wasn't Em's place to rat out her friends, especially when she'd tagged along with them most of the time.

Emmeline snapped her seatbelt into place while he walked around the front of the truck and climbed in the other side. Tonight would be the first time the four of them had been together in ages. She'd been looking forward to it for weeks. It wasn't every day a gal got to watch one of her friends sing his heart out in front of thousands of adoring fans. The last time she'd seen Knox play in person, it had been at a side stage at the Texas state fair. He'd come a long way since then and was now headlining his own shows.

"I was hoping to say hi to your mom. How's she been doing lately?" Justin asked.

"Good. She's at a garden club meeting. They're hoping to raise enough money to sand down the statue and put a fresh coat of paint on Queenie the giant zucchini this summer. I guess they're tired of everyone thinking she's a cucumber."

Justin pointed out the window as they passed the eyesore of a landmark that had been sitting on the edge of town for decades. "Have they considered tearing the damn thing down?"

"And take away Blewit's one claim to fame as the zucchini capital of the US?"

"I suppose it's better to have people think they're coming to visit the world's largest cucumber than to not have anyone come visit at all."

Em wasn't sure she agreed with that, but her mom had to have something to focus on besides taking care of her dad. Time for a change of subject.

"Are you excited to see Knox perform?" She twisted to face Justin, studying him through the dark shades she'd slid over her eyes. They hadn't spent too much time together since he got injured. He'd been in a lot of pain since then, a shell of the guy whose smile used to make her light up inside like the Fourth of July.

"Hell, yeah. It's been too long since we've all been together." His fingers drummed along with the beat of the song on the radio. "How was the last day of kindergarten this year?"

She settled her hands over her belly, trying to tamp down the mixture of relief and regret that always hit her hard on the last day of school. "Good. I got four bouquets of dandelions, three loaves of zucchini bread, and two proposals."

"Two proposals? Anyone I need to check out for you?"

His faux concern made her laugh. "Not unless you're in the habit of shaking up five-year-olds."

"I don't remember ever having a crush on a teacher. Even if I did, I never would have had the balls to make a move." Justin fiddled with the radio dial. "Kids these days have got some big cojones."

"I even got a ring." She held her left hand out, showing off the bread tie one of her students had presented her with that afternoon.

"Let me see that." Justin reached for her hand and held it up, his gaze bouncing back and forth from the road to studying the paper-wrapped wire. "Man, he really went all out, didn't he?"

Emmeline pulled her hand back with a laugh. "I don't think he had a very big budget to start with."

"The kid's definitely got big balls. To propose with a ring like that . . ."

"It's not about the ring, it's about the intention behind it, right? He's a sweet kid. I'm going to miss him next year." The end of the school year was always bittersweet. She started off every August with an unruly passel of kids and by the time June rolled around, not only had they learned how to read, they'd also learned how to treat each other with kindness and respect. At least most of them.

"Don't go getting all sappy on me, Em. I know how you get when you have to say goodbye. It's not like they're going far, though. Just a few classrooms over to first grade." Justin shot her a knowing grin. "Cheer up. Tonight's about letting loose and having a good time, right?"

"Who says I'm not going to have a good time?" she challenged. "My summer vacation starts tonight. I'm not the one who has to get up early tomorrow morning for a workout with my personal trainer."

"Good point. Maybe I should have rescheduled."

Emmeline reached over to snag his cowboy hat off his head, then settled it on her own. "That just means that you'll have to keep it low-key and keep track of the rest of us tonight."

"Seeing as how Knox has an entire management team to keep tabs on him, and Decker's bringing his new girlfriend, I guess that means you'll have my full attention."

Emmeline smiled in response, as a hint of something she didn't recognize fluttered against the walls of her belly. She was just excited. It had been a while since she'd spent an evening out with the guys. Had been too long since she'd spent much time with anyone over three feet tall. Nothing to get too worked up over. Justin was right. Tonight was about cutting loose and having fun, and all of them could use a night like that.

2

⌒ ♡ ⌒

Justin

The arena bulged at the seams with the number of fans who'd shown up to hear Knox sing tonight. Justin kept a hand on Em's shoulder as they struggled against the current of a nonstop stream of people.

"That way." He pointed to a small sign off to the right. "I think we can get to the suite level over there."

Not wanting to lose Emmeline, he reached for her hand. She laced her fingers with his and squeezed. A surge of desire shot through him. He lived for the moments he could be this close to her, feel this connected. They might just be good friends to her, but to him, she was his everything.

He'd just never had the guts to tell her.

Until he had something to offer beyond his unfaltering love and halfway-decent looks, he was hell-bent on keeping his feelings to himself. He shot a glance to the bread tie on Em's left ring finger. How sad was it that even a five-year-old had bigger balls than he did where Emmeline was concerned?

They cleared the throng of people, and Emmeline let go

of his grip. "Wow. I can't believe all these people are here
to see Knox."

"I hope it doesn't go to his head," Justin joked.

Em shared a smile. "No chance of that."

Wasn't that the honest truth? Knox was by far the most
humble, gracious superstar Justin had ever met. That
wouldn't mean much if he'd been the only country-western
star Justin knew, but some of the bull-riding events brought
in massive crowds and huge names. Justin had met his share
of performers whose egos rivaled the size of the arenas they
played.

"You ready to meet Decker's latest love?" Justin stopped
in front of the door to the suite. A small sign to the right
read "Wayne Holdings." A woman's high-pitched laugh
came from the other side of the door. According to Decker,
she was "the one." If only he hadn't already said the same
thing about a half dozen other women over the past five
years, Justin might be inclined to believe him.

"Are we ever ready for anything Decker does?" Emmeline asked.

"Good point. Ready or not . . ."

The door flew open. Decker stood in front of them, all
dressed up in a pair of shiny lizard cowboy boots and a
shirt with enough starch in it to stand up by itself. "Get in
here, you asshole."

"Good to see you, too." Justin gestured for Emmeline
to go first.

Decker wrapped his arms around Em, pulling her into
a giant bear hug and lifting her off her feet. Justin's chest
twinged at the sight of the two of them in a tight embrace.
Though Decker swore his feelings for Em had never
strayed past platonic, he sure as hell enjoyed putting on a
show and seeing how riled up he could make Justin.

Choosing to ignore Decker's blatant attempt at making him jealous, Justin nodded to the tall, slim brunette who stood off to the side. "Hey, I'm Justin Forza. You must be Melissa."

"Miranda." She reached out to shake his hand.

His stomach twisted. Fuck. Miranda. Melissa. Who could keep track?

"Miranda, baby. These are two of my dearest, oldest friends. Meet Justin, one of the top-ranked bull riders in the world, and Emmeline, the sweetest kindergarten teacher this side of the Mississippi."

"It's nice to meet you both." Miranda smiled.

"Nice to meet you, too." Emmeline gave Miranda a hug, then scooted past them to check out the suite. "Damn, Decker. So, this is how the other half lives, huh?"

More like the top 1 percent. Justin had a little insider knowledge of what kind of cash the Wayne family's oil business had been raking in over the past few years. It made hime wish joining the company would be a more appealing option, especially if the chance to secure the world championship title and the cash prize that went with it disappeared.

"Welcome. I figured it would be more comfortable to watch the concert from here than backstage." Decker spread his arms wide. "Bar's to your right. Catering will be up with some food in a little bit. Make yourselves at home."

Emmeline set her purse down on a leather club chair. "Got anything without alcohol in that fancy cooler of yours?"

"Em, let loose a little. You've got the whole summer off and don't have to drive anywhere tonight." Decker gave her his patented puppy dog eyes. Justin had seen the look work on a countless number of women over the years, but Emmeline had always been immune.

"Fine. You wanna party like it's your twenty-first birthday again?" Emmeline moved toward the bar, glancing at

Miranda on the way. "Did Deck ever tell you about the time he got so wasted he directed someone to his professor's house instead of his own when they tried to take him home?"

"Hey, now. The past is the past." Decker cleared his throat. "No need to bring stuff like that up now."

Justin laughed to himself. Poor Decker. He should know better than to rub Em the wrong way. She had enough dirt on all of them to ruin any chance they had of a respectable future.

"What happened?" Miranda asked.

"Nothing happened." Decker took her hands and led her to the area of the suite overlooking the arena floor. "Have you been here for a Mavericks game? You can see Porzingis dunk from this seat right here."

Justin sidled up next to Emmeline at the well-stocked bar. "What do you think?"

"Of Miranda? She seems nice so far." She pulled down two glasses from the shelf and poured a few fingers of his favorite whiskey into each. "Here, let's toast."

"What do you want to toast to?" He lifted the crystal tumbler etched with the Wayne Holdings logo.

Her lips curled up into a grin that warmed his belly like he'd already swallowed a sip of whiskey. "You decide."

He could think of a dozen things he'd like to say. *To you, the most beautiful woman I've ever met, both inside and out. To me, to securing the title so I can get my dad off my back and finally figure out how to tell you how I feel. To us, to the possibility of what the future has in store.*

But he couldn't say any of that. Not now and maybe not ever. He raised his glass. "It's been a long time since the four of us were in the same building together. How about we toast to us? That each of us gets exactly what we need."

Em clinked her glass against his. "I'll drink to that."

He took a generous sip of whiskey, relishing the burn as it slid down the back of his throat. Em held the glass up to her lips, her gaze focused on the amber liquid. Then she lowered it, locking her eyes on his.

"I'm curious. What exactly is it you think you need, Justin?"

Emmeline

Emmeline didn't mean to put him on the spot. Not before the concert even started. Not with Decker trying to romance his latest conquest around the suite. The way Justin's brows knit together and his jaw set in a tight line told her he hadn't been expecting the lighthearted conversation to take a serious turn.

He opened his mouth like he wanted to say something. Before he had a chance, Decker elbowed him in the ribs. "He needs the title, isn't that right, J-Bone?"

"Yeah, right." Justin cocked his head, studying her.

"Forzas aren't quitters," Decker said, lowering his voice to mimic Justin's dad. "Your dad's not going to stop riding your ass until you secure that world championship. I think this is your year, though."

Emmeline pasted on a smile. Of course. She'd hoped that Justin's most recent injuries might have made him reconsider putting his life on the line every time he got on the back of a bull, but if she knew one thing for sure, it was that bull riders didn't make decisions from a place of common sense. If they did, her daddy never would have gone back to riding with a severe concussion. Never would have taken the ride that left him permanently saddled with the effects of a traumatic brain injury.

"Thanks, man." Justin turned toward Decker and took another sip of his drink.

"Plenty more where that came from." Decker tipped the bottle to add more whiskey to Justin's glass. "Forzas aren't quitters, you know."

Justin laughed, but Em could see the tightness in his jaw, the glint of hardness in his eyes. She wanted to grab him by the shoulders and shake some sense into him. Couldn't he see he was on a path of self-destruction? Knowing him, his dad would bully him into returning to the ring before he was ready. She'd lost count of the number of broken bones, sprains, and concussions he'd had over the years. Her only hope was that he'd return to competing and finally snag that stupid title. Maybe then he'd come to his senses.

"So how do all y'all know each other?" Miranda sidled up next to Decker.

"Let's see." Decker draped a possessive arm over her shoulders. "I've known Justin since what . . . we were about two weeks old?"

"You were two weeks old, I was five weeks old." Justin turned toward Miranda. "Our moms were roommates in college and got pregnant around the same time."

Decker leaned close to Miranda. "He likes to hold it over my head that he's a couple of weeks older than me."

"Somebody's got to keep you in line," Justin said.

Em shook her head. She'd heard this routine enough times over the years that she could recite it by heart. "Yeah, since Deck doesn't have any siblings, we have to keep him humble."

"Hey"—Decker nodded—"it's not my fault my parents got it right the first time. Justin here's got a brother and a sister, and Emmeline's got a younger sister. I guess my folks figured why keep adding kids to the mix when they already had the perfect son."

Em let out a sharp laugh and landed a playful knock on Decker's forehead. "Excuse me, is there room for anything else in there besides your ego?"

Used to her teasing, he gave her a wink. "Always room for a dressing-down by you, Ms. Porter."

"Ugh. Don't call me that. It's traumatizing." She rolled her eyes. "I'm looking forward to just being Emmeline over the summer."

Sensing a weakness, Decker did what he always did . . . wedged his way in like a pseudo–big brother would and tried to exploit her discomfort. "The under three-feet-tall crowd getting to you?"

"Never. It's just nice to have the next couple of months off." After she cleaned out her classroom tomorrow, she'd have two and a half months to herself. Much-needed time to catch up on her reading, get some projects done around the three-bedroom bungalow she'd purchased last summer, and visit her younger sister down in San Antonio.

"How about you, Justin? When's your next event?" Decker's teasing grin faded. He seemed just as worried about Justin's next move as Em. She might be able to use that to her advantage at some point. Maybe if the two of them ganged up on him, Justin would reconsider returning to the tour.

"Sometime this summer, I hope. Shoulder's still giving me a little trouble, but I think I can work through it." He rolled his shoulder like he wanted to prove he hadn't lost any mobility. "Hey, I think the opening act's about to start."

"Grab a refill." Decker moved to the bar, taking Miranda with him.

Emmeline's gaze trailed over her best friend. Justin looked like he'd healed. The scar on his forehead from where his head had bounced off the metal bars of the bucking chute had faded. If she peeled away his shirt, there would be minimal evidence of the surgery he'd had to put a pin in his shoulder. But some scars couldn't be seen on the outside.

He knew how she felt about rodeo events, bull riding in particular. If he wanted to talk to someone about things, she'd never be his first choice. Something was bothering him, though. They'd been friends for over twenty years, and, unlike Decker, who put on a front, and Knox, who wore his heart on his sleeve, Justin fit somewhere in between.

The first strains of an electric guitar reverberated through the stadium. Emmeline followed the others to claim a seat facing the stage as a trio of blinged-up women strutted out in high-heeled cowboy boots.

Justin plopped down into the seat next to her and rested his cowboy boots on the railing. "Maybe we should have watched from backstage."

Em's eyes widened as a giant disco ball lowered from the roof in the middle of the arena. It spun slowly, sending sparkles flying around the perimeter of the building. "Poor Knox."

"'Poor Knox' is right. No wonder he wasn't crazy about us coming to the show tonight. Looks like they've turned him into a modern-day rhinestone cowboy."

Em winced. "Hopefully it's just the opening act. Surely he won't take the stage in a pair of bedazzled chaps or anything."

"Bedazzled chaps?" Justin eyed her from under the brim of his straw Stetson. "I think I know what to get him for Christmas now."

"You wouldn't dare." She landed a playful swat on his arm.

He bit his lip and reached for the spot where she'd landed the slap.

Her chest squeezed. "I'm so sorry. That's your hurt shoulder, isn't it?"

"I'm fine, Em. Don't be silly."

The stage exploded into a dazzling display of lights, matched with a deafening twang from a steel guitar. Justin faced forward, his attention drawn by a tall redhead parading around on the stage. If he didn't want to talk about it now, Em wouldn't force it. But sooner or later, he'd have to talk to someone. Because one thing was sure, he wasn't ready physically or mentally to return to the ring. She just needed to figure out how to get him to admit it.

3

∾⊸♡⊸∾

Justin

"That was some kind of a show." Justin grabbed Knox's hand and did the half-hug thing guys did when they wanted to offer more than a handshake.

"It's ridiculous." Knox's grip tightened. "I feel like a fucking dancing monkey on this tour."

Justin got out of the way so Em could give Knox a hug. She had to rise up on her tiptoes to get her arms around his neck. Just like with Decker, his chest tightened at the sight of her wrapping her arms around another man, even though he knew they were only friends. What was he going to do if she found someone who wanted more before he had the chance to tell her how he felt?

He shifted his weight from one foot to the next. Not going to go there. He couldn't. The idea of Emmeline Porter spending the rest of her life with anyone besides him was too awful to think about. Sure, she'd had boyfriends over the years. She attracted men like bees to honey. Thankfully, she hadn't fallen for any of them. She'd always said she'd never settle. Too many of her friends had married their high school sweethearts or college boyfriends, afraid if they didn't say yes to the guy in front of them, they'd never get another chance.

Not Em. She'd sworn she'd rather stay single than commit to anything less than true love. But lately, it seemed she was getting antsy. Her closest girlfriend got engaged last fall, and the wedding was later this summer. Her younger sister was expecting her first baby in about a month. Though she said she'd hold out for happily ever after, Justin knew her well enough to recognize the glimmer of hope in her eyes when she talked about bridesmaids' dresses and becoming an aunt. It was only a matter of time until some cowboy came along and caught her eye.

"Y'all want to hang out for a bit or can we get the hell out of here?" Knox asked.

"Your show, your call," Justin said.

"I've been craving a chimi from Terlinga's for the past six months. I need to wash away this stink and do a quick meet and greet, but we could head there after." Knox lifted his cowboy hat off and wiped the sweat away with a towel.

"We can wait for you if you want." Decker craned his neck to look past Knox's broad shoulders. "I promised Miranda she'd get to meet some country stars tonight."

Knox gestured behind him. "Suit yourselves. You can wait for me in the greenroom. I've got to take a quick shower before I shake hands with anyone. I'll send the band in to introduce themselves."

Justin wandered over to the stocked bar. Damn, Knox had definitely risen through the ranks from the last time Justin had been backstage at one of his shows. It had been a tiny dive bar in College Station and the backstage area was really just the closet where they stored the cleaning supplies. He fixed himself a club soda and grabbed a lemonade for Em.

Decker, Miranda, and Emmeline had made themselves

comfortable on a pair of sofas that faced each other. He handed the bottle of lemonade to Em and sat down next to her.

"This is the life, huh?" Decker popped the top off a beer.

"I don't know." Em crossed her legs, drawing Justin's attention to her embossed leather boots. He'd always loved that she preferred cowboy boots over heels.

"What's not to love?" Decker asked.

Em glanced around the room. Life-sized cutouts of Knox in various poses stood around the perimeter. "This just doesn't seem like him. Did you hear that new song he played toward the end?"

"The one with the guy beatboxing?" Decker asked.

"Yeah. Knox grew up on Johnny Cash and Conway Twitty. His music's starting to sound like a weird version of country-western hip-hop."

She was right. Justin thought about that for a minute. It had been a while since he'd checked in with Knox. The man had been on tour for the past seven months though, so it's not like they could have grabbed a beer and watched a Rangers game together.

"He just doesn't seem happy." Em shrugged.

"So maybe he's not just strumming his six string." Decker waved his arms around, gesturing to the closest cardboard cutout of Knox. "He's got more going for him by dressing up like Cowboy Ken and singing whatever the record label wants him to than he ever did playing the songs his grandpa raised him on."

"Money's not everything, you know." Em's mouth screwed into a frown.

She could tell Decker that until she was red, white, and blue in the face, but it wouldn't change the way he felt about things. Or the way his priorities fell.

Maybe if her dad hadn't gotten injured and hadn't had to raise their family on his monthly disability checks, she'd feel differently. Ends never seemed to meet at her house when they were kids. Not until Em got a job her sophomore year of high school and started helping with the bills. Em might say it didn't matter how much money a man had in the bank, but Justin knew she craved security as much as Knox needed the spotlight.

Decker pushed up from the sofa to wander around the room. "Money might not be everything, but it sure as hell helps, doesn't it, Justin?"

Justin's head snapped up. He didn't need to get thrown in the middle—a place he often ended up, thanks to Decker and Em's conflicting views. He was saved from having to reply by the trio of women who'd opened for Knox entering the room.

They introduced themselves as the Strum Sisters. Triplets. Though if he looked close enough, they didn't seem to look much alike beyond their long red hair. Probably another play by Knox's record label to generate some buzz. Justin wasn't a stranger to the way the media twisted and turned things to suit their needs, but at least he didn't have to bow down to a manager. Besides his agent, his dad had always handled things for him. Bull riding was a family business, and Justin was lucky his dad happened to have a lot of experience.

He kept quiet in his corner of the couch, taking everything in like he always did, biding his time until he could make his move and get his own future back on track.

Before he knew it, Knox returned. "Y'all ready to go? I'm starving."

"I've got a limo waiting. Think we'll all fit?" Decker asked.

A limo. Of course, he did. "The restaurant's only a few blocks away. Can't we walk?" Justin asked.

"Not in those shoes." Decker nodded toward Miranda's strappy stilettos.

"I'll walk with you," Emmeline offered. "The fresh air will do me good."

"See y'all there." Decker shot him a smirk. If you don't get lost along the way."

Emmeline

Emmeline linked her arm with Justin's as they headed away from the giant arena. He'd seemed off all night. More quiet than usual. More reserved. More serious.

"Cat got your tongue?" She nudged him with her hip, trying to get him to open up a bit. He could be a hard one to read sometimes. If left to his own thinking, he could think himself down into some pretty dark places. Places where he shouldn't go.

"Nah." He dismissed her concern with a quick shake of his head. "Just thinking about Knox. Seeing him play tonight wasn't exactly what I expected. Do you really think he's selling out?"

"Only Knox can answer that."

"I suppose."

She squeezed his arm, wondering if now might be the right time to broach the subject she'd been wanting to talk to him about for the past couple of weeks. She'd meant to bring it up before, but there never seemed to be a right time. Out of the three men, Justin was the one she talked to most often, especially now that he was back home. When he'd been riding bulls, he spent 95 percent of his time on the road, either competing in events or traveling back and forth between. But even with him being home for the past couple of months, they still hadn't seen each other as much as she would have liked.

Sometimes she felt like he was avoiding her. He knew how much she hated rodeo events. Knew how much that lifestyle had taken from her family. He also knew how she felt about him following in his dad's and brother's footsteps. Though she tried to understand, she couldn't. Justin wasn't cut from the same cloth as his older brother Jake. Though they both followed in their dad's footsteps when it came to bull riding, Justin didn't subscribe to his dad's all-or-nothing way of thinking like his brother did. He'd been avoiding talk about his return to the circuit. If she wanted to get a straight answer, now might be the best time to press for one.

"Got big plans this summer?" She slowed her stride on purpose, not wanting to run out of sidewalk before she had the chance to steer the conversation somewhere serious.

"I've got PT on my shoulder to look forward to and hopefully some time at the lake with Decker and Knox." He hip checked her with a quick bump. "I'm hoping you'll have time to squeeze me in sometime between when Georgie's baby arrives and Keisha walks down the aisle."

"You know I'm never too busy for you." They'd been friends since the day they met and had always been there for each other. That wouldn't stop now, not even if he was being bullheaded about riding bulls.

He looked ahead as he answered. "Good to know some things never change."

"Sometimes some things need to change."

"I see." He clucked his tongue. "Is that what we're going to do tonight, Em?"

She stopped and let her arm fall away from his. "What do you want me to say? You can't seriously be thinking about getting back up on a bull this summer. You might be fooling Knox and Decker, but you're nowhere near healed up enough to even consider it."

"And you know all about shoulder injuries now?" His eyes narrowed just a little, the teasing tone long gone from his voice.

"I know you're still in pain. I know your dad's been pushing you. I know you've got some sort of death wish." She crossed her arms over her chest, challenging him to deny it.

"I don't expect you to understand." He adjusted his cowboy hat, pulling it lower over his eyes.

Her heart squeezed. "I do understand, at least part of it. Your dad's been pushing since you started mutton busting. But just because he won a title, it doesn't mean you have to kill yourself to try to get one too."

"Yeah, he got a title, then Jake got a title. If I don't keep the tradition going, I may as well change my last name." He glanced down at her, his gaze connecting with hers barely long enough for her to see the hint of humiliation in his eyes. "I can't let them down."

There was nothing she could say or do to change his mind. She'd learned that about Justin over the years. Once he set his sights on something, he wouldn't let up until he'd reached his goal. It might be an admirable quality if he'd directed his focus on something a little less likely to cause a permanent injury.

"I wish you'd reconsider." She linked her arm with his again, her way of backing off a bit.

"I wish you'd stop bugging me about it."

"Touché. How about a truce?" She whirled around to

face him. "I'll stop bringing it up if you promise me you won't commit to an event until you're fully healed."

Justin clenched his jaw and shifted his gaze to a spot over her shoulder. "'Fully healed' is a pretty subjective term."

She poked him in the stomach. "Fine. When a doctor clears you. Is that better?"

"Sure. I won't get back on a bull until I'm cleared by a doctor." The hard lines around his mouth eased. "Is that what you want to hear?"

"Shake on it?" She thrust her hand out.

"I'll do you one better than that. Let's hug on it." He opened his arms, his mouth curving up into that playful grin of his that made her toes curl. But this was Justin, her best friend. Hugs from best friends shouldn't induce toe curling.

She flattened her toes inside her favorite cowboy boots and snuggled against his chest. His arms embraced her, making everything right in her world, at least for the moment.

Justin had that effect on her. No matter what was going wrong in her life, no matter how hard of a day she'd had, the moment he wrapped her in his arms, it all faded away.

"Should we catch up to the others?" Justin pulled back. "Wouldn't want them to think we got lost on the walk over."

"Sure." Reluctantly, she let him go. He might think he'd won the battle, but she hadn't given up on trying to get him to see things her way. After all, that's what friends were for . . . to help each other navigate the twisty turns life threw in their path. What kind of a friend would she be if she gave up that easily?

4

Justin

Sandwiched into a corner booth with Em on one side and Knox on the other, Justin breathed in the mouthwatering scent of sizzling fajitas and let being in a place he liked with the people he loved soothe his troubled soul. Terlinga's had been one of their favorite places to visit back in high school. They'd spend the day out on Lake Ray Hubbard on one of Decker's dad's boats, then grab their fill of authentic Mexican food before heading home.

Being back here with three of his favorite people in the whole wide world made the problems waiting for him at home fade into the background. He took a long draw on his tea and focused his attention on the conversation going on between Knox and Decker.

Decker dipped a still-warm tortilla chip into the bowl of salsa in the center of the table. "I'm just saying, if you don't want to play the kind of crap they're telling you to, then why don't you walk away?"

"Just walk away?" Knox spread his arms out as wide as

he could in the cramped space of the booth. "You think it's that easy?"

Decker finished chewing and shrugged. "Personally, I'd ride that money train until the tracks came to an end, but if you're determined to sabotage your own success . . ."

"Some of us don't have Daddy's cash to back us up if we change our mind about things." Knox's jaw clenched, along with his grip on the bottle of beer.

"Come on, y'all." Emmeline's gaze bounced back and forth between the two men. She always played the peace-keeper in their testosterone-fueled trio. "How long has it been since the four of us got together? Let's not waste time with a pissing contest."

"You know you'd be the one to lose in a pissing contest, right?" Justin couldn't help but poke fun. She used to get so jealous that the three of them could take care of business just about anywhere when she'd oftentimes have to head off alone to find the ladies' room.

"How about we change the subject from bodily fluids to figuring out what kind of appetizers we want to order before the server comes back," Em suggested.

Justin stifled a laugh. Though Em was the youngest of the four of them, she'd always been the most mature.

"Queso flameado for sure. The big bowl." Decker slung an arm over Miranda's shoulder and ran a finger over the laminated menu. "And an order of the guacamole prepared table side. What else do y'all want?"

"Just keep the beer coming." Knox tipped his bottle toward Justin. "Your turn to get dogpiled. What's going on with your run for the championship title?"

Great. He'd gone from tempering the fire between Knox and Decker to ending up in the hot seat. Before he had a chance to downplay his injuries, Em spoke up.

"You know Justin. He's pretending like he didn't almost

die and counting down the days until he can climb right back up on a bull again." The look on her face dared him to disagree. It was like she'd somehow taken every look of disappointment he'd ever received in his life and swirled them all together into one big frown.

"That's not exactly true." His fingers fiddled with the straw wrapper. Em was only trying to protect him, but she had no idea how important it was for him to get back to what he needed to do.

"Let's count your most recent injuries." She held up her pointer finger. "One. A severe concussion. What's that come to? Three in the past two years?"

Justin pressed his thigh against hers, a silent request to change the subject. But she was on a roll.

Her middle finger went up. "He also had surgery on his shoulder to repair his rotator cuff."

Knox winced. "Damn, I've heard a torn rotator cuff hurts like hell."

"Yeah, well, we know Justin never does anything half-assed. What did the doctor say"—she bit her lip and dramatically shifted her gaze to the ceiling—"something like you shredded it to the point he was amazed your arm was still attached?"

"Can y'all excuse me for a minute?" He didn't want to listen to Em go through the rundown of all the ways he'd abused his body over the years.

Knox slid out of the booth so Justin could get up. Out of all his friends, Knox understood the sacrifices a man had to make to follow his dreams. He'd turned his back on everything he loved for a shot at making a living with his music. Sure as hell had paid off for him. He'd sold out the entire arena tonight and had back-to-back shows lined up across the country for the next several months.

"She just worries about you." Knox waited for Justin to pass before he slid back into the booth.

"Yeah, I know." He couldn't help that a bull put an end to Emmeline's dad's career or that her father struggled with the aftereffects of a permanent injury. She had a right to her feelings. Truth was, she had reason to be concerned. Justin had lost track of how many bull riders had come up through the ranks over the years only to fade away when a bad landing put an end to their career.

He couldn't let that happen to him, though. His dad expected him to continue the tradition of keeping the Forza name in the headlines. Bull riding was all Justin knew. He'd barely graduated from high school and never gone to college. If he quit bull riding tomorrow, his dad would probably disown him or maybe cut him out of the family business. Without a title to his name, he wouldn't have much value being associated with the bull-riding school his dad and Jake had started. If that happened, there'd be no way he could afford to give Em the life she deserved.

Hell, even if he did win the title, the prize money wouldn't go very far if he wanted to secure a future for the two of them. Not when he had his eye on a little tract of land not far from the ranch where he was raised.

Em deserved a hell of a lot more than he would ever be able to give her, but he'd do his best. He'd either get back to the competition this summer or have to wait until January to start over. He wasn't sure his heart, or his battered body, could wait that long to finally tell her how he felt. That meant whether he was 100 percent ready or not, he had to find a way to get back into the circuit.

His body could heal if he got injured again. But his heart—there was no way his heart would ever recover if he didn't get the chance to come clean with Emmeline.

Emmeline

"We need to do something about Justin." Emmeline narrowed her eyes and turned her gaze from Decker to Knox and back again.

"Like what?" Decker leaned against the back of the booth and pulled Miranda tight against his side. "Knowing him, he's got a plan. He's always thinking a couple dozen steps ahead."

She huffed out a breath. "Not this time. I can feel it. His dad's messing with his head, and it's going to get him killed."

"You mean the whole 'Forzas aren't quitters' bit?" Knox asked. Finally, someone was taking her seriously for a change.

"Exactly. Mr. Forza won his title, what, thirty years ago?" She was rounding up. He'd won multiple titles, the last one being twenty-eight years ago. How could she not have the year memorized when memorabilia from his last year of competing covered the walls and every horizontal surface in the house Justin grew up in?

"Give or take a couple of years." Decker shrugged. "What does that have to do with anything?"

"Things have changed since then. Nowadays, the bulls are bigger. The scoring is harder. Back when his dad was riding bulls, the competition wasn't nearly as fierce."

"But Jake won his last title, what, five years ago now?" Knox asked. "Things aren't that different now than they were then."

Emmeline didn't want to acknowledge Justin's older brother's win. As the oldest, Jake didn't have a choice but to chase after that title like a coonhound tracking down a fox. Once Jake snagged it, Justin felt obligated to follow in his older brother's footsteps, no matter how different they were. His sole goal in life had been set in stone like their dad had chiseled it into bedrock himself.

"When Jake won, it meant that Justin had to make a go of it. You know how their dad is. I don't even know if Justin likes riding bulls anymore." Thank goodness Justin wasn't sitting next to her when she said that out loud. Even if he hated bull riding more than he hated the veggie pizza she made him try on occasion, he'd never admit it. He was a legacy rider. It was in his blood, and, as far as she knew, he'd never considered doing anything else.

"Whether he does or not, you know he won't give up. He's got to carry on the family tradition." Knox swept a napkin over the ring of condensation that had formed around his beer bottle.

"I know what that's like." Decker nodded toward Miranda, then shifted forward to lean his elbows on the table. "My dad has certain expectations as well. I didn't have much of a choice about joining the family business."

Em rolled her eyes. "It's not the same. Justin could get himself killed chasing after his dad's dream. What's the worst that could happen to you? You stub your toe while checking on one of your dad's oil rigs?"

"Hey, that's not fair." Decker jutted his bottom lip out like one of her kindergarteners who'd just scraped his knee on the playground.

She caught Miranda's smile as Em covered Decker's hand with hers. "You're right, I'm sorry."

"Deck would be more likely to get his Italian loafers dirty than get hurt." Knox teased. "Come on, bro, you know we love you."

"They're Spanish leather, not Italian." Decker popped a chip in his mouth, and all was forgiven. That was the beauty of hanging out with the guys. Hurt feelings never lasted long, and when they put something behind them, they meant it.

"I think you're right about Justin." Knox clasped his hands together. "He's been spending so much time around his dad, I'm not sure he even knows what he wants right now."

Finally, a voice of reason. The tight band around Em's heart eased a bit at the idea of Knox and Decker helping her force Justin to see the light.

"So, we need to get him out of the house for a couple of weeks?" Decker asked.

"It would give him a break from living under his dad's thumb. Why don't you invite him to tour with you?" Emmeline focused on Knox. "Get him out of town and a change of scenery. Maybe once he's away from his family, he can figure out if he really does want to go back to competing."

"I don't know." Knox reached up and rubbed the back of his neck. "My schedule's pretty tight. He'd be more than welcome to join me on tour, but we wouldn't have much downtime to braid each other's hair and share our deepest wishes."

"Don't be a jerk," Em said.

Miranda hadn't said much of anything since they entered the restaurant. Emmeline had almost forgotten she was still there. "We could invite him to go to Colorado with us."

Decker's smile froze. "I don't know if that's such a good idea, babe."

"Why not?" She bumped her shoulder against his. "Justin's your friend, and if he needs help, you should try to be there for him, shouldn't you?"

"I bet he'd like Colorado," Knox said.

"There's only one bedroom in the condo where we're staying. I doubt he wants to sleep on the couch. Besides, if I'm there with you, there's not going to be a whole lot of talking going on." He leaned over to nuzzle his lips against Miranda's neck.

Emmeline resisted the urge to toss a handful of tortilla chips at him. "So, then what? We just hope for the best?"

"What about you, Em?" Knox's chin tucked against his chest and he eyed her from under the brim of his hat. "You've got the summer off. Why don't you get him out of town for a week or two?"

"Me?" She put her hand on her chest. "But I've got Keisha's wedding coming up, and my sister's going to be having a baby, and—"

"I know just the place." Decker slapped his palm down on the table. Emmeline jumped, along with several sets of heavy silverware.

"I can't afford a Decker Wayne–style getaway." Emmeline readjusted the silverware that had scattered thanks to Decker's enthusiasm. They didn't have the same standards when it came to vacations. While she did everything on a budget, she'd be willing to bet her entire life's savings that he'd never even traveled in coach.

"What if your Decker Wayne getaway was on me?" Decker waggled his dark brows. "Dad just bought a place on some island down by South Padre. Couple hundred yards of private beach."

Em's stomach flip-flopped. An island getaway with a private beach? That sounded way too good to be true. "Are you serious?"

"Yeah. Dad's going to have the whole thing redone before he takes wifey number four down this fall. You'd have the whole place to yourselves."

Her head spun with the possibilities of how she could

fill long, sunny days on an island. On a lounge chair with a good book. Combing the beach for shells. The yes hovered on the tip of her tongue. "That sounds great, but how in the world would we ever get Justin to agree to go on vacation with just me?"

Knox let out a soft laugh.

Before Em had a chance to ask him what the heck that was supposed to mean, Decker slapped the table again. She jumped, her knee slamming into the underside of the table.

"You need to cut that out."

"Sorry, I forgot to tell you the best part. When I was checking into the place to see if it would be a good investment, I learned something. I don't think you'll have any trouble convincing Justin to go down for a visit. Remember the name Chick Darville?"

Em trolled through her memory. "Chick Darville? Isn't he a bull rider?"

Knox let out a low whistle. "Not just a bull rider. The guy's legendary."

"It's where he retired." Decker gave her a smug grin. "You tell Justin he'll have a chance to shoot the shit with Chick for an afternoon, and you won't have to drag him with you . . . he'll row all the way there in a dinghy if it means getting face time with his idol."

"Hmm. I think y'all might be onto something." She turned a bright smile on the two men and Miranda. "Let me look into it and make sure Mr. Darville will be there. If it all works out, it looks like I might be heading to the beach this summer."

5

Justin

Justin eyed his reflection in the wavy glass of the bathroom mirror. It was no secret the past few months had been rough on him. The dark circles under his eyes were evidence of that. It was kind of hard to fall asleep at night when he couldn't clear his mind. Maybe he needed to get away for a bit. Just a few days off the grid to refocus.

He turned on the tap and splashed cold water on his cheeks. The stress was getting to him, and the last thing he wanted to do was take it out on the ones he loved. Em only wanted the best for him. Of course she'd be worried.

Maybe he'd see if Knox and Decker wanted to head out to Big Bend for a long weekend of camping. They'd had the opportunity to do that in the past, and he always came back feeling refreshed and ready to take on whatever obstacle was sitting in front of him. He needed to reframe things, that was all. With the added pressure from his dad and being worried about losing his chance with Em, it made sense that he'd feel off.

Feeling sure about next steps, he left the men's room

and returned to the table. Em held her phone in her hand and was snapping pictures of the bowl of tortilla chips in the center of the table.

"You're just in time." Knox slid out of the booth so Justin could take his seat. "I think Emmeline's finally lost it."

"You're just jealous." Em adjusted the bowl of chips and snapped another photo.

"I'm not jealous of a rock." Knox let out a chuckle as he settled back on the seat.

"A rock?" Justin asked.

Em reached out and grabbed something from the middle of the table. "Justin, meet Mr. Rocky Von Poopster."

"You've got to be shitting me. The rock has a name?" Decker reached for his beer.

Justin eyed the pinkish rock in Em's palm. "This is Rocky?"

"Yep. The one and only." Her eyes sparkled.

"Why does your rock have a name, and why the hell are you taking pictures of it on the table with our food?" Decker leaned against the back of the booth.

"He's my classroom's pet rock. I'm in charge of him this summer and promised the kids I'd add pictures to his social media accounts. Obviously, they picked out his name."

"Obviously." Justin held out his hand to take the rock. "It's nice to finally meet you in person, Rocky."

"You're talking to a rock," Decker pointed out.

Justin ignored him. Em had talked about Rocky before, but since the kids took turns taking him home during the school year, this was the first time he'd seen the odd-shaped rock outside of the images posted to Rocky's very popular social media accounts.

"Rocky's not just any rock," Em said.

"You're right. He's got a bit of an odd shape to him, doesn't he?" Knox leaned closer.

Em grabbed the rock out of Justin's hand. "He's a little sensitive to his shape. Best not to comment on it."

"He looks like a dick." Knox let out a laugh.

"He does not." Em's cheeks pinked. "I'll have you know Rocky's been a beloved member of my classroom since we found him on the playground my very first year of teaching."

"He really does." Decker picked up the rock and flipped it one way, then the other.

Justin took a closer look. The damn rock did have a bit of a phallic shape. "I think they're right, Em."

"You've got him sideways, that's all. He should really sit upright." She slipped the rock into a small bag and zipped it closed.

"What happened to having a class guinea pig or hamster?" Knox asked.

Justin was glad the spotlight had moved past him to settle on someone else, but he was sorry it was Em's turn in the hot seat. Based on the way the skin across her chest bloomed into an unnaturally rosy color, she wasn't enjoying the focus on her classroom's mascot.

"Too many kids have allergies. I'm not allowed to keep anything live in the classroom." She slid her margarita closer to the edge of the table and bent over to take a sip.

"That's too bad." Decker didn't let Em's glare faze him. "We always had class pets back in grade school."

Knox ignored him, which seemed like the best option under the circumstances. "It wasn't a class pet, but remember that time in chemistry when we found a rattlesnake in the back of the room?"

"Yeah, you jumped onto your chair like a big baby while Justin and I tossed it out the window." Decker pulled Miranda tight against him. "I should have kept it and made myself a pair of snakeskin boots."

"You were the one on top of the chair," Em reminded them. "The only one who didn't panic was Justin."

Justin remembered that afternoon well. It was the day he realized he was 100 percent head over heels in love with Emmeline. She'd been the one to open up the cabinet at the back of the room to get an extra container for their lab project. The beaker had shattered into shards when she noticed the unwelcome visitor slithering out of the darkness.

Justin had reacted without thinking. He jerked her out of the way as the snake struck, and it caught the leg of his worn jeans instead. Thankfully, he'd been wearing his work boots, and the fangs didn't penetrate the leather. A bite from a rattler probably wouldn't have killed her, but it would have hurt like hell. The teacher had tried to grab it with the hook he used to pull the overhead screen down but missed. Justin took it and somehow managed to fling the snake out the open window.

Em had been shaken up but uninjured. That's when it struck him. If anything had happened to her . . . he still couldn't bear to think about it, even all these years later. That was the day he knew for sure she held his heart in her unknowing hands. He should have told her then and saved himself over a decade of misery. But even then, he knew their lives would follow different paths. By that point, her dad had already been injured, and Em had made her vow.

"I figured you'd win Homecoming King for that stunt," Knox said.

Justin shook his head. "That was never my scene."

"Only because you spent your afternoons riding bulls

instead of throwing passes for the football team. I know we could have made state junior year if you hadn't quit." Decker shook his head.

"I'd rather have a belt buckle for winning first place than a crown for winning Homecoming King."

Knox lifted his hands off the table as their server set down a bowl of Terlinga's famous flaming cheese dip in the middle of the table.

"I haven't had this in forever." Knox didn't wait for the alcohol to burn off the top of the dip before he shoved a chip into the bowl. "Y'all have no idea how lucky we are to be from a place where the food's so good."

"Is that what you miss most when you're on the road?" Em's mouth curved up in a lopsided smile.

"For sure." Knox tried to talk around a mouthful of chips.

"So much for us then, huh?" Em's thigh brushed Justin's as she shifted to face him. "He gets a taste of fame and fortune, and all he misses is the food. At least I know you miss us when you're gone."

Justin brushed a hunk of hair back that had fallen over her shoulder. She was joking, but he could hear the half-buried truth under her words. He could have blurted it out right then and there. Told her exactly how much he missed her when he was on the road. How he pictured her face every night while he prayed for sleep to come. How he dreamed about a day when he wouldn't leave at all.

"Aren't you going to get some of that dip before Knox inhales it all?" Emmeline nodded toward the rapidly disappearing bowl of cheese dip.

Justin took one of the small appetizer plates and handed it to Em. "Ladies first."

6

❦

Emmeline

Em tried to stifle a yawn, but it had been a long day. She'd been up since before dawn to get everything ready for the last day of school. Every time she closed her eyes it felt like sandpaper rubbed over them. It was getting harder and harder to open them back up.

"You sure you don't want to stay on the bus tonight?" Justin's arm rested on the back of the seat next to her, and she leaned close so she could hear him over the music blaring through the back of the limo.

"Don't you have an early appointment in the morning?"

"Yeah. It's probably best if we head back tonight."

Knox had invited them to stay on the tour bus since they hadn't seen each other in so long. He was heading out tomorrow morning for a show down in Austin, so it might be the last time they'd see him for the next few months. But she wouldn't be very good company tonight. It was already late, and she'd probably conk out as soon as her head hit a pillow.

Justin's fingertips skimmed her bare shoulder as he brushed her hair away. Her eyes drifted closed again, and she leaned into him, letting his scent surround her. He smelled like home. Always had and probably always would. She didn't sleep well when he was on the road. But with him right beside her, she knew he was safe.

"We're almost there, Em." His breath tickled her ear while goose bumps pebbled the skin on her arms.

"I just want to keep my eyes closed for a few more minutes." She snuggled closer, picking up the steady *thump-thump-thump* of his heartbeat. When she did meditation yoga and the instructor told her to envision her safe spot—somewhere she could picture herself when she got overwhelmed—this was exactly what Em had in mind.

The limo came to a stop.

"You awake?" Justin's warm breath brushed against her ear.

"Yeah."

"Good. I'm not sure I'd be able to carry you out of the limo." He pulled his arm away from her back, and she sat upright.

"Wouldn't want to add to your injury. If you can't lift me, don't you think that's a sign you might not be ready to start riding again?" She hated herself for saying the words out loud but couldn't stop herself. Sooner or later he had to acknowledge the risk of what he was thinking about doing.

Justin waited until the others climbed out, and then stepped onto the pavement and held out a hand for her. "Can we give it a rest for tonight? I'm tired, and all I want to do is head home and get a good night's sleep."

She bit her lip. "I'm sorry. You know I'm only busting your ass because I care, right?"

"I know." He closed his eyes for a moment. When he opened them again, he had a tight smile on his face. "Let's say our goodbyes and hit the road."

"All right." She looked at the giant tour bus, wondering what it would be like to live on the road. Knox had been chasing his dream for the past few years, never spending more than a night or two in the same place. Justin did the same, at least up until he got hurt.

What would it feel like to wake up in a different town every day? To never feel settled anywhere? When she used to talk to Justin when he was on the road, half the time he didn't know what town he was in. Before her dad got hurt, he lived the same kind of life. They never knew when he'd be stopping home on his way from one rodeo to the next. He'd missed out on so much over the years . . . birthdays, family events, so many milestones she and her sister passed while they were growing up.

She didn't want that for her friends. Justin was so bull-headed that he couldn't see the damn forest for the trees. She'd pushed hard enough for tonight, but she wasn't giving up on trying to get him to see things her way.

"I wish y'all didn't have to leave so soon." Knox held out his arms for Emmeline, and she stepped into his embrace.

"Block some time on your calendar to come home for a bit." She gave him a squeeze. He was like the big brother she'd always wished for. She worried about him on the road. Besides his manager and bandmates, he didn't have anyone looking out for him. Based on the show he put on, his career was heading in the opposite direction of what he'd had in mind when he set out for Nashville a half dozen years ago.

"I'll try." He pulled back and lowered his voice. "Don't worry about Justin. We'll figure something out, okay?"

Em nodded as she turned to Decker.

"Got a hug for me, too?" Decker opened his arms.

"Of course." She leaned in, whispering so Justin didn't overhear. "Did Justin say anything more to you about when he might return to riding?"

Decker shook his head. "I don't think he's going to quit. Our best bet of knocking some sense into his head might be getting him down to Paradise Island to talk to Chick."

"That's what I was afraid of. How am I going to convince him to take a week or two off?" Her mind spun through possibilities. Justin wasn't stupid; he'd suspect something was up if she suggested the two of them take off on a trip together.

"You find out if Chick's still there. Leave the rest to us. Knox and I will figure something out." He pulled back and squeezed her shoulder. "You know we're just as worried about him as you are, don't you?"

"Yeah." Em released her grip. "Be careful with Miranda, okay?"

He looked down at her, humor flashing through his eyes. "You afraid I'm going to break her heart?"

"No. I'm afraid she's going to break yours." She swept her gaze over the three men. They were her family, just as much as her parents and her younger sister. True, they could annoy the hell out of her at times, but that's what family did. She loved them with a fierceness she couldn't explain.

"See y'all on the flip side." That was Justin's way of saying goodbye. She'd never actually heard him say the word. He'd once told her that he hated the thought of saying goodbye to his loved ones every time he left town, so he'd stopped. It was too final. He preferred to leave things open-ended with the anticipation that there would always be a next time.

With a heaviness in her heart, she climbed into Justin's truck. When would the four of them be able to get together again? Unless she came up with a way to get Justin to see reason, they might not have a chance.

No. That wasn't an option. Justin's dad might claim the phrase *Forzas aren't quitters*, but he had no idea how far Em would go to keep his son from doing something stupid.

"Well that was fun." Em settled into the bucket seat. "Do you think Knox sleeps well on that bus?"

"Hell, Em. When you're used to being on the road, you can fall asleep anywhere, with anyone." He glanced over and gave her a grin.

That fluttery feeling returned to her belly. The thought of Justin falling asleep on the road, all by himself, made her stomach roll over.

But he'd also said "with anyone."

She wasn't naive enough to think that he hadn't taken advantage of the buckle bunnies who hung around the fringes of the rodeo scene, always looking for a cowboy to bag. Justin was smart, though. He wouldn't fall for just anyone. In all the years she'd known him, she could count the number of girls he'd dated on one hand. He'd never had time for dating, not with the rigorous training and workout schedule he'd kept.

Maybe Knox and Decker would be able to talk some sense into him. Both of them seemed just as worried, though it would be up to her to put a plan into play. Decker's offer from earlier in the night didn't sound quite as feasible without the cloud of tequila fogging her brain. Could she really convince Justin to escape to a private island with her? He'd never voluntarily take time off without a damn good reason.

The radio played softly as the truck ate up the ribbon of highway that stretched ahead. Em must have dozed off for a bit. When she woke, Justin had brought the truck to a stop in her driveway.

"Come on, I'll walk you up." He left the truck running while he scooted around and opened her door for her.

She got out and took slow steps to her front door. "Thanks for the ride."

"You're welcome. Don't stay up too late."

"I won't. I'm going to post a few pictures of Rocky from the concert, then I'll turn in." There was a cute one of Rocky in the suite with a stage full of pyrotechnics exploding in the background. The kids would get a kick out of that.

They reached the door and Justin held out his arms to give her a hug. "Good night, Em."

"Good night." She wrapped her arms around him. "Are we still on for tomorrow?"

"Yeah." He pulled back first. "I've got PT early, then an appointment with Dr. Lindell at ten. I'll head to school after that."

"Thanks." She put her hand on the doorknob. "Hey, Justin?"

"Yeah?"

"I know it's only for a little while, but it's good to have you home."

"It's good to be here. See you in the morning." He waited until she slipped into her apartment and shut the door before heading back to his truck.

Admitting it was good to have him home shouldn't have made the flutter in her belly resume, but it did. What was it about Justin being back that made her feel like an awkward middle schooler all over again?

It had to be hormones. Ever since her sister told her she was pregnant and her friend got engaged, the ticktock of Em's biological clock had grown louder. She'd started looking at the few available men in Blewit through a new lens . . . the one with the I-wanna-have-babies-someday filter. Someday still seemed far away, but with her twenty-ninth birthday right around the corner, it was creeping closer.

She was a modern-day woman and knew she didn't need a man to be a mom. But she was also somewhat of a traditionalist and would prefer to bring up a baby in a two-person household where they could co-parent.

Whoa.

She was getting way ahead of herself. Justin would never qualify for her list of give-me-your-sperm candidates. How could he when she never knew which ride might be his last? If she could convince him to walk away from bull riding, though . . . then he could be a real contender.

7

Justin

Justin winced as he pulled his shirt back over his head and waited for Dr. Lindell to speak. Though he could handle the pain in his shoulder, he was still lacking the range of motion he needed to be considered 100 percent. The next few minutes would seal his fate. Either he'd get the green light to rejoin the circuit or he'd have to wait until next year to start another run for the world title.

"Well?" He didn't like the way the doc's mouth turned down at the corners. It couldn't be a good sign.

"You're doing great. Your shoulder's healing well, especially after such a significant injury."

"But," Justin prompted. There was definitely a *but* coming. He steeled himself to hear the words that would end this year's run.

"But"—the doc lifted his gaze to peer at Justin over the rim of his glasses—"you had major surgery. You're right on track, but I think you still need a few more weeks before you get back to competing."

Justin's shoulders sagged as the breath he'd been holding seeped out of his chest like a balloon deflating. "A few weeks? Like three?"

"Let's schedule another check-in at the beginning of July. We ought to know by then whether you'll be ready to get back to riding when things start up again in August."

"Yeah, okay." Justin hopped off the exam table, his stomach churning. How was he going to break the news to his dad? "Thanks, doc. I appreciate it."

Dr. Lindell shook his hand. "If you keep up with your PT, I'm sure you'll be ready to go before the end of the summer."

The end of the summer . . . there was no way he'd be able to make up the points if he had to sit out the whole month of August. That meant another year gone, another chance to win a title and relieve himself of his family obligation would pass, and he'd still be biding his time before he could tell Em how he felt.

His phone rang as soon as he walked out of the doctor's office. "Hey, Dad."

"What's the word from Dr. Lindell? Did he clear you to compete? I've been talking to Blaster Energy Drinks and they want to come on board as a new sponsor. I'm talking a six-figure deal for the rest of the season."

Justin's stomach rolled. His dad was all about the sponsorships. Yeah, it was a great way to supplement his earnings from riding, but sponsors tended to dry up when a cowboy wasn't competing.

"Doc wants to see me in a month." Justin waited for the inevitable explosion.

"A month? What the hell is he thinking? You can't sit out another month, son. You're already falling behind."

"I know. But what am I supposed to do?"

"You're supposed to do what bull riders do. What your brother did the year he won. Man the fuck up."

Justin's chest squeezed. He didn't want to repeat history. As proud as his brother was to win the title that year, it had cost him. He'd gone back to riding before he was ready and still walked with a limp thanks to a knee injury he'd sustained. The doc had warned him not to head back until his knee was ready, but Jake hadn't listened.

"I've got to go, Dad. Can we talk about this when I get home?" He needed time to process, to think.

His dad didn't answer, just disconnected. The reason his dad was hard on him was due to how he'd been raised. His methods worked for others. After he won the championship, he'd started training bull riders. He'd been successful over the years, but it wouldn't mean shit if his own sons weren't able to win.

The pressure might have broken another man, but Justin had carried the weight of his dad's expectations on his broad shoulders his entire life. He'd figure out a way to make this right. He didn't have a choice. With a steely resolve settling in his chest, he tried to figure out his next move.

Since he knew he'd be in town today, he'd volunteered to help Em clean out her classroom. Her smile would make him feel better, even with the sucky news the doctor had delivered.

There were only a few cars in the parking lot at the elementary school. It felt weird to walk through the halls of the same building where he'd attended preschool through sixth grade. Everything seemed so big back then. He walked by the principal's office and his gut twinged at the memory of spending so many afternoons sitting on a hard wooden chair right outside the door.

He hadn't raised too much hell in elementary school—that came later in high school. But between him, Knox, and Decker, they'd managed to get into enough trouble that he knew the inside of the principal's office better than most.

Arriving outside of Em's classroom, he paused. She had the radio on and was singing along to one of Knox's older songs. They must have turned off the air in the building, because it was hotter than hell, and Em had her hair piled on top of her head in a messy updo. Her hips swayed back and forth as she pulled colorful pieces of paper down from around the whiteboard. He'd give just about anything to put his hands on those hips and pull her tight against him.

A hot-pink tank top left her shoulders bare. Her skin usually tanned to a deep golden brown in the summers. She obviously hadn't had a chance to spend much time in the sun yet.

Damn, she was a sight. He could have stood there all day watching her, but the song ended, and she turned around, almost like she could feel his eyes on the gorgeous curve of her fabulous backside.

"Hey. Are you going to come in or stand there like a creeper all day?"

He let out a laugh. "I was just trying to compare what it felt like to sit here when Mrs. Cravich stood at the board versus what your students might feel like having you as a teacher."

Emmeline grinned. "Mrs. Cravich finally retired a few years ago."

"About time, don't you think?" The woman had been old when he'd had her, and had to have been at least eighty when she finally retired.

"Get in here. I can't reach the stuff at the top of the board, and I'm too lazy to go get a ladder."

"So, you want to use me for my height?" He wished she'd want to use him for something else, but he'd take it, for now. Any chance to spend time with Em alone was worth it.

"Your height for sure, but I bet I can think of a few other things I can use you for."

"Oh yeah?" He'd bet his truck that they weren't thinking along the same lines, but he'd help her any way he could. She'd always been it for him, and if it took him until he was as old as Mrs. Cravich, he'd keep trying to find a way to be worthy of her.

Emmeline

Emmeline bit back a grin as Justin tried to wedge himself into one of the student desks in her classroom. With his help, she'd almost gotten all of her things packed up. After a quick bite to eat, she'd be done and wouldn't have to return to the building until the end of August.

"Here, I made up your favorite." She pulled a sandwich bag out of the insulated lunch tote on her desk.

"You made brisket and beans?"

"When do you think I'd have time to smoke a brisket?" She tossed him the bag. "It's that barbecue chicken salad you said you loved."

"Oh." He pulled the plastic bag open. "That's good, too."

"But not as good as brisket, huh?"

He rubbed a hand over his abs. "Nothing's as good as your brisket, Em."

"Nothing?" She couldn't help but tease. The look he got when he talked about food made her want to laugh. His eyes closed halfway, and he looked like she suspected he might on the verge of a big O. Not that she spent much time thinking about Justin's O face. But if she did, the look he got when mentioning her brisket would be the one she pictured.

"Well, I can maybe think of one thing I might enjoy more." His mouth twitched into a teasing grin. "Maybe two."

"Is that so?" It was nice to see him smile. He'd been so down lately she'd do about anything to earn a grin or laugh. "Care to share? Does it have anything to do with a certain busty brunette being back in town?"

Justin took a bite out of his sandwich. His brows knit together, and he shook his head. "What do you mean?"

"I heard Simone Plevitt's back in town." Em didn't particularly care for Simone, but she might provide a welcome distraction for Justin. At least for now.

He shook his head. "I hadn't heard."

"I don't think she's ever gotten over you turning her down for senior prom." Em remembered that night like it had been only a few months ago, not over a decade. Where had the time gone? What did she have to show for being ten years out of high school?

"That was a good night." Justin took a swig of the jar of sweet tea she'd packed. "We should do it again sometime."

"No way." Heat danced across her cheeks thinking about it. She, Justin, Knox, and Decker had gone with a bigger group of friends. Dinner at the steakhouse had been fun, but they'd spent only an hour or so at the dance. Then Decker had made the suggestion they head out to the lake and go swimming off the dock of his dad's club.

They'd been picked up by lake patrol for indecent exposure for skinny-dipping in the lake. The only reason her parents hadn't found out was that Decker's dad smoothed it over with the club management and now had a patio named after him at the clubhouse.

"I'm worried about you." Justin set the last bite of sandwich down.

Worried about her? She almost choked on a celery stick. "Why in the world would you be worried about me?"

"When's the last time you had a little fun?" His eyebrows rose.

"That's easy. I had a blast at Knox's concert last night."

"Okay, before that. When's the last time you had a night that rated a ten?" She wished she could say something that would wipe that knowing smirk right off his scruffy mug. But one of the drawbacks of being friends with a guy who'd known her since second grade was that he could always tell when she tried to tell a little white lie.

Her hesitation was all the ammo he needed. "I've been having fun."

"When was your last ten night?" Justin leaned back as much as he could in the small desk and crossed his arms over his chest.

"Rating nights is overrated." She mimicked his position.

"That's a weak argument, Porter. You want to talk about hearing things? I've heard you haven't shown your face at Lloyd's in months. You deserve to have a little fun, you know." His grin spread across his face.

"I hate Lloyd's." It was the kind of place a person would expect to find in a town the size of Blewit. The kind of place where the smell of cheap beer had soaked into the floor over the years and the same folks could be found any night of the week, drowning their sorrows in a bucket of beer or sometimes a shot of cheap whiskey.

"You might hate it, but it's all we've got unless you want to drive closer to Dallas. From what I've heard, the only time anyone's seen you out is when you show up at the Legion with your dad for the meat raffles."

She lifted a shoulder in a half-hearted shrug, not willing to admit that the last time she'd been out was on a blind date a few weeks ago. There were some things she just didn't want to share with Justin.

"So? I've been busy. Teaching kindergarten isn't for the faint of heart. Besides, I won the big meat prize at the Legion a couple of Friday nights ago."

"The big meat, huh? You know I've got a million different dirty jokes I'm trying to hold back, right?"

She leaned in, her cheeks heating. "I'd be disappointed if you didn't."

"Do I even want to know what they stuffed the big meat prize pack with?" His eyebrows lifted.

She tapped her fingertips against her lips. "There may or may not have been a brisket in the big meat prize pack."

"Seriously?" The look in his eyes switched from teasing to hopeful.

"And a couple good-looking rib eyes, but we already ate those." She dipped her celery stick in the plastic container of blue cheese dressing. "Maybe if you stop giving me grief about not going out, I might be inclined to fire up Dad's smoker and fix that brisket for you."

Justin clasped his hands together over his chest. "Damn, Porter, you sure know your way straight to my heart."

"So, you'll stop pestering me about my love life, or lack thereof?"

Justin reached across the desk, holding his hand out to her. "Come on, Em. You're acting like you're on the verge of getting your AARP card, not a couple weeks away from your twenty-ninth birthday."

Instinctively, she slid her palm against his. "I'm an old soul. Hanging out at the same bar with the same people I've known since we used to sip juice boxes isn't my idea of a good time."

"What is your idea of a good time?"

The mood inside her classroom shifted. Justin eyed her with a mixture of heat and curiosity in his eyes. If she didn't know better, she might think he was making a move on her. But this was Justin. Her Justin. The same guy who carried her half a mile home when they were kids and she wiped out on her scooter. The same guy who crawled through the window when she had the chicken pox so he could catch them, too, and he wouldn't have to go to school without her.

Movement by the door to her classroom pulled her attention.

"Knock knock. Just wanted to stop in and tell you to have a good summer." Mrs. Richmond, the principal who'd been around since Emmeline and Justin attended Kennedy Elementary, stuck her head through the doorway. "Sorry, I didn't know you had a helper."

Justin pulled his hand away. "Hi, Mrs. Richmond."

"Justin Forza?" The older woman adjusted her thick glasses. "I should have guessed that was you. It's about time the two of you started seeing each other."

"Oh, we're not together." Emmeline was quick to correct any assumption Mrs. Richmond might have leapt to in her head. It wouldn't do any good for word to get out that she and Justin had been holding hands at school. "We're just friends."

"If you say so." She moved into the room with the aid of her walker. "I'm off to Minnesota to spend the summer with my daughter. I can't take the heat here anymore."

"I hope you have a good time." Em glanced at Justin.

"I don't suppose you'd be willing to help me grab the last two boxes I need to take out to my car?" Mrs. Richmond jerked her head toward Justin. "I know your shoulder's injured, but I figure you've still got use of your arms?"

Justin slid out of the desk and picked up his trash. "I'd be happy to give you a hand."

Em breathed out a sigh as the two of them left the classroom. She wasn't sure what to call the feeling that passed between them, but it set her on edge.

On edge wasn't a very good place to be if she planned on finding a way to get Justin alone on a tropical island.

8

Justin

Justin climbed out of the passenger seat of his dad's truck and braced himself for the evening ahead. He would much rather have been catching a movie with Em or sitting on a barstool at Lloyd's, but bailing on tonight's junior rodeo event wasn't an option.

"That rep from Blaster Energy Drinks said he'd try to make it tonight." His dad pulled out a can of chew and offered it to Justin.

"No, thanks." He'd never been interested in the stuff, even though he'd rarely seen his dad without a lump lodged against his gum line.

"If he asks about when you're coming back, you let me do the talking, you understand?"

"Yes, sir." Justin wouldn't argue with his dad in public. If things went south, they'd have a chance to exchange words on the ride home. Family was family, no matter what, even if he didn't always agree with the bullish way his dad handled his business.

"Chin up, son." His dad held the door to the arena open,

letting Justin enter first. "We're about to resurrect your career."

Justin stepped into the crowded arena. The smell of fresh-popped popcorn greeted his nose. Something earthy mingled with it—the scent of dirt and mud and bulls. He didn't want to attend the local junior rodeo championship any more than he wanted to scrape cow shit off his boots, but sometimes obligations took priority.

"We've got seats behind the chutes." His dad handed over a ticket. "I'm going to make the rounds and see if I can rustle up that rep. I'll come get you if I find him."

Justin slid the ticket into his back pocket as he caught sight of his brother heading their way. "You didn't tell me Jake was going to be here tonight."

"There's my boy." His dad might be a hard-ass when it came to his kids, but he turned into a giant teddy bear at the sight of Jake's two-year-old son.

"Hey." Jake handed his mini-me over to their dad. "He wants to see the big cows. I figured that was a good job for Grandpa."

"They're bulls, Lucas. What the hell have you been teaching him? How's he going to grow up to be the next Forza world champion if he doesn't know the difference between a dairy cow and a bucking bull?"

Jake's wife handed her father-in-law a teal sippy cup. "Make sure he drinks a lot of water. We're working on potty training and he's been holding it."

His dad hefted Lucas into his arms. "Come on, big guy. Grandpa needs to teach you how to pee standing up."

Justin shot a look at his older brother as their dad walked away with Lucas laughing in his grip. "You think that's going to work?"

"Tough love, that's his way." Jake put an arm around his wife. "Seemed to work for us."

His brother might think so, but Justin wondered. What would their lives be like if their dad hadn't pushed so hard? He probably never would have had the courage to climb onto the back of his first bull. Might have flunked out of high school without his dad riding his ass about his grades. He loved his dad, he and Jake both did, but sometimes he wondered how he might have turned out if his dad had done a little less pushing and a little more encouraging.

"Should we go find our seats? I don't want to waste a second of being kid-free." Justin's sister-in-law, Sienna, tightened her arm behind her husband's back. "Did Jake tell you we've got number two on the way?"

Justin glanced from Sienna's smile to Jake's beaming grin. "Seriously? When?"

"Due in November. Hopefully, he or she doesn't arrive while you're riding in the finals." Jake clapped Justin on the back, and the three of them moved toward the end of the arena to find their seats.

His brother had won back-to-back titles seven years ago. He'd retired from bull riding when he was twenty-nine and now helped their dad with training others to follow in his giant footsteps. He had two world titles under his belt, a wife, a healthy son, and a baby on the way. There'd never been any doubt in Jake's mind about choosing a different path. His future had been set into motion the day the doctor told their parents they had a son.

Justin wished for the kind of conviction Jake had possessed. Even after an injury that would have sidelined a lesser man, his brother pushed on. He'd already married Sienna by that point. Maybe it was her unwavering faith in him that made the difference. Whatever it was, Justin didn't have it.

"Here we are." Jake waited for Justin to head down the steps to their seats first. His limp made steps a little challenging.

Justin looked back to see his brother lean on Sienna as he navigated steep stairs. Had it been worth it? He'd never asked Jake the question in a direct way, and now he wondered. If he had it to do all over again, would he make the same choices? Would he have gone back to bull riding against doctor's orders? Risked his life and a permanent injury for one more title?

"Guess who I ran into." His dad stood at the entrance to their row of seats. "Lucas and I will have to visit the bulls later. Justin, can you join me? There's someone I want to introduce you to."

"Excuse me." Justin shuffled past Sienna while Lucas reached out for Jake. "I'll be back in a few."

"Hurry or y'all are going to miss the first ride." Jake settled his son on the seat between him and his wife.

"This will only take a few minutes." His dad tapped on the top of Lucas's pint-sized cowboy hat. "We'll be back before you know it."

With a sinking feeling in his chest, Justin braced himself for the conversation ahead.

His dad led him to a room overlooking the arena. As they entered, a thin young man in a bright orange shirt headed their way, the Blaster Energy Drink logo emblazoned across his chest.

"Justin Forza, it's a pleasure to meet you." He held out his hand. "I'm Turner Dobson, vice president of marketing for Blaster Energy Drinks."

"Nice to meet you, too." Justin took the man's hand in a tight grip.

"Sounds like we have a lot to discuss. Will you join me?" Turner pulled out a chair at a table for four.

Justin and his dad did the same, and the three of them sat down in unison.

"Turner's been eager to catch a word with you, son."

"Monty tells me it won't be long before you're back on track to make a run for the title." Turner motioned a server over.

Justin had been behind the scenes at events like this before. The riders provided entertainment in the ring while the real business happened in conference rooms and suites around the perimeter.

"What can I get you, gentlemen?" A woman in tight jean shorts and tall cowboy boots stopped by the table.

"How about a round of beer?" Turner asked.

"Just water for me." Justin gave the server a tight smile. "I don't want to mess up my training schedule."

His dad's nod signaled his approval. They'd done this song and dance routine before. Even though Justin had no problem enjoying a drink with his friends the night before, if the sponsor thought he was already in serious training mode, it would increase whatever sponsorship offer he might make.

"Sounds like you're serious about getting back to the chase," Turner commented.

"Forzas aren't quitters." His dad clapped Justin on the back. "Justin ought to be cleared by the doc in just a couple of weeks, isn't that right, son?"

Justin drew in a breath through his nose. His dad had never been one to heed doctor's orders, but a couple of weeks was a big difference from what Dr. Lindell had said this morning. "That's right."

"Great news." Turner pushed up his shirtsleeves. "I think we've got a lot to talk about. Should we get started?"

Emmeline

Em had just pulled the covers up to her nose and settled into bed with one of the books from her nightstand when her phone rang. The opening notes to "Save a Horse (Ride a Cowboy)" blared. She fumbled for the phone, cursing herself for letting Justin pick out his own custom ringtone.

"How'd it go?" Pressing the phone to her ear, she slid an old ticket stub into the book to mark her place.

"Same old, same old." Justin let out a long sigh. "Dad's pushing me to sign a new sponsor."

"The energy drink people?" She could barely keep them all straight. When Justin went out to ride, his shirt was covered with so many patches and sponsor logos that there was barely a plain stretch of fabric.

"Yeah. They're offering a ton for the rest of the season. Plus, an unlimited supply of Blaster."

She laughed. "Have you tried it yet? Is it even any good?"

"It's all right. I like your homemade sweet tea better."

Her heart swelled at the compliment. "Why thank you. I think it's the two cups of sugar you like, though. It doesn't have anything to do with me."

"That's not true. My mom made it with the recipe your grandma gave her, and it doesn't taste anything like yours. I think you put something special in it."

"It's just Lipton, a little bit of lemon, and a shitload of sugar."

"Maybe that's what's different. I bet Mom used a cup to measure, not a shitload."

"That's probably it." Em snuggled under the covers. "The Porter family has a secret stash of measuring tools. It's either a shitload or a crap ton. You can't find utensils like that at your local Williams Sonoma."

"Williams what?"

She wrinkled her nose, enjoying teasing him. "It's a kitchenware store. You know, for that room in a house where normal people prepare food?"

"Nope, never heard of it. I thought food came in cartons and foam containers, straight from the front seat of a delivery truck. Though, you sure do know your way around a kitchen."

As if his trainer would ever let him survive on nothing but takeout. Em had always been a sucker for a kind word, especially when someone praised her cooking. "Fine. I'll make a brisket for you. How about Sunday dinner?"

"I thought you'd never ask."

She could practically hear the smile of victory stretch across his mouth. "Liar. You've been begging for an invite for weeks. I've got a couple of conditions, though."

Justin groaned. "I knew there'd be a catch. Lay it on me, Em. What do I have to do?"

"You've got to help. A man should know how to make a few meals for himself, and—"

"Hey, I cook for myself."

She could picture the defensive look on his face—the swell of his lower lip sticking out and the crease between his brows. She'd seen the look often enough. She knew that one by heart. "Beanie weenies from a can don't count. Do you want me to share my big meat win or not?"

His laugh came through the phone, soft and low, and warm enough to send a flush of heat over her chest. "Yes, I want the big meat."

She wouldn't start trading innuendos about big meat. Not when she was in the middle of her longest dry spell. The only "big meat" she'd seen lately was the summer sausages on the shelves at the Super Save. "As I was saying before I was so rudely interrupted, you've got to help. We can cook at my parents' house. Their kitchen has a lot more room, and I'll get credit for feeding all of you in one fell swoop."

It would do her dad good to spend some time with

Justin and might even work in her favor in the other direction, too. Having Justin around her dad might remind him of what could go wrong if he jumped back into competing. They'd both known bull riders whose careers had ended too soon. Most of them because of a debilitating injury they'd have to deal with for the rest of their lives.

"I'm in. What time do you want me there?"

"Let's aim for eleven. It's a small brisket but will still take about four or five hours on the smoker." Plenty of time for him to be reminded of how her dad's injury affected his daily life.

"Wait, how small is small? You know bigger is always better, right?"

She rolled her eyes. He still had the sense of humor of a twelve-year-old. What did it say about her that she almost laughed? "According to some people. Do you want my free brisket or not?"

"As long as there's enough for some leftovers." Justin let out a low, long moan. The kind of moan a woman might expect to hear if she'd been getting up close and personal with his own "big meat." The sound sent something bouncing around in her belly. "Nothing like a little leftover brisket with beans for lunch the next day."

"You make it sound absolutely pornographic."

"Oh, hell no." His voice dipped even lower. "Em, there's nothing better in this world than your brisket. Not even sex."

And there they were . . . just two lifelong friends talking about big meat and sex with a moan or two mixed in. As much as she wanted to call him on it, unfortunately, she had to agree. She hadn't had any sex lately, not unless she counted the couple of times she'd reached for her battery-operated boyfriend.

"I didn't know a guy would ever admit to anything

being better than sex." She was skirting some dangerous ground with Justin. As much as she wanted him to find a reason to stay off the back of a bull, she wasn't sure how she'd feel about him having a girlfriend. It had been years since he introduced her to a woman he was dating. Unlike Decker, who always seemed to have a new woman on his arm, and Knox, who'd fallen so hard once that he'd sworn off relationships for life, Justin fell somewhere in between.

"Obviously, those guys haven't had your brisket. So, eleven on Sunday at your parents' house. Can I bring anything?"

Em ran through the list of menu items her mom had always served with brisket. She'd make up the beans, probably roll out some biscuits, and maybe fry up some okra if her mom had any ready in the garden.

"How about dessert? Think you can manage to pick up some lemon bars or cookies at the bakery on your way over?"

"You want me to bring store-bought treats when you're treating me to my favorite home-cooked meal?"

"I didn't say you *had* to pick it up at the store. I'd just like whatever you bring to be edible." Knowing Justin, the only way to ensure the latter was if he followed her recommendation of visiting the bakery.

"I'll see if Jenny will help. She owes me one."

"For what?" Em couldn't imagine how Justin could have earned a favor from his sister. She'd left the ranch to go to college in Dallas and had been working for a fancy event planner ever since graduating.

"For stuff."

"Stuff like . . ." Em pressed.

"I told her I'd get one of her friends tickets to a pro

rodeo event later on this summer. No biggie. I'll see you Sunday, okay?"

"Yeah, see you Sunday." She hung up and set her phone back on the nightstand. Flipping her book open to the page she'd been on before the call, she tried to focus. The words swam before her eyes, a scribble of black ink on a creamy background.

She didn't feel like reading anymore. It wasn't even ten yet, and she'd planned on diving into her book and enjoying a couple of hours of losing herself between the pages of a fictional life . . . a life more exciting, more romantic, more everything than hers.

"Dammit." She tossed the covers back and got out of bed. Decker's offer had been playing through her head for the past couple of days. Talking to Justin tonight, it seemed his return to the ring was inevitable. Unless she could find a way to help reprioritize, he'd take that sponsorship and to hell with the consequences. There had to be something she could do.

She flipped open her laptop case and pulled up a search page. Then she typed in the name Chick Darville into the search bar.

9

Justin

Justin pulled into the Porters' driveway at precisely eleven o'clock on Sunday morning. He'd always been on time. He had to be when a few seconds meant the difference between making a ride or losing out on the chance. Too many times he'd seen competitors get knocked out of the money round for not making it to the arena on time. He picked up the wide, low pan holding the Texas sheet cake his sister had made last night. The smell of chocolate and pecans made his stomach growl as he headed toward the door.

"Well, hey there, Justin. Come on in." Mr. Porter held the screen door open as Justin approached. "What have you got there?"

"Oh, it's a Texas sheet cake. My sister made it, and I thought I'd bring it over for dessert."

"Does she use buttermilk in the icing?" Em's dad nudged his nose into the air like he was trying to sniff out the recipe.

"Yes, sir. I believe she does."

"And fresh pecans?"

Justin nodded.

"Well then come on in."

It was good to see Em's old man up and moving around. Ever since his injury, he had good days and bad. Looked like today was off to a good start.

"Thanks, Mr. Porter." Justin wiped his boots on the welcome mat and stepped inside.

"I've told you before, call me Matt, son. Em's in the kitchen. She tells me she's going to teach you how to smoke a brisket today." Matt's mouth lifted up on one side. Justin had been around the Porter place enough growing up that he knew Em's dad lived by an outdated attitude that a woman's place was in the kitchen.

"Yes, sir. I figured it was about time I learned how to make my favorite meal." Justin glanced toward the kitchen, but Em's dad wasn't done with his side of the conversation yet.

"You just need to find yourself a woman who can make it for you." Matt crinkled his nose and winked. "Though don't tell Emmeline I said that."

Justin was pretty sure Em already knew her dad's beliefs when it came to the domestic roles men and women ought to play in a household.

"I won't say a word," Justin promised.

"Don't let him go filling your head with nonsense." Em's mom Marguerite stepped into the living room from the hall. "Hi, Justin. I'm so glad you're joining us for dinner tonight."

Justin welcomed her hug. She'd always been the touchy-feely type, a stark contrast to his own mother's style, at least what he could remember about her. She'd bailed on all of them when Justin was in grade school. Having a rodeo cowboy for a husband didn't work for everyone. That was another reason he needed to be done with the tour before he could expect Em to take a chance on him. "It's good to see you both."

"Let me take that for you." She held out her hands for the pan. "Emmeline didn't tell me you were bringing anything."

"Oh, it's just a sheet cake. My sister's in town for the weekend and she made it last night."

"How's Jenny doing?" Mrs. Porter led the way to the kitchen in the back of the three-bedroom ranch home Em and her sister grew up in.

"She's doing well. Still up in Dallas and talking about starting her own event-planning business."

Em stood at the counter, her back facing him. She had on a pair of denim shorts and a T-shirt with cherries printed all over it. At the sound of his voice, she turned.

"Good timing." She held out a giant chef's knife to him, handle first. "We need to trim off the fat and get this in the smoker."

"I'll leave the two of you to it." Mrs. Porter set the cake down on the counter. "Good luck, Justin."

"Thank you, ma'am." He headed toward the sink to wash his hands.

"So you talked your sister into making a cake for you?" Em asked, the knife still in her hand.

She was a sucker for chocolate, always had been. He used to be able to bribe her for help with his math homework with a Hershey's Kiss, or when he ran out of those, a handful of chocolate chips.

"Yeah. I left half at home for Dad and brought the rest over here. No big deal."

"No big deal?" Em set the knife down and peeled back a corner of the foil. She leaned down and closed her eyes, inhaling the sweet scent of chocolate cake with chocolate icing. "Oh my god, this smells so good. Maybe we need to skip over dinner and dive right into dessert."

Justin slid the pan away from her and tucked the foil

back in place. "Think of it as a reward for what we're going to go through over the next few hours."

"Fine." She turned back toward the raw slab of meat sitting on the cutting board. "One of these days I'm going to have dessert first, though."

"You rebel." He tried to picture the rule follower he'd always known bucking tradition. The only time she'd ever come close to cutting loose was the night of their prom when they all went skinny-dipping. And look how that turned out. Since then Em had toed the line. The thought of getting caught doing something she shouldn't kept her out of trouble through college. Now that she was a teacher, she said she had to set a good example for the kids.

No doubt her wild side was still there. It had just been buried under a tall, teetering stack of obligations and responsibilities.

"Are you going to mock me, or do you want to learn how to smoke a brisket?" She planted a hand on her hip and studied him, her green eyes twinkling with humor.

"Lead the way, Chef Porter." He picked up the knife and grabbed hold of the meat.

"You want to leave a little bit of fat for flavor, but you can trim off the big pieces like that one there." Em pointed and he sliced where she directed.

When he was done trimming, she had him cover the cut of meat with a mixture of fresh-ground pepper and kosher salt.

"I started the smoker before you got here. Let's go check the temp, then get this baby going." She led the way to the back deck, where wisps of smoke floated from the sides of her dad's old smoker.

Justin did what she said, checking the temp, making sure there were enough chips to feed the flames, and finally, adding the cut of brisket to the rack.

"Do we get to take a break now?" he asked. "All that hard work has me craving some of that sweet tea I know you've probably got in the fridge."

She turned on him, her lips curled into a sassy grin. "All that work? We still have beans to heat, cornbread to bake, and cabbage to shred for my grandma's famous coleslaw."

Justin put a hand on her shoulder and steered her toward the sliding glass door. "One glass of tea won't take much time at all, and it might just earn you another sniff of Jenny's chocolate cake."

"You drive a hard bargain." She shrugged out from under his hand. "Somebody ought to make sure that cake's edible, you know. Add a pinch off the corner so I can test it, and you've got yourself a deal."

"As long as I do the pinching." He could think of several other things he'd rather pinch for Em than the corner of a chocolate cake, but none of those things were on the table. When he was with the guys the other night, Decker mentioned something about seeing Em out on a date at a local steakhouse. The need to ask her about it weighed on his mind, but that wasn't the kind of thing he could work into the conversation. At least not without making her wonder how he'd heard about her date and why he'd suddenly taken an interest in her love life.

They'd never kept things from each other before, which meant maybe the guy she went out with wasn't serious at all. Or it could mean the exact opposite. What if Em had found someone she really liked but didn't want to tell him because she knew it would mean pulling back? His stomach rolled with his indecision.

"You coming?" Em stood in the doorframe of the sliding glass door.

"Yeah, right behind you." He followed her into the house. Tonight. After dinner, he'd see if she wanted to sit on the swing on the front porch and he'd ask her if she was seeing anyone. If she said no, nothing would change. He swallowed hard, not wanting to consider the alternative. If she said yes . . . damn, he didn't know what the hell he'd do if she said yes.

Emmeline

Justin pushed back from the table and clasped his hands over his stomach. "That was absolutely delicious. Probably one of my top five meals, maybe even top three."

Warmth flooded Em's cheeks at the praise. "You did most of the cooking."

"I only did what you told me to do." He took in a deep breath. "I'm so full, I don't think I could eat another bite."

"We still have dessert," she reminded him.

"Texas sheet cake," Mom said. "I can't remember the last time someone made me dinner in my own kitchen."

Em's gaze drifted between her parents. Her dad was having a good day. The tremors that usually got the best of him, especially around mealtime, seemed to be held at bay. She'd been a little worried about how he'd feel trying to eat an entire meal in front of Justin. The last thing she wanted was for him to feel embarrassed or uncomfortable, especially in his own home.

"Think you could make me some coffee to go with that cake, sweetheart?" Her dad asked.

"Of course." Em got up from the table and stacked her dad's plate on top of her own.

Justin pushed back from the table. "I'll help with dishes."

"Why don't you men head into the family room?" Mom suggested. "I'll help clean up and we'll bring dessert and coffee to you."

"Come on, Justin." Her dad slid his chair back and stood.

"You sure?" Justin looked to Em. She nodded. Her dad probably wanted to get him alone to relive the glory days. He'd always been invested in Justin's career. She'd been waiting for the conversation to turn toward bull riding during dinner, but her dad was probably saving it for after.

"You go on ahead. I'll come save you in a few minutes."

Justin followed her dad from the dining room, and she stared after him.

"You should invite him over for dinner more often," Mom said.

"He hasn't exactly been around much over the past ten years." Em set the dirty dishes down on the counter.

"He's here now."

"Exactly. That's why I invited him."

"That's not what I meant." Mom gave her that kind of look that said what she meant went way deeper than what she said.

Em wasn't sure how to take it. "What do you mean?"

"I mean"—Mom set down the dishes and reached for Em's hands—"maybe it's time you and Justin need to think about whether or not you can see each other as more than friends. Don't take this the wrong way, sweetheart, but your brisket's not that good."

"Mom!" Em jerked her hands away from her mother's.

Her mom put her hand on the counter. "There's nothing wrong with your cooking, but if all a man like Justin wanted was a home-cooked meal once in a while, he could head down to the Smokestack. Now I know your dad enjoys his company, but why do you think Justin keeps coming back?"

Em squinted at her mother. "Justin and I have known each other for over twenty years."

"That's right." Mom put the stopper in the sink and turned on the hot water.

"We're friends, that's all." Even the idea that there could be something more between them seemed too ludicrous to say out loud. There may have been a time back in high school when she thought about him as more than a friend, but that had passed. While the other boys stayed after school to play baseball or took girls mudding in their trucks, Justin headed home to train with his brother and dad.

Years of working on his family's ranch turned his body into a mass of muscles. He changed from the scrawny smart-ass to a guy who drew more than a few of her friends' attention, and for a sliver of time she thought maybe they could take things between them a step further. Then she came to her senses and realized that would be the best way to ruin their friendship. And who would get custody of Decker and Knox when they broke up?

No, she and Justin would never work out. Not because she didn't enjoy his company. Not because they didn't share the same sense of humor. Definitely not because they couldn't finish each other's sentences. When she thought about the kind of man she wanted to spend the rest of her life with, Justin Forza checked all the boxes.

All of them except one.

Even if she found him irresistibly attractive, even if she thought he was the most hilarious man alive, he was a bull rider.

"Mom, I don't know why you'd even think such a thought. Out of everyone in my life, you ought to know I could never fall for a bull rider. Just look at what Daddy's put you through." Em braced herself against the counter and glanced over at her mother.

"Honey . . ." Mom reached out as if to smooth Em's hair away from her cheek.

"Don't." Em stepped away. "I'll be back to clean up in a few minutes. I need to get some air."

She found Justin and her dad poring over old photo albums in her dad's office. It was good to see her father sitting behind his big oak desk. He hardly ever ventured through the doorway anymore. He'd told her once it was too hard to be reminded of what he'd lost.

"That right there was a ride for the record books." Her dad's finger skimmed over a page of old photos. "I thought that bull was going to knock me into next month."

Justin shook his head, his eyes full of admiration. "They inducted that bull into the hall of fame a couple of years ago. There were only a handful of guys who managed to get their eight seconds on his back. You were one of them."

Em clasped her hands together as her dad's face lit up from within.

"That bull you rode the second round in Cheyenne was from his line," her dad said.

"Habanero's Heat?" Justin asked. "I rode him for eighty-four points."

Seeing the two of them bonding over their rodeo days cemented the thought in her brain. Justin would never give it up, never walk away on his own. It would take something like the accident her dad suffered through—or maybe something even worse—to get him to see how he was putting his life in danger every time he climbed onto the back of a bull.

Decker's offer rattled around in her head. It might be

the only chance she had of saving Justin from himself. Before she let herself think about the ramifications, she cleared her throat, announcing her presence.

"Guess what I just did?"

Justin and her dad glanced up, the two of them like peas in a pod.

"What's that, sweetheart?" her father asked.

"I won a trip to some island off the coast of Texas. Ten days in paradise and I need someone to go with me. Justin, are you interested?"

10

Justin

"Tell me again about this trip you won." Justin sat on the swing on the Porters' front porch with Em next to him. "You said it was a contest of some sort?"

"That's right." Em's fingers combed through the fringe of the throw pillow she held on her lap.

"Where did you hear about it?"

Em pushed the swing with her foot and they drifted backward. "It's a teacher thing. One of my students must have nominated me and I won."

"That's great. You deserve some downtime. Are you sure you can fit it in this summer, though? When's Keisha's wedding?" He couldn't understand why she couldn't save the trip for sometime later when she could find someone else to go with her.

"The wedding's not until the end of July. With Georgie's baby due in August, if I want to go, I really need to go soon." She tucked a foot up underneath her. "Don't you want to come with me?"

Ten days with Em in a tropical paradise? The very idea

made him want to run home and pack a bag right then and there. "I don't know. I've got training and PT if I want to get back to competing in the next few weeks."

"You could train down there. We could run on the beach together and you could still meet with your trainer through a virtual appointment."

"Why the rush?" The thought of spending time alone with Em on some faraway island begged him to say yes. Especially now, when he might be running out of time. But his dad was counting on him. How could he leave when there was so much at stake?

"I thought it would be fun to spend my birthday somewhere different with you." Em shrugged.

Justin's stomach churned. She hated celebrating her birthday. For her, the date didn't just mark the day she was born. It was also the day of her dad's last ride. The one that put him into a medical-induced coma for six weeks and left him a shell of the man he'd been before.

That day seemed like it could have been a few months ago instead of almost twenty years. His mom had dropped him and Em off at the community pool that day to meet up with Knox and Decker. The four of them spent the afternoon playing Marco Polo and getting yelled at by the lifeguards to stop running on the deck.

Em's mom wasn't supposed to pick them up until four but had shown up just after two with tearstained cheeks and Georgie in the back seat. Word spread fast through a town the size of Blewit, and by dinnertime everyone knew the worst had happened.

Her mom had jumped on the first flight to Denver and Em's grandma and grandpa came to stay at the house. With her birthday overshadowed by the tragic accident, Em didn't get to blow out candles or unwrap a single gift. Justin rode his bike six miles to bring her a Little Debbie zebra cake. He was the only one who even remembered it was her birthday.

Since then, he'd made it a point to try to be in town for her birthday, or at least send her something obnoxious to let her know he was thinking about her on her special day. This year, he had the opportunity to do more. She was giving him the chance to spend time together—something he'd been dreaming about for years.

How could he turn her down?

"Let me talk to my dad and my trainer and see what I can figure out. You said it's all expenses paid?" He looked up to where some industrious spider had built a web that covered the corner of the porch.

"That's right. Oh, and guess what I heard about the island where we're going."

He didn't like guessing games. "You know I'm no good at guessing. Just tell me."

"Does the name Chick Darville mean anything to you?"

He must not have heard her right. "I'm sorry, who?"

"Chick Darville." Em waved a dismissive hand. "His name came up on a list of famous residents of Paradise Island."

"*The* Chick Darville?" Justin's mouth gaped. "The only man in history to earn two perfect rides?"

"Oh, wow. That's impressive. I just knew he was a bull rider."

Justin got up from the swing. "He's not 'just a bull rider,' he's one of the best who's ever competed."

"What happened to him?"

"No one really knows. He won back-to-back world championships, then disappeared. I thought he moved down south and started training riders. Dad told me once he thought he moved to Brazil. Why would he be living on an island off the coast of Texas? That doesn't make sense."

"Maybe you can ask him yourself if you meet him." Em shrugged.

"When do you need to know if I can go with you or not?" If her offer hadn't already been so damn appealing, it was now. Justin had to figure out a way to carve out the time to go. Ten days alone with Em at the beach, plus the chance to meet one of his idols, was a once-in-a-lifetime opportunity. He wasn't stupid enough to pass that up.

"The sooner the better. I don't have anyone else to ask. Keisha's got too many things to do for the wedding, and Georgie is too pregnant to travel. You're my last hope."

"If I can't go, you could always ask Decker or Knox." Justin didn't want to turn her down, but he also didn't want Em to miss out on the trip if he couldn't figure out a way to make it happen on his end.

Em got to her feet. "Knox is too busy on tour and there's no way Decker would go without Miranda. You saw the two of them the other night. They're practically joined at the hip. You know how he gets when he starts dating someone new."

"Yeah, he gets pretty intense."

"If it works out for you to go, great. If not, no hard feelings."

"What about your mom? A girls' trip?"

"Like she'd leave this close to her first grandchild's arrival?" Em shook her head. "She's already got a bag packed just in case Georgie goes into labor early. There's no way she'd go so far away right now."

"Okay." Justin put his hands up, palms out. "I get it. I'll see what I can do. Ten days is a long time to be away right now. I'm not sure my dad will go for it, but I'll see what he says."

"Sounds good." Em followed him to the edge of the porch, her bare feet slapping against the wooden floorboards.

He looked down, the sight of her pink-painted toes making him wonder what they'd look like buried in sand. Would ten days in paradise make any difference in the way she saw him? This was his chance to spend some time alone with her and maybe the perfect opportunity to finally come clean about his feelings.

"I'll see what kind of mood he's in when I get home tonight."

"Hold up a sec." Em disappeared through the front door and returned a few minutes later holding a brown paper lunch bag. "I packed up some leftovers for your lunch tomorrow. Brisket, beans, coleslaw, zucchini bread . . . it's all there. Except for the cake. That's staying here with me."

He took the bag and pulled her in for a hug. "Thanks, Em. I had a good time tonight."

"Dinner's on you next time," she muttered against his chest.

Maybe a birthday dinner. He could almost feel the ocean breeze blowing over their skin as he pictured them sitting on the beach for a candlelit dinner to celebrate. Surely the place they were staying would have a chef who could whip up some kind of surf and turf, and he'd follow it up with a slice of chocolate birthday cake to commemorate her big day.

"You got it." He gave her shoulders a final squeeze, then grabbed his hat off the table. "Talk to you tomorrow?"

She nodded and waited for him to back down the driveway before she headed inside.

Justin turned toward home, already thinking of how he could frame a beach vacation as an opportunity his dad couldn't turn down. But all he could think about was Em.

Em in a swimsuit standing in the surf. Em in a towel fresh out of the shower. Em in a sexy nightgown leaning over him on the single bed in their hotel room.

Damn. Come hell or high water, he was going to figure out a way to join her on that vacation.

He had to.

11

Emmeline

Em clutched the armrest of the narrow airplane seat. She'd never minded flying, but this trip was putting her to the test and they'd been in the air for only forty-five minutes. Thanks to a summer thunderstorm, the tiny plane had bounced around before getting up above the clouds. Nothing seemed to faze Justin. He had his seat leaned all the way back next to her and the soft sounds coming from his mouth sounded an awful lot like light snoring.

She supposed he got used to sleeping in a variety of conditions during all the time he spent on the road. Hadn't he told her as much the night they went to Knox's concert? It had been only a couple of weeks ago, but it felt like months. So much had happened since then.

Before she forgot, she pulled the pink rock out of the side pocket of her purse and lowered her tray table. The kids would get a kick out of seeing Rocky midflight. She leaned him against the back of the seat in front of her. He toppled over before she could snap the photo.

"Need a hand?" Justin cracked an eyelid.

"Sorry, did I wake you up?"

"Nah. I was just catching a few winks before we land. Here, let me prop him up." Justin set Rocky upright and nestled a bag of honey-roasted peanuts on either side of his base to hold him steady.

Em rolled her eyes. "If he didn't look like a penis before, he sure does now, sitting between two bags of nuts."

Justin laughed. "Hell, I didn't think about that."

"Right." Em drew out the word. "Sure, you didn't."

"Honest." Justin gave her a playful elbow to the ribs.

"Maybe I'll wait until we get there and just take a picture of Rocky by a palm tree." She slid him into the velvet pouch she kept him in and tucked him back into her purse.

"I can't believe you brought a rock with us on vacation." Justin pushed the button to raise the back of his seat.

"The kids look forward to his adventures. Rocky's got more followers on social media than any of my accounts."

"Are you sure it's just kids who are interested?" Justin asked. "You've got to admit, Rocky could attract a certain kind of audience."

"I don't think there's an audience of people who are attracted to penis-shaped rocks," Em whispered.

"You might be surprised." Justin tried to stretch out his legs, but the narrow space didn't allow for much room.

Em shifted her feet to the left. "You can share my foot space if you need to. One of the benefits of being five foot two is not needing much in the way of legroom."

"Thanks, Em." He moved his left leg and extended it into the space in front of her seat. "Have you figured out what you want to do while we're there?"

"Yeah, actually I made a list." She leaned forward, reaching for the bag at her feet. "I figured you didn't have time to look into any of the outings since you've been so busy."

Justin leaned over and pulled the bag out for her. "You've got short arms too."

"Thanks for pointing that out. Not all of us were blessed with long limbs." Something about Justin's legs stretching over to take up her personal space set her on edge. Not in a bad way.

But this was just Justin. Justin who used to put garter snakes in her backpack and tie the laces of her sneakers together so she'd trip when she got up from her desk. She obviously needed to start dating again if the sight of his foot next to hers had her thinking about him as anything beyond one of her oldest and dearest friends.

"Hey, I like your short arms and legs. It means more room for me when I sit next to you on a plane."

"Stop trying to make me feel better." Em snatched the notebook out of her bag, more thrown by her own reaction than Justin's teasing.

He tapped his fingers against his thigh. "What kind of activities do they have at the resort?"

"Hmm?" Em couldn't believe she'd gotten him to come this far. What was he going to do when he realized there was no resort, just a two-bedroom bungalow Decker's dad had bought as a vacation home? She'd struggled with whether to tell him over the past few days. As far as she knew, there had never been lies between them. But was it warranted when a little white lie could mean the difference between life and death?

That might seem extreme, but that's how she viewed the two options facing Justin. Either he walked away from competing, turned his back on the burden of expectation his dad had saddled him with for all these years . . . or . . . he returned to competing and risked a lifelong injury, possibly even death.

She could justify the little white lie by telling herself he needed time away from the influence of his dad to make a decision. But what was he going to do when he found out?

"Is there snorkeling? Do they have one of those swim-up bars where you can sit in the pool and order a drink? I'll be ready for an ice-cold beer when we get there. How about you?" He waved a hand in front of her face. "Earth to Em."

"Sorry. I was trying to remember the name of a place a friend told me we should go for dinner." She flipped open the notebook, revealing a page full of scribbled notes.

Decker had sent her a text with the address of the house and the key code for the front door. They'd have to stop at the store on the way there if they wanted to pick up some food. Maybe she could ease Justin into the truth by stopping at a bar or restaurant on the way. And what? Getting him liquored up so he wouldn't care that she'd lied to him about winning a trip for two?

"About those activities . . ." Justin prompted.

"Yeah, um, let's see. There's zip-lining if you want to try that. I also found a place where we can rent four-wheelers and visit a turtle sanctuary. I thought that sounded pretty cool."

"Leave it to you to want to save the turtles on vacation." He was teasing, but the gentle smile he gave her showed her he didn't mean anything by it.

"If it weren't for dumbasses tossing their plastic stuff into the ocean, the turtles wouldn't need to be saved," she shot back. "You've been known to save an animal or two. Didn't you bring home a seven-legged tarantula and almost give your mom a heart attack in fifth grade?"

He shrugged. "It was right after we read about that girl who saved a goose by building it a fake wing. I thought I'd make him a prosthetic leg out of Popsicle sticks and he could go on to live a happy, full, spidery life."

"It's a miracle you didn't get bitten and lose your arm." He was always putting others first, even the eight-legged kind. It was no wonder he was willing to risk it all to try to win that championship for his dad.

"Hey, do they have big bugs on the island? I read that some of the spiders down in Padre can be as big as a dinner plate."

Em shuddered. "Please tell me you're joking."

"Fine, I'm joking. But I bet they have snakes. You remember the time Decker and I went camping by the Neches River? He picked a spot right along the water to set up our tent."

Em had lost track of all the antics her friends had gotten into over the years. "What happened?"

"A bunch of cottonmouths thought it was the perfect place, too. I've never run so fast." He let out a laugh.

"With all the crap you've pulled, it's a miracle you're still alive. You know that, don't you?"

He studied her with eyes that could go from blue, as bright as a cloudless sky, to a light green that reminded her of the jade pendant her dad had brought back from a rodeo he'd traveled to in Alaska.

"Look, Em, I know you're worried about me."

"I'm not the only one." She shut the notebook and held it to her chest. Her heart thumped so hard she could hear the *boom-boom-boom* echo through her ears.

Justin rested his hand on her thigh. "I'm going to be okay."

Her gaze settled on the back of his hand. The weight of it on her leg made her hyperaware of his touch. His hands were strong, capable, his fingers long and straight. Except for the ring finger on his left hand, which he'd broken back in grade school.

The feel of his hand on her thigh caused an unfamiliar sensation deep in her belly. Like a shot of whiskey burned all the way down, the feeling seemed to burn its way up.

Heat flickered in her stomach, then slowly made its way up her chest, across her neck, over her cheeks.

"Hey, is that where we're headed?" Justin moved his hand and leaned toward the window.

Em took in a shaky breath and glanced out the small oval window. They'd been flying above the clouds since they took off. Now the plane had started its descent. The wispy clouds gave way to the bright rays of the sun. She squinted against the glare of the reflection on the water.

"Looks like it." They'd be on the ground in fifteen minutes. It was too late to turn back. For the millionth time since she first mentioned the trip to Justin, she hoped with all her heart she hadn't made a mistake.

Justin

Justin snagged his duffel from the baggage carousel, then set it next to Em. "I'm sure yours will be out any minute."

"I hope so." Em rocked back on her heels while they waited. She'd always been more anxious than him.

"Relax. We're supposed to be in vacation mode now, aren't we?"

She attempted a smile, but the nervous glance she cast at the bags passing on the conveyor belt told him she hadn't succumbed to the pull of the beach yet. Granted, the Brownsville airport wasn't exactly his idea of paradise, either. Em said something about catching a shuttle to a ferry that would take them where they needed to go. He hadn't paid too much attention to the details. This was her trip, and he was happy to follow her lead.

Once he'd made up his mind to take her up on her offer of ten days off the grid, ten days of getting his head and his heart back in line with his goals, he couldn't wait to board the plane. His dad hadn't been quite as enthusiastic until Doc Lindell gave his blessing. Then he got on board when the doc said some time away might speed up his recovery process. Justin fully expected his dad to meet him at the airport the day they returned and drive him over to get on the back of a practice bull that night. With his dad champing at the bit to sign that new sponsor, it wasn't an unrealistic expectation.

"It's not here. I think they lost it." Em nodded toward the carousel where the last couple of lonely bags circled. "Looks like most of the other passengers have claimed their bags. I don't think any more are coming."

"It was a direct flight. How could they have lost it between DFW and here?" Justin glanced around the newly constructed terminal. "Let's go check with the lost luggage office and see if we can fill out a claim."

Em trailed behind as he made his way over to the counter.

Fifteen minutes later, they'd located her bag. Too bad it was still sitting on the ground at Dallas Fort Worth International Airport. The clerk filled out the paperwork and told them to check back the next day. Em's shoulders sagged, and Justin figured it would be up to him to cheer her up. A giant margarita might be a good way to start.

"Where are we supposed to meet the shuttle?" He slung the strap of his duffel over his shoulder and waited while she consulted her notes.

"Ground transportation is that way." Em tucked the notebook in her bag. "Let's get out of the airport and maybe we can find a place to grab a bite before we head over to the island."

"I'm sure they'll have more people coming in tomorrow. We can pick up a toothbrush and a pair of pj's for

you, and I bet they'll have your bag at the resort before
we're ready to head to the beach in the morning."

"Yeah, hopefully." She smiled, but it didn't reach her
eyes.

Something was going on with her, and Justin intended
to find out exactly what it was. She'd sold him on the trip,
saying it would give him a chance to clear his head, but
maybe she was the one in need of some downtime. Em did
such a great job of putting up a front that he sometimes
forgot about everything she had going on.

Em came to a stop by a sign for Padre Transportation.
"This is it."

"Where's the bus?" Justin glanced up and down the
curb, where hotel shuttles and a variety of buses and vans
idled.

"I don't know. I'm sure another one will be along soon."
She checked her watch.

Justin's stomach growled.

"Are you hungry? I've got some protein bars in my bag."

"Yeah, those peanuts didn't make much of a dent."

She held out a peanut butter and chocolate protein bar.
"Here you go. I'm sure it won't be long before the shuttle
gets here. There's a great restaurant I want to try right by
where the ferry docks, so don't ruin your appetite."

"You know me, Em. I can always eat." He peeled the
wrapper back and worked his way through the protein bar
while they waited. He'd worn his standard jeans and cowboy boots on the plane. Now the heat engulfed him, making him eager to switch into a pair of shorts and some
flip-flops.

Em's foot tapped on the concrete curb and she checked
her watch for the umpteenth time.

"Is this the only way to get to the ferry?" Brownsville,
Texas, wasn't so small that there couldn't be another way.

"You want to call the resort and see if they can give us an alternate?"

She slid her phone out of her pocket. "Give me just a minute, okay?"

"I'm already on island time. Take as long as you need."

Em tapped on her phone and paced the stretch of sidewalk. The woman needed to relax. She was on summer vacation. He couldn't remember the last time he'd had more than a day or two off, unless he'd been recovering from a major injury. He'd always liked it that way, but he might be able to get used to this.

While Em held the phone to her ear, he set his bag down on a nearby bench and leaned back against the concrete pillar behind him. He pulled his cowboy hat down over his eyes and closed them, then breathed through the pain radiating out from his shoulder. His dad focused more on the physical aspects of bull riding: building strength, flexibility training, and reaction times. Over the years, the physical part became second nature.

Now Justin spent more of his time and effort on the mental aspect of the ride. His shoulder might not be at 100 percent, but he was used to working around injuries. If he could get his head in the game and figure out how to get into the right mindset, it wouldn't matter what kind of physical issues he had to deal with. Riding a bull was 10 percent talent, 10 percent luck, and 80 percent being in the right headspace.

The next week and a half would give him the time and space he needed to work on the piece that had been missing. Em was right to push him into taking this break. By the time he got on the plane to head home, he planned to be in the exact frame of mind he needed to get back into the competition.

He opened his eyes and shot a glance to where Em

stood, the phone pressed to her ear. Her shoulders curved forward a bit and her teeth held her bottom lip captive. Maybe he'd also find a way to hint at his feelings while they were here.

He was so close to reaching his goal, so close to being where he needed to be to come clean with her. But what if she didn't feel the same? What if she wasn't open to the idea of exploring a relationship beyond friendship? Things were always so comfortable between them, he'd never doubted they could easily slip past the boundaries of friendship and into new territory. He just needed to find a way to convince her to give him a shot.

She tucked her phone back into her bag. "Come on, Justin. I just found us a ride."

12

Emmeline

The taxi bounced over a pothole in the middle of the road, sending Em flying into Justin's side. They'd been in the car for forty-five minutes but had yet to catch a glimpse of the ocean. A traffic jam on the way out of the airport tied them up for a half hour and now an accident up ahead threatened to set them back even more.

"How much farther to the ferry?" Justin asked.

The cabdriver glanced in the rearview mirror and held up his hand. "Five minutes."

Justin leaned close. "Hasn't he been saying that for the past twenty minutes?"

Em closed her eyes and breathed in the scent of gasoline and exhaust. In addition to not having very good shocks, the cab she'd picked also didn't have air-conditioning. Sweat beaded along her hairline and trickled down her back. It seemed like the universe was out to get her. Or at least out to make sure she had a hard time getting Justin off the mainland.

He was rolling with it, though. She thought it would be

difficult to convince him to leave his daily training sessions and physical therapist at home. She'd almost caved and told him the truth about her plan on more than one occasion, but then something flipped. He went from making excuses about why taking time off to go play at the beach wouldn't work, to actually looking forward to it.

Studying him across the back seat of the cab, she wondered what had changed his mind. He leaned against the seat and gazed out the window. The hot breeze ruffled his hair. For a split second, she wanted to reach out and smooth it away from his forehead. His eyelids hovered at half-mast and a relaxed smile played across his lips.

If she didn't know him better, she might think Justin was just a tourist on a well-earned vacation without a care in the world. The only things he was missing were a Tommy Bahama shirt and a pair of Ray-Bans.

So what if things hadn't gone smoothly so far? They had a lot of time stretching ahead of them and she'd be foolish not to use it. Her worry for Justin might have been the reason that brought her to the southern tip of Texas, but she could use the time away to figure out a few things for herself. Such as coming to terms with the fact she'd be twenty-nine next week.

She always thought she'd be married by now, settled into a three-bedroom ranch house on a couple of acres. There'd be room enough for a horse or two, but not so much land that she'd have to spend more time taking care of the property than enjoying it. Her parents hadn't always lived in town. When she was younger, they'd lived on almost two hundred acres. Her dad ran a small cattle operation and rented the rest out to a local farmer up the road.

Em and her sister used to love spending the summers running around the ranch, exploring the creek that divided the property, and taking care of the calves that were born each spring. All that changed toward the end of her dad's career. Before he suffered his debilitating concussion, he'd had other injuries. The kind that prevented him from putting in the kind of physical labor that living off the land required.

They'd sold the ranch and moved into town. That's when she'd met Justin. He'd saved her in so many ways the first day she walked into the classroom and he tugged on her braids. Being the new girl in a school where everyone had known each other since preschool terrified her. Then Justin took her under his wing. Decker and Knox didn't have a choice, since both of them thought Justin had lassoed and hung the moon.

Now it was her turn to save him.

"Whatcha thinking about?" Justin turned toward her.

"Nothing much."

"Come on, I know that look." He made a fist and reached out to playfully knock on her temple. "There's a lot going on in there, I can tell."

She'd never admit what she was really thinking. It would freak him the hell out if she said she was worried about turning twenty-nine and having so little to show for it. He didn't need the added pressure. His brother Jake had been younger than Justin was now when he'd won back-to-back world championships. There was no doubt in Em's mind that Justin already felt like he'd failed since he'd be thirty in the fall and hadn't managed to clench a title.

"I'm wondering what kind of fresh fish I should order for dinner." She'd keep things light, at least for now.

"Hmm. That sounds like it deserves some serious consideration. Do you think we'll have a chance to go fishing while we're down here?"

Her stomach twisted. She had to tell him the truth. That there was no resort, no fancy hotel with unlimited activities, no all-you-can-eat beachside buffet.

"Did I ever tell you about the time my dad took Jake and me deep-sea fishing off the coast of Florida?" Justin set his elbow on the doorframe and rested his cheek on his hand.

Eager for a change of subject, Em cocked her head. "Nope, I don't think you have."

"You know what an ass my dad can be," Justin started. "The man is hell on wheels and like a devil when he gets on the back of a bull."

Em nodded. That was a fairly accurate description of Mr. Forza as far as she was concerned.

"Hell, he got on that boat and spent the whole time hanging overboard. Jake and I had a blast, reeling in one fish after another. The captain said he'd never seen anything like it. We barely had to toss the line into the water before a grouper or a snapper would hop on it and almost jump into the boat."

"And your dad missed it all?" Em asked.

Justin chuckled. "Took him three days to be able to stand up straight without holding on to something. He's got no sea legs at all. Sure can make a man humble when he finds himself so far out of his element he doesn't know what hit him."

Em sat with that thought for a moment, an image of Justin's dad with his head hanging over the bow of a boat playing through her brain.

The taxi came to a stop. Em glanced out the open window and caught a whiff of something salty and damp. They'd reached the ferry. One step closer to having to come clean with Justin.

Justin

Justin wrapped a hand around a post and leaned over to peer into the ocean. The sea spray hit his cheek. He could taste the salt in the air.

The last time he'd been near the ocean might have been the fishing trip he'd been telling Em about. Except for a few events in Florida each year, he didn't get the chance to compete anywhere near a beach. Now, with the turquoise water of the Gulf of Mexico underneath him and the promise of ten days of relaxation stretching ahead, he wondered why he hadn't taken time off like this before. The sun hovered at the edge of the horizon, sinking into a blur of reds and oranges and yellows. They'd been traveling most of the day. It would be nice to kick off his boots and find somewhere to put his feet up.

"Look, I bet that's where we'll dock." Em came up next to him, her arm stretched out toward a blurry spot off in the distance.

"How can you see that far? All I can make out is a darker spot surrounded by what looks like miles of beach."

"I might have short arms, but I've got twenty-twenty vision." She smirked, her lips curving up into a smile.

The boat motored closer to the shore. Besides another couple on the other side of the deck, they were the only people on the ferry. Justin figured anyone else heading to the resort must have caught an earlier boat.

"Hey, Em, any idea how many resorts are on the island?"

"Um, I'm not sure . . ."

The man looked up. "Sorry, I couldn't help but overhear. There aren't any resorts on the island."

Justin glanced over. "Excuse me? This is Paradise Island, right? We're staying at the . . . what's the name of the place we're staying, Em?"

Her eyes grew wide. "Um, it's not exactly a resort."

Not exactly a resort. What did that make it?

The man stood and held out a hand to help the woman next to him as the boat slowed and approached a wooden dock. "There aren't any commercial properties on the island except for vacation rentals and a few restaurants. Are you sure you got on the right ferry?"

"Yes, we're on the right ferry. Thank you." Em grabbed Justin's arm. "Hey, can I talk to you for a second?"

The man nodded. "Enjoy the rest of your evening." Then he and the woman with him moved past them to stand at the front of the boat.

"What's going on?" Justin studied Em's eyes, trying to figure out what she might be hiding.

"Not here. Let's get off the boat first." She tugged him toward the ramp that stretched from the dock to the boat.

He followed, the carefree attitude he'd been trying on falling by the wayside. A muscle in his jaw twitched, and he took in a breath through his nose. The smell of something cooking on a grill drifted past, making his mouth water. The only thing he'd eaten all day were two bags of peanuts and a protein bar.

Em turned around, her mouth drawn in a tight line. "About the place we're staying."

"We do have somewhere to sleep tonight, right?"

"Yes."

"Good." At the moment, that was all he cared about. That and getting something that smelled like a fresh-grilled burger into his stomach as soon as possible. "Let's figure out where that smell's coming from and you can fill me in over a loaded burger. Deal?"

"Deal." She wrapped her fingers around his arm, and he took off, letting his nose lead the way.

The pavement gave way to a gravel trail. Justin followed it through some scrubby bushes until the gravel turned into sugar-fine sand. They emerged onto a stretch of beach surrounded by squatty palms and a variety of other vegetation that blocked out the rest of the island. A structure sat about a hundred yards ahead. Smoke from a barbecue drifted into the air.

"That's where we're heading." Justin set off across the expanse of sand that separated him from the divine scent.

The building came into focus as they got closer. Bright teal siding provided protection on one side while the other opened up to a view of the ocean. The grass roof made him think of a giant tiki hut on the beach, which was exactly what it looked like. Strings of twinkle lights sparkled and outlined the perimeter of the seating area, and the low country music coming from the speakers made him feel right at home.

"Are you hungry, Em?" He stopped at the edge of a well-worn deck.

"Starving."

"Me, too. I'm going to find out where we can sit and how to get some food." He set his bag down on the sand and headed toward the covered bar. His stomach twisted as the smell from the grill grew stronger. The interior of the building glowed from strands of twinkle lights crisscrossing the ceiling. Justin was too intent on figuring out how to get dinner to pay much attention to his surroundings.

A woman with dark, curly hair grabbed two menus as he approached the bar. "Feel free to sit anywhere. I'll be over in a few minutes to take your order."

"Thanks." Grateful for the menus, he turned and made his way back to Em.

"Do you want to sit closer to the water?" She looked out at the tables by the edge of the eating area.

"How about that table over there?" Most of the tables surrounded a firepit in the center of the beach, but Justin eyed one sitting a little farther out. It would give them a bit of privacy while he pulled the truth out of Em. Clearly there was something she wasn't telling him. She'd been acting strange all day, and he was ready to get to the bottom of it.

"That's perfect." She led the way across the beach. Sinking into the chair, she kicked off her shoes.

"Feel good?" The sight of her swirling her bright-pink-painted toes around in the sand made him wish again that he hadn't worn his boots.

"Feels amazing." She tilted her head back and looked up at the sky. "You should take off your boots and try it. Your blood pressure will drop by at least twenty points, I swear."

Before he had the chance to respond, the bartender with the curly hair came over. She had on a pair of cutoff denim shorts and a bright, floral tank top. "Welcome to A Cowboy in Paradise. I'm Claudia and I'll be taking care of you tonight. Can I start you off with something to drink?"

"What'll it be, Em?" He waited for her to order first.

"What's your most popular frozen drink?" Em hadn't even glanced at the menu. Kudos to her for tapping into her dormant adventurous side.

"Well, there's the Bucking Beachcomber. We layer piña colada with daiquiri, then add a layer of blue Bahama Mama on top."

"That sounds delicious." Em nodded. "I'll take the largest one you've got."

"And for you?" The bartender turned her attention to Justin.

He'd been about to order a beer, but something frozen sounded good. "Why don't you give me one of those, too?"

"You got it. I'll be back in a few with your drinks." She turned toward the bar.

"I didn't know you liked frozen fruity cocktails," Em said.

"When in Rome . . ." Justin leaned over to kick off his boots. He set them upright in the sand next to his chair, then peeled his socks off and tucked them into his boots. Sinking his toes into the sand, which was still warm from the sun, he let out a deep, appreciative sigh.

"I told you it would feel good."

"You were right." He lifted his gaze to catch hers. "Now why don't you tell me what the hell we're doing here and where we're staying."

13

◦ ❤ ◦

Emmeline

Em tried to swallow, but her throat had gone dry. She knew this moment would come. Justin wasn't stupid, and it was only sheer luck and the fact he was so tired that he hadn't asked more questions before now.

"So, we're not staying at a resort, exactly."

His eyes narrowed the tiniest bit, and his jaw went tight. "I kind of figured that part out already. Want to tell me where exactly we *are* staying?"

She wasn't ready to give him all the details. If he knew Decker and Knox were involved, he'd probably swim back to the mainland and walk all the way home if he had to. Best to let it out a little at a time. She was sure that once he'd had a few days with nothing but the sun and the surf to keep him company, he'd realize how much he needed a break. Then she could start broaching the subject of his return to the ring.

"It's a vacation home." That wasn't a lie. Decker said his dad was going to remodel and use it as a place to vacation.

"So, you won a stay at a vacation home?"

"That's right." It would be easier to let him jump to his

own conclusions. Her stomach twinged. She didn't like lying to her best friend, even if it was in his best interest. It wasn't exactly a lie, though, and she did plan on telling him the whole truth.

Later.

After he'd had a chance to relax. He'd been so stressed since he got injured. He deserved some time away from the pressure.

"Why did you tell me we were going to a resort?" Justin fiddled with the paper napkin ring that had been wrapped around his silverware. He'd always had a tendency to fidget, especially when he was uncomfortable.

"I didn't say we were going to a resort." She bit her lip and shrugged a shoulder. "You just assumed."

"You let me assume. Why?" He shifted his glance from his fingers to her face. His eyes drilled into her, pinning her in place.

"Here we go. Two Bucking Beachcombers." Claudia set their drinks down on the table. Saved by giant cocktails.

Em reached for her glass. Holy hell. When she asked for the largest size they had, she wasn't expecting a container the size of a fishbowl. It was going to require two hands to lift the monstrosity anywhere near her lips.

"Have you had a chance to look over the menu?" Claudia asked.

"I'll take the Western Rancher salad." Em handed over her menu.

"The Bronc Burger for me, please. Medium-rare, with fries on the side." Justin gave the server a warm smile.

"I'll have those right out. Just so you know, we have live music tonight. Our house band will start up in about twenty minutes."

"Great, thanks." Justin glanced toward the covered bar area.

Em followed his gaze to where a couple of men in cowboy hats were setting up their equipment in a corner that had been cleared of tables and chairs. "This seems like a nice place."

"Yeah." Justin let out a soft laugh. "Leave it to us to find a country-western bar on the beach. I guess I was expecting something a little more tropical, and a little less boot scootin'."

Em hadn't planned on stopping at A Cowboy in Paradise on their first night on the island. When she'd done her search for Chick, she was surprised how easy it was to find him. Turned out he'd retired to Paradise Island and opened up a bar. The same bar where she and Justin now sat. She'd scanned the place when they arrived, but hadn't noticed anyone resembling the grizzled old cowboy she'd seen online.

Justin took a sip of his gigantic drink. "Mmm. This is pretty good. What do you think?"

Em nodded. "Really good. We probably could have shared one, though. I don't think I'll be able to come close to finishing this."

"Why not? Neither one of us has to drive tonight. We've got nowhere to be, nobody breathing down our necks, no plans, right?"

"True." She watched as he lifted his drink and took another long draw on the straw. His Adam's apple bobbed up and down as he swallowed. His carefree attitude wasn't fooling her. He wanted answers. Answers she wasn't prepared to give quite yet.

"Are we staying far from here?" Justin toyed with his straw.

"Not too far. I think it's about a mile up the road."

"Are we walking? I didn't see any cars when we got off the ferry."

Em shifted in her seat, wishing for a change of topic. "No cars are allowed on the island, but we can catch a ride on a golf cart or a horse-drawn carriage. I think they use those as taxis."

Justin leaned against the back of his chair. "Is there anything else you want to tell me about this trip?"

Butterflies batted their wings against the walls of her chest. If she came clean now, what would he do? Would he spend the night right here on the beach and take the first ferry back in the morning? Would he understand she had his best interests at heart?

She needed more time. He might be upset when she told him she'd tricked him into this trip for his own good, but she was counting on him understanding her motivation after he'd been here for a few days. No, she couldn't tell him everything yet. She would, she promised herself. There had never been lies between them, and she didn't want to start.

She reached out, cupping her giant drink with her hands and drawing it toward her mouth. "Nope. Nothing else to tell."

"Okay then. To having a great time together." He lifted his glass and leaned forward to clink it against hers.

The tension bled from her body. Her muscles relaxed as she touched her glass to his. "To having a great time."

Justin

"I can't eat another bite." Justin pushed his plate away. "That has to be one of the best burgers I've ever had."

Em nibbled on a bite of salad. She wasn't even halfway through her meal, but he'd inhaled his. The only thing left he hadn't quite finished was the monster drink he'd ordered.

"Better than Terlinga's?" Em asked.

He let out a soft laugh. "Don't tell anyone, but yeah, even better than Terlinga's."

"Wow. That's high praise. We'll have to come back so I can get a burger next time."

"Consider it done." They'd have time. Time to do whatever they wanted over the next week and a half. And maybe during that time he'd find the courage to feel her out about the possibility of them building a future together. He didn't want to rush, didn't want to push Em into a corner. But he didn't want to lose her, either.

He still didn't quite believe her story about winning a vacation. There was something else going on, something she didn't want to talk about yet. He could tell by the way she got that deer-in-the-headlights look when he asked for details.

Knowing Em, she was probably going to try to convince him not to go back to competing. She'd done it before, though in subtle ways. As much as she might think she was being discreet, there wasn't anything super subtle about her. At least not with him. He knew all her tricks, had seen her bend others to her will over the years. Hell, she had the power to wrangle a whole class of kindergarteners into submission. A grown man would be helpless against her.

But not him.

He leaned over and pulled his socks out of his boots. They'd be done and ready to head out soon. As eager as he was to get to the bottom of Em's intentions, he was also dead tired. There wasn't anything he could do with new information tonight. Might as well get a good night's sleep and see what tomorrow would bring. Knowing Em, she wouldn't be able to keep a secret from him for long.

The socks felt stifling on his feet after wiggling his toes in the sand. There would be plenty of time for that in the days ahead. He pulled his boots on and took another sip of his drink. It was going down way too easy.

"Hey, should we get a picture of Rocky in the sand before the sun goes down?" he asked.

Em's eyes lit up. "I thought you hated Rocky."

"I'm not his biggest fan, but he doesn't need me, he's got hundreds of five-year-olds who want to see him at the beach, right?" He'd play along with Em's game for now. But he was going to get to the bottom of things between them soon.

"That's right." She reached into her bag and pulled out the rock. "How about one with him in the sand and then one with him leaning up against the sign at the bar?"

Justin wrapped his fingers around the rock. "I'll take care of that while you finish your salad. Sound good?"

She nodded.

He got up from the chair and walked toward the water, his boots sinking into the sand. From here, he had an unobstructed view of the ocean. The waves crashed against the shore, sending salt water racing toward his feet. He jumped back before the water washed over the toes of his boots.

A few stars already twinkled in the sky above, and the sun was rapidly disappearing beyond the horizon. If he wanted a picture of the rock without having to use a flash, he'd better hurry. He set Rocky down, wedging him upright in the wet sand. As the waves raced toward shore, he snapped a photo. How could anyone see the rock jutting up toward the sky and not think it looked just like a petrified dick? Maybe he still had the sense of humor of his twelve-year-old self, or maybe Em needed to find a new rock.

"Did you get it?" She called to him from where she still sat on the beach.

"Yeah." He glanced down to grab the rock, but it was gone. The waves had retreated, pulling the sand and shells and everything else they'd just deposited on the beach back into the ocean. Oh shit. He couldn't lose the rock. Em would strangle him. Strangle him, then drown him.

He searched the stretch of wet sand where the rock had been just a couple of seconds ago. The only evidence it had been there was an indent from where he'd jabbed it into the sand.

"Did you want to get one by the bar?" Em asked. She was getting up from her chair. Any moment she'd be heading his way and see he'd lost her class's pet.

He couldn't let that happen. Tucking his phone into his pocket, he swept his gaze over the beach. Something tumbled on the sand a few yards away on his right. Justin jogged over to it, his heart clenched tight, hoping he hadn't fucked up. It was a small piece of wood. While he stood over it, the water swept over his feet and drew the wood back into the sea.

Fuck. His boots were meant to handle cow shit and mud, not a dip in the ocean.

"Can you text me the picture you took so I can post it?" Em's voice came from behind him. She was only a dozen feet away.

"Yeah, sure." Justin squinted, begging for a glimpse of the damn rock. The beach stretched out on either side, smooth and undisturbed. There was no sign of Rocky.

"Let's get a picture by the bar next." Em reached him, her palm extended, expecting him to hand over the rock she'd taken care of for the past seven years.

"Um, I don't know what happened to Rocky." Justin gritted his teeth and braced himself for her reaction.

"What do you mean?"

"I mean, I set him down right there"—Justin pointed to the spot where he'd wedged the rock into the sand—"then I snapped a picture. You said something, and I looked away for just a second."

"You lost my rock?" Her eyes widened.

This wasn't good. Not at all. "I didn't lose him. The waves must have pulled him into the ocean."

Em shifted her gaze to the waves, which continued to batter the beach. "Rocky's out there somewhere?"

He funneled a hand through his hair, at a total loss over how to fix this. "I'm sorry, Em. I only looked away for a second. It's got to be here somewhere."

"I've had that rock since the first day I started teaching." Her voice came out flat, devoid of emotion.

"I know." He moved toward where the waves hit the shore, and then bent over, peering into the frothy water.

Em joined him. "You think it was somewhere around here?"

"It's got to be. He's heavy, right? It's not like he could have gone far. He has to be here somewhere." The fact that he'd started referring to the rock as a "he" instead of an "it" wasn't lost on him. But Rocky was important to Em, and that meant he was important to Justin as well.

Em pulled out her phone and turned on her flashlight. Shining it into the water, she slowly swept it from side to side. "We've got to find him, Justin. I can't believe you lost him. The kids are going to be heartbroken."

His chest squeezed. "We'll find him. I'll find him. I promise."

It wasn't the kind of promise he ought to make. Rocky could be buried under twenty pounds of sand by now. The ocean was relentless, taking what it wanted and covering up its tracks with every wave that crashed upon the shore. But he had to say something to reassure her. In the grand scheme of things, losing a rock into the ocean wasn't something to get all bent out of shape over. But Rocky wasn't just a rock.

And Em wasn't just anyone.

A flash of something white caught his eye in the light from Em's phone. He reached out and grabbed it. His hand closed around the precious rock.

"Hey, Em. I got it. I found him."

14

⌒~♡~⌒

Emmeline

Large palm trees stretched over the gate and a screen of dense bushes prevented them from seeing anything beyond the concrete wall facing the street. Em tapped the code Decker had given her into the keypad to the right of a tall iron gate. They'd caught a ride on one of the island golf carts and now stood in front of the drive that presumably led to the house where they'd be staying. She'd wanted somewhere private where Justin could step out of the limelight and figure out what really mattered. Based on what she'd seen so far, this place was going to be perfect.

The keypad turned green. A lock clicked, and she pushed the gate open and then stepped into a well-landscaped garden. Tall grass swayed in the gentle breeze. The scent of honeysuckle tickled her nose while the sound of running water drew her attention to a fountain farther along the path.

"Wow, this is something." Justin's comment came from over her shoulder as he followed her into the yard. "It's like a private oasis."

That's exactly what it was, and Em sent a silent thank-you to Decker for offering the use of the house. Solar lights along the edge of the path lit the way to the door. She glanced at her phone to confirm the code for the front door was the same as the gate before typing it in on the pad.

"You ready to see the inside?" She turned and looked at Justin. Light from the moon behind him sharpened his features. Hopefully, he wouldn't be too angry when he found out she'd tricked him to get him here.

"Yeah. Just let me slide my boots off first. They're still sopping wet from my trek through the ocean." He set his bag down and bent to pull his boots off his feet.

"I'm sure there's a hair dryer here. We can dry them off and they'll be good as new." She hoped that was true. She'd never heard of anyone taking a dip with their boots on before and wasn't sure what salt water might do to the leather.

"It's fine, Em. I'm the dumbass who wore his boots on the beach." At least he'd found the rock. She wasn't sure what she would have done if she'd lost Rocky.

With Justin standing barefoot behind her, Em swung the door to the house open. She felt around on the inside wall for a light switch. Finding nothing, she stepped inside and pulled out her phone.

"How do you think we turn on the lights?" Phone in hand, she flipped on her flashlight app and pointed the light at the wall. "They said it was a smart house. Do you think that makes a difference?"

"Maybe we just ask nicely," Justin joked. "House, please turn on the entryway light."

The crystal chandelier overhead sparkled to life. Em let out a laugh.

"You've got to be shitting me." Justin tilted his head back and studied the fixture.

"I saw something like this on one of those home renovation shows once, but never in real life." She was too practical to want a house with all the bells and whistles. Eventually, something would break, and it would probably require a visit from an engineer to fix it.

"I wonder what else this house can do." Justin gave her a lopsided smile. "House, play me some Kenny Chesney."

The first bars of "Somewhere with You" trickled through hidden speakers.

"Well I'll be damned." Justin padded through the entryway, his feet slapping against the travertine tile. "House, turn on the light in the family room."

Em closed the door before following him into a huge open-concept living area. A few lamps flickered to life, casting a warm glow through the room. A wall of windows covered in floor-to-ceiling shades lined the back of the house.

"House, open the shades," Em instructed. A whirring noise sounded, and the shades lifted. It was too dark to see beyond the glass. "I wonder what kind of view they've got out the back."

"Based on everything else around here, it's got to be spectacular." Justin stood in the middle of the room. "Where do you think the bedrooms are?"

Em glanced around the circular room. "You want to try that hall over there, and I'll try this one?"

Two halls led from the room, one closer to the kitchen area and one closer to where she stood by the giant TV screen sitting on a built-in shelf. The walls were a pale beige, almost sand colored, and the decor blended classy elegance with a casual beach look.

"Let me know what you find." Justin headed down the hall on his side of the house.

Em turned to explore her side. "House, please turn on the hall light."

Wall sconces illuminated the short hall. The first door led to a guest bathroom. She continued on toward the doorway at the end. Soft light filtered in through the windows and Em stepped forward. The shades were open, providing her first look at the backyard. Twinkle lights wound through an arbor that sat over a hot tub right outside the window.

She turned around, noticing the king-sized bed. The house honored her polite request to turn on the bedroom light, and she sucked in a breath at what she saw. A vaulted ceiling stretched two stories overhead. She glanced up, but there wasn't a ceiling at all. Two huge panes of glass provided a view of the night sky above. It was like the whole ceiling was one giant skylight.

"Justin, you've got to see this." She moved toward the door to get his attention, but he was already coming down the hallway.

"It can't be more incredible than the bedroom on the other side."

"Look up." She pointed, and he tilted his head, his gaze shifting to the glass ceiling.

"Wow. Where did you find this place, Em? It's amazing." He moved past the bed to check the view out the bedroom windows. "There's a hot tub out there. I bet that would feel incredible after the long day we've had. You want to go in?"

She wasn't ready to tell him exactly where she'd found this place and there was no way she was getting in the hot tub. "I don't have a swimsuit, remember?"

"You can use a pair of my shorts and a T-shirt if you want."

She shook her head. "I think I'll wait for my bag. Do you want this room or the other?"

Justin shrugged. "Your call. You're the one who won a vacation; you get to pick. Though you might want to check out the other room before you decide."

"Good idea." She backtracked through the family room and down the other hall, with Justin following.

The room on the other side was just as large, though there was no glass ceiling. Instead, it had a sliding glass door that opened up to a private patio with a large swing hanging from a beam overhead.

"This is like a private little sitting area, isn't it?" She perched on the edge of the swing. It had a giant cushion, like one of those swing beds she'd seen while searching Pinterest for inspiration for the screened-in porch she wanted to build. What would it be like to own a place like this? According to Decker, his dad owned a couple of vacation homes around the world but hardly ever visited. Seemed like a waste.

"I think that's exactly what it is. Do you want the glass ceiling or the private sitting area?" Justin crossed his arms over his chest and grinned. "It's a difficult decision, but there really isn't a bad choice, is there?"

"Not really." Em leaned back and stretched out on the cushion. "I'll take this one. You can sleep under the stars."

He lowered himself to the edge of the swing. "I think I might sit in the hot tub for a little bit before I turn in. You sure you don't want to join me?"

"I'll sit outside with you if you want, but I'm not going to get in." A full day of traveling had caught up to her. Even the idea of changing her clothes seemed like it would take too much effort. "If my luggage doesn't come tomorrow, I'll head back to those shops we passed on our way in and find a new swimsuit."

"Suit yourself. Meet you out back in five?" he asked.

"You got it." Em watched as he disappeared around the corner, and then picked up her phone to fire off a text to Decker.

Em: The house is gorgeous. Thanks so much for letting us use it.

Three dots blinked, signaling Decker was typing out a response.

Decker: No prob. Have you told him the truth yet?

Em: No. We just got here!

Decker: Good luck. I know y'all will have fun.

Em: I hope he's not too mad at me.

Decker: Look in the cabinet by the fridge for a little something he might enjoy.

Em got up and headed to the kitchen. She pulled on the handle of the cabinet next to the refrigerator and it swung open. A bottle of Justin's favorite whiskey sat inside.

Em: You shouldn't have.

Decker: Trust me, he's going to need it when you come clean.

Em's throat went dry. Hoping Decker was underestimating Justin's ability to deal with the truth, she found two glasses and filled them with ice and water from the dispenser on the fridge. With plans to sit with Justin for a few minutes before making an excuse to turn in, she headed out onto the patio, her fingers crossed that talk didn't turn toward the real reason they were there.

Justin

Justin eased into the hot tub, sinking into the steamy bubbles that would hopefully soak all of his aches and pains away. Though he couldn't see beyond the edge of the patio in the darkness, the ocean had to be close. He could taste the salt on his tongue every time he inhaled. For a moment he tried to forget his time in paradise probably came with a catch, and told himself to relax and enjoy it.

He closed his eyes, letting the warm water soothe his shoulder pain. Since they'd been traveling, he hadn't done any of his exercises, and it was stiff.

"Need me to loosen that up for you?" Em asked as the glass door slid closed.

Yes. Start with my shoulder, then work your way around to my front and drop a little lower, please. He stifled that thought and cleared his throat. "Nah, you don't have to do that."

"I don't mind. Just don't get me wet."

Just what he needed . . . thoughts of getting Em all wet drifting through his head. Why did every word coming out of her mouth send blood straight to his dick?

She set a glass of ice water in the cup holder by his hand and perched on the edge of the hot tub. "Scoot over here, and I'll rub your shoulder."

"You really don't have to, Em." Thank goodness for the coverage of the bubbles in the hot tub.

"Now, Forza." Her voice didn't leave room for negotiation.

He moved from the reclining bench he'd been sitting on to the upright seat in front of Em. The first touch of her fingers on the tight muscles at the back of his neck made him want to melt into her.

"You're tight."

He bit back the "that's what he said" joke on the tip of his tongue.

"Is it too hard?"

"Huh?" His voice came out sounding strangled.

"The pressure?" She dug her thumbs into his traps. "Let me know if I'm hurting you."

He wanted to reach back and pull her into the tub, settle her on his lap, and show her just exactly how hard he was. But he took in a deep breath instead and silently recited the name of every bull he'd ridden in the past two years to distract him from how good her hands felt on his skin. How sweet she smelled, even after a full day of traveling. How she might taste if he ever got the balls to press his lips to hers.

She worked the muscles on his neck before moving over to his shoulder. "Your scar's healing well."

"Yeah." He glanced at what remained of the proof of his incision. "Still ugly, but not nearly as bad as it was."

"Come on, you know the girls think it's sexy." She traced the scar with her fingertip.

Every nerve in his body lit up as her finger skimmed over his skin. "You sure you don't want to soak for a few minutes?"

"No. I think I'm going to turn in. It's been a long day. Do you have everything you need?" She stood and stepped down from the side of the hot tub.

Did he have everything he needed? Yes and no. Yes, he had what he needed to get through another night. He had a suitcase full of clothes, had remembered to pack his toothbrush and deodorant. But did he have what he really needed?

He wanted to tell her no, that what he really needed was standing right in front of him but had always been just out of his reach. Wanted to tell her that not a day went by without him thinking about what it would feel like to hold her in his arms. Wanted to tell her that everything he did, he did with her in mind so that he might finally reach a day when he would deserve her.

But instead of saying any of that, he nodded. "Yeah, I'm good."

She reached out and tousled his wet hair. "Don't stay up too late, J."

"I won't." He waited while she grabbed her glass and disappeared back inside. Then he pushed himself up and out of the water to sit on the side of the tub. Steam rolled off his body as it came in contact with the night air. He snagged the towel he'd brought out onto the patio with him and wrapped it around his shoulders.

Sitting down in a chair at the glass-topped patio table, he reached for his phone. His notifications had been going off for the past hour, but he'd ignored them. He hadn't wanted to face the outside world.

Two missed calls from his dad and one from Jake. He flipped to his text messages.

Dad: I got an offer from Blaster Energy Drinks. Call me.

Justin pulled up a transcript from the voice mails. Same thing. His dad wanted him to call right away so they could finalize the sponsorship. Jake wanted him to call their dad. Same old, same old. The two of them were cut from the same damn cloth. Justin had always felt like he didn't quite belong.

While Jake blindly followed their dad without questioning his intentions or tactics, Justin had never fallen into line. Jake was the golden boy. The one who'd secured junior championships, who'd graduated from high school early so he could join the tour and travel across the country in his quest for a world title.

Their dad had put him on such a high pedestal that no one could touch him. And Jake came through. He mastered every challenge set in front of him, conquered every injury, and returned to the competition stronger than he'd been before. When he won his second championship and retired, he'd taken the Forza legacy further than any of them could ever imagine.

And now it was Justin's turn.

If he failed, it wouldn't be just his dad he'd be disappointing. He'd let his older brother down, too.

He had a chance to finally come through for both of them. How could he say no? He fired off a text to his dad saying he'd call in the morning, then responded to Jake so he'd know he was on top of things.

He dried off as best he could and entered the stone-cold silence of the house. The sound of the ocean breeze and chirping crickets faded when he closed the door. He tiptoed to the kitchen and set his glass down on the counter. Then he peeked down the hall toward the room Em had taken. The hall was dark. No crack of light drifted out from under the door.

If he knocked on the door and asked if they could talk, she'd let him in. But this was something he couldn't talk to her about. He knew where she stood when it came to his return to the tour. She was against it. How could she be anything but when bull riding had taken something so precious from her? It had stolen the dad she knew and sent back a man who battled mood swings, who couldn't stop the tremors from overtaking his body whenever they wanted, who'd become a shell of the man he was before.

It wasn't fair to ask her to be a sounding board. So, he turned toward the bedroom with the glass ceiling, prepared to spend another night alone in his bed.

Wishing he could hold her in his arms.

Wishing he could make her understand.

15

Emmeline

Em tossed the covers away. She'd been lying in the dark for the past two hours, trying to force herself to sleep. But sleep wouldn't come. She could chalk it up to being in a strange house or being overtired from such a long day, but deep down she knew the real reason sleep was evading her.

She'd lied.

Seeing Justin relaxing in the hot tub, feeling the tension leave his shoulders as she dug her thumbs into his broad back, her stomach had twisted into knots. Now her emotions were so tangled up inside, she doubted she'd be able to fall asleep even if she had access to one of the over-the-counter sleep aids her mom kept in her nightstand.

Em had found them one day while looking for a nail file. Her mom told her to go into the bedroom and look on the bedside table. Em didn't see one there, so she'd pulled open the drawer, thinking it might have fallen inside. The number of prescription bottles had caught her off guard. She'd had to look up most of the names. One pill was for depression, two were for anxiety, and another was a muscle relaxer. The only bottle Em recognized was the sleep aid she'd seen commercials for on TV.

She'd closed the drawer and returned to the kitchen without a nail file, figuring she could deal with her hangnail once she got home. She still hadn't broached the subject with her mom, but it made her wonder how long her mother had been relying on prescription meds to get by.

She didn't want that to be her life.

She also didn't want Justin to end up like her dad. The number of pills her dad took on a daily basis boggled her mind. Pills to keep the tremors at bay, pills to help with muscle spasms, pills to regulate his blood pressure . . . that's what she was trying to save him from.

Convinced she wouldn't be able to fall asleep, she got up from the bed. Maybe fifteen minutes in the hot tub would draw the tension out of her own shoulders. Since she didn't have her luggage, she'd fallen asleep in her panties and shirt. She slipped her underwear off and left it on the bathroom shelf next to the bra she'd removed earlier. Then she pulled her shirt over her head and wrapped one of the big, fluffy towels around her torso, tucking the corner in right between her breasts. She pulled her hair up into a high ponytail and ventured out into the hall, hoping like hell Justin wouldn't be getting up to grab a glass of water in the middle of the night.

The sliding glass door opened without making a sound, and she breathed in the scent of chlorine from the hot tub. A slight breeze blew over her shoulders. She shivered, despite the warmth in the air. Even with the breeze from the ocean, it still had to be over eighty degrees outside.

Justin had clipped the cover back in place after he got out of the hot tub, so she flipped it open. It was heavy and landed with a thump. Her heart hammered, and she waited for the light in his bedroom to come on. The room he'd taken faced the patio, but the shades were drawn. Nothing happened.

Drawing in a calming breath, she slid the cover to the ground and dipped her fingers into the water. The digital thermometer displayed the water temperature at a balmy ninety-nine degrees. That ought to be good for drawing the tightness from between her shoulder blades.

She climbed up the steps and eased her feet into the water. Oh, that felt good. She lowered herself in, tossing her towel toward the table when the water hit her thighs and then sinking in completely. She didn't want to risk the noise the jets would make if she turned them on, so she picked one of the deep corner seats and settled in.

Tilting her head back to rest against the edge, she looked up at the inky black sky. A half-moon covered by clouds provided little light and Em tried to remember names of the constellations she'd learned about in high school. The vine-covered arbor overhead blocked her view, but she could make out a few stars sparkling in the darkness.

As she soaked in the quietness, she let her thoughts shift to Justin. He was all she could think about lately. She just wanted what was best for him, and she was convinced his dad didn't want the same. He was only concerned about the reputation of the family business. If Justin secured a world championship, she could only imagine what that would do.

Mr. Forza already had a reputation for training some of the best bull riders that had come out of Texas over the past twenty years. He'd made a living by pushing young men to the brink of exhaustion and bullying them into giving their all even when they didn't have anything left to give. That might work for some, but his bullish ways sure seemed to be taking their toll on her best friend.

Justin had been distracted over the past few weeks. The

weight of everyone else's expectations had been weighing on him. She could see it in the lines around his eyes, the strain that seemed to keep his jaw clenched tight whether they were talking about his training schedule or something as simple as the weather.

Em swirled her finger around in the water, wishing there was an easy fix. Part of her wanted to shake some sense into him, force him to look at her dad and face the future that seemed certain if he kept pushing himself past his limit. The other part of her wanted to pull him tight into her arms and appeal to his sensitive side.

There was so much more to him than the way he rode a bull. He had an incorrigible sense of humor that always made her laugh. He'd deny having a soft side until he was blue in the face, but she'd seen it in the way he took his time signing autographs for his youngest fans. More than once he'd lingered long after the stands had emptied, until every last kid who wanted a picture had been satisfied.

She also happened to be only one of a few people who knew that he made a habit of donating to local charities in each town where he rode. He'd kept that nugget of info away from the media, not wanting the extra attention it would bring if someone found out.

When she thought about the kind of man she wanted to spend the rest of her life with, it was Justin's face that kept popping up in her mind. In her head, she knew that was impossible. She'd never considered exploring a relationship past the edges of friendship.

He was a bull rider, and the one attribute she refused to even consider when it came to dating or falling for someone was being associated with a rodeo in any way. Okay, maybe if a guy sold tickets or worked for a stock contractor, she might consider it. But anyone who had any tie to participating in any event was off-limits.

She couldn't handle the kind of heartache she'd seen her mom deal with every single day of her life. Couldn't handle not knowing who her dad was anymore since he got hurt. Couldn't handle putting her heart on the line eight seconds at a time while she held her breath to see if someone she loved would make it through another ride.

The hot tub wasn't working. All she was doing was working herself into even more of a tizzy. She'd be better off lying in bed and at least pretending she might fall asleep soon.

She looked up, one last glance at the dark night sky above. Movement along the vines intertwined with the arbor above caught her eye. She squinted, peering into the darkness, trying to make out the fuzzy form that seemed to creep closer. Was that a . . . no . . . She shook her head, not willing to entertain the thought that there could be something so terrifying crawling right above her head.

Justin

Justin stood next to the window, his attention captured by Em's silhouette. He'd been unable to fall asleep. The feel of Em's touch on his shoulders kept playing through his mind. The sensation of her fingers kneading the muscles at the back of his neck had felt incredible. And now, watching her relaxing in the hot tub not even ten feet away, all he wanted to do was go to her.

He'd turned and taken several steps toward the door to the patio at least three times already. Every time he got close enough to wrap his fingers around the door handle, he stopped himself. What good would come out of telling Em how he felt about her? He couldn't do that to her, not while he was still planning on returning to competing.

But hell, when she'd slipped the towel from around her body and set it on the patio table, he hadn't been able to look away. Even in the dark, her curves illuminated only by the light of the moon as it filtered through the arbor overhead, she was the most stunning woman he'd ever seen. He wanted to go to her, skim his palms over her soft skin, and tell her he'd been in love with her for years.

Instead, he'd watched from the window. He knew it was wrong, yet he couldn't seem to tear his gaze away. He'd seen her in a swimsuit, seen her in skimpy tank tops and short shorts, but he'd never seen her without a stitch of clothing on. Now he drank her in, as if he'd never be able to get his fill. He'd never get enough when it came to Em. And that was the truth that felt like a permanent burr in his backside. Knowing he'd never get enough, knowing that even if he came clean with her today and they fell into each other's arms, he'd already wasted so much time.

He tapped his forehead against the wall. If he hadn't been so worried about making noise and getting caught watching her like a fucking Peeping Tom, he would have banged his head hard. He was either the dumbest asshole who'd ever lived or the most selfless bastard. Either way, it meant Em wouldn't be his. Not until he could walk away from the rodeo life and be the man she wanted . . . the man she deserved.

Air seeped into his lungs on a deep inhale, doing nothing to slow the rapid beat of his heart. He should go back to bed. Leave Em to her middle-of-the-night musings and try to get some sleep. He was about to turn away from the window and leave her in peace when she let out a muffled shriek.

He pushed the window covering out of the way and pressed his face close to the glass. Em stood on the patio, water running down her naked limbs. She'd left her towel on the table, but she hadn't reached for it. While he waited, not knowing whether to reveal himself by running out to the patio to find out what was going on, she hopped from foot to foot and put her hand over her mouth.

She was scared of something. The table with her towel on it sat between where she stood on the edge of the patio and the door of the house. Justin strained to make out what she was staring at. Something on her towel moved. Something big. Something with eight long legs and a fuzzy body the size of a goose egg.

He bit back a laugh and slid the door open, trying to keep his eyes from straying to Em's naked form. "Do you need some help?"

Em yelped . . . a high-pitched sound like one of the donkeys on his uncle's ranch might make when it spotted a coyote looking for an easy meal. "Oh my god, cover your eyes. Don't you dare look at me."

"What the hell's going on out here? You're going to wake up the whole island if you keep that up." He put his hand over his eyes to give her the privacy she wanted. No way would he tell her he'd been watching her for the past fifteen minutes, like a pervy kid spying on his favorite babysitter.

"Spider. A big one. It fell off the arbor and landed on my towel." Her voice bordered on the edge of hysteria.

Justin peeked at the tabletop through a crack between his fingers. A furry spider stood in the center of the bath towel. He'd seen enough of them around the ranch to recognize it for what it was. "Just a tarantula, Em. You know they're more scared of you than you are of them."

"I don't see him standing naked on the edge of a patio," Em said.

Justin chuckled. "Are you naked? I hadn't noticed."

"Just get rid of it. Hurry." She spoke in a loud, harsh whisper.

"I can't do anything with my eyes covered. I'm going to have to look." He waited for her to agree. Even in her rattled state, she had to recognize that he'd have to uncover his eyes if she wanted him to deal with the spider.

"Fine. But don't look over here. I'm serious, Forza." She practically growled out the words.

"You got it." He removed his hand from his eyes and inched toward the table. Where had the spider gone? "You want to flip the light on so I can see?"

"I'm not moving until you tell me you've caught that giant beast."

The moon disappeared behind a bank of clouds. "Em, I can't see shit. It's too dark out here. I'm turning on the light."

"Don't. You. Dare."

He stood tall, letting his hands drop to his sides. "How do you expect me to catch something I can't see?"

Her voice came out small, like she was trying to make herself invisible. "I swear, Justin, if you look over here, I'm going to die. Drop dead right here on the spot and you'll have to tell my parents."

"Run inside then."

"I'm not going anywhere. What if it jumped off the table and I step on it?"

"Then go stand behind the bushes."

"And bare my ass to the neighbors? Are you kidding me?"

"You're right. Let's just hang tight until the sun comes up and see if I can find it then. Is that what you want?"

"Nooooooooo." She drew the word out, her voice cracking at the tail end.

His heart squeezed. She was scared. Spiders had never been her thing. He'd seen her hunt for worms to go fishing and handle garter snakes the same as him, Decker, and Knox. But she'd always been a scaredy cat when it came to spiders. Didn't matter if they were a harmless daddy longlegs or a black widow, she turned into a shaky mess when confronted with any kind of arachnid—a weakness he'd used against her once when he threatened to fill her backpack with spiders if she ratted him out for skipping homeroom in ninth grade.

"Calm down. I'm turning on the light so I can see where it went."

"Do you have to?" An anxious resignation replaced the panic that had laced through her tone.

"Yeah, I do."

"Fine. Make it quick, though. Please."

He bit back the smile that threatened to split his lips. "I promise."

"And, Justin?"

"Yeah?"

"If you so much as even think about glancing over here . . . I'll . . ."

"You'll what?" He cocked his head, waiting for the empty threat.

"I'll make you wish you hadn't."

16

❦

Emmeline

Light filtered through the slats of the window shades, forcing Em to open her eyes. She'd barely slept a wink. How could she, when the mortification of being caught naked on the patio by Justin held her in its heated grip? Her skin burned like she'd spent hours in the sun. That was the after-effect of what should have been a quick, relaxing dip in the hot tub.

Even now, hours after he'd scooped the spider off her towel and carried it to the edge of the fence line, she could feel the heat of his gaze on her skin. He promised he hadn't looked. Even covered his eyes as he handed her the spider-free towel and waited until she'd escaped to the privacy of her bedroom before he entered the house.

Still, he'd seen her.

She knew it.

He knew that she knew it, too, which made the whole morning-after thing beyond awkward. Wasn't it last night that she'd been fantasizing about what it might feel like to run her hands over his chiseled chest?

The air kicked on, blowing a cool blast of air over her

bare legs. All the ice in the world couldn't save her from the burning embarrassment she was going to face when she saw him. She'd always been a fan of facing difficulties head-on and getting them out of the way, so she forced herself to get up and dragged her body to the bathroom.

Her hair had dried in a matted, chlorine-ridden mess. Chunks stuck out all over her head, making her look like some sort of suburban Medusa. She splashed some cool water on her face and patted it dry with the clean towel she'd grabbed as soon as she got inside last night.

Time to face the music. Actually, time to face the cowboy. With any luck, Justin was still in bed, sleeping off the shock of seeing his best friend in her birthday suit. She pulled on the clothes she'd worn the day before, and cracked open the bedroom door.

Silence greeted her. Hopeful she'd have a chance to caffeinate before facing Justin, she tiptoed down the hall toward the kitchen. She'd just picked up the glass carafe of the coffeepot and turned toward the sink to fill it when she caught sight of a man-shaped form in the doorway of the kitchen.

The carafe crashed to the tile floor, shattering into a billion tiny pieces.

"Jesus, Em. What the hell? Are you okay?" Justin made a move toward her, glanced at the glass scattered in front of his bare feet, and stayed put.

Her heart pounded so fast it might burst out of her chest and take off running out the door. "I'm sorry. I thought you were still in bed. You scared me."

"Are you okay?"

"Yeah, I'm fine." She put her hand to her forehead. What in the world was wrong with her? Why was she so jumpy?

"Don't move. I'm going to go put my boots on and grab a broom to clean this up, okay?"

Em's gaze swept along the tile. Glass covered the area around her feet. "Don't worry. I don't think I can take a step in any direction without getting cut."

"I'll be back in just a second." He held up a finger, then spun around to retreat to the bedroom.

She let out a long-drawn-out sigh. Maybe this trip had been a mistake. Nothing had gone right since they got on the plane yesterday. First, her bag got lost. Then the delay with the shuttle. She wouldn't even let herself think about the mishap with the spider that left her cowering on the patio naked.

Naked.

In front of Justin.

Eager to escape before he returned, she evaluated her options. She could try to jump onto the counter. If she made it without cutting up her foot, she could crawl across and try to hop over to the kitchen island. She'd be home free from there.

"I'm coming." Justin came through the door, his feet encased in the cowboy boots that had taken an unexpected dip in the ocean last night.

Before she could react, he'd swept her up in his arms and cradled her against his chest. She wasn't a teeny tiny little thing. Her mom always said she was big-boned thanks to her sturdy German ancestors, but Justin held her like she didn't weigh any more than a bag of feathers.

"You're going to hurt your shoulder. You'd better put me down." She pressed on his chest, her palm firm against his chiseled pec.

"Don't worry. I've got you." He carried her back to the bedroom where she'd tossed and turned all night long.

When he reached the bed, he released her from his arms. She bounced once, then reached up to push him away. Instead of retreating, he fell on top of the mattress.

"You want to tell me what's going on?" He shifted, putting an arm behind his head while his boots hung off the edge of the bed.

She pulled her knees to her chest, feeling the slightest bit defensive. "What do you mean?"

"I mean, there's an elephant in this room and the sooner we confront it, the sooner we can put it behind us."

"I don't want to talk about it." She drew her knees tighter against her and wrapped her arms around them.

"So, I saw you naked last night. No big deal." Justin held her in his gaze, his blue eyes as cool as the bay they'd crossed on the ferry yesterday afternoon.

She rolled her eyes and rested her chin on her knees. "It's a big deal to me. I understand in the grand scheme of things, you've probably seen lots of naked women. I'm just one more female body to you, but—"

"Good grief. Is that what you think?" He got up from the bed. His fingers went to his belt buckle. The one he'd won during his first professional rodeo. "If it'll make you feel any better, I'll strip down to my birthday suit right here and now."

Her throat constricted but she jerked her head up and tried to laugh it off. "That sounds like a great idea, but I don't think it's going to make it better."

"Why not? I figure you've shown me yours, so I'll show you mine and we'll be even." He pulled the end of his belt free and started working on the button of his jeans.

She couldn't watch, but she also couldn't look away. Words formed but she couldn't force them past her tongue. He'd lost his mind if he thought showing her his bare ass would lessen her embarrassment about last night.

But underneath her sheer and utter mortification, a tiny part of her wondered . . . what would Justin look like without a stitch of clothing? She'd seen him shirtless countless times. Had even caught him in his boxer briefs once when Knox and Decker had pranked her into walking in on him right after a ride.

While she sat there, speechless, he jerked down his zipper and slid his jeans down his hips. Heat bloomed on her chest, rolling up her neck in a crimson wave. She couldn't let him go through with this, and yet, she wasn't sure she wanted to stop him.

Maybe just a teeny, tiny peek would make her feel better.

He kicked off his boots and his jeans followed. "You ready for this? I want you to take a long look, so we'll be nice and even."

The waistband of his underwear slipped down, revealing a stark tan line. "I don't understand how this is going to fix anything."

He slid the band farther down his hips and Em couldn't sit there and watch any longer.

She jumped up and grabbed for his briefs, the only thought running through her head that she needed to stop him from taking them off.

She didn't think he'd move. She didn't think she might accidentally touch something she hadn't intended on touching. But as she lunged for him, trying to prevent him from sliding the elastic band printed with "Calvin Klein" past his butt, he jerked them down.

Her hands grappled for his boxer briefs, but they were gone. She fell forward, stumbling into him. His hand wrapped around her arm as her fingers touched something else. Something rigid. Something that felt a whole lot like something she shouldn't be touching at all.

She didn't look down, she couldn't. So instead, she looked up.

Justin

"Em, please take your hand off my . . ." He tilted his head back. "I need you to move your hand."

She cleared her throat, the warm breath from her shaky exhale brushing right across the head of his cock. His rock-hard, eager-to-engage dick.

"Oh my god. I'm so, so, sorry." She grabbed hold of his hips and pulled herself up from the awkward position where she'd landed, half kneeling, half standing, her cheek smashed against his pelvis.

Justin removed his hand from around her arm and reached down, his fingers grasping for the briefs hugging his ankles. He'd wanted to even the score but hadn't planned on this. His cheeks burned, sweat beaded along his brow. What the fuck was he supposed to do now?

"I, uh . . ." Em's gaze shot from the ceiling to the dresser behind him to the doorway to the bathroom. "I wasn't expecting that."

His pants back where they belonged, hanging low on his hips, concealing his raging erection, he scrubbed a hand along the back of his neck. "I wasn't expecting that, either. I was just trying to make you feel better."

"By showing me your huge dick?" Her eyes popped, like one of those old-timey cartoons where the character's eyes boinged out of their sockets on a long spring.

His brain sputtered, too many thoughts crowding into his head all at once. "Did you just say I have a huge dick?"

"What? I did not." She looked like she'd gone a little overboard with her blush, the way color flushed her cheeks.

"But you did." His embarrassment receded just enough for him to think about what she said. "You said, 'By showing me your huge dick.'"

"I don't think so." Em climbed off the bed and started to pace. "I said I wasn't expecting that."

"Right, and then I said I was just trying to make you feel better. And you said something like 'by showing me your huge dick.'" He waggled his eyebrows, preferring to defuse the situation with humor than talk about what had really just happened.

"Fine." She put her palms up in the universal sign for surrender. Or maybe she just wanted him to shut the fuck up and stop talking about his dick. Either way, she clearly didn't want to argue. "I might have said that."

"It's okay, Em. I mean, words don't come easy when talking about big Justin." He rebuckled his belt as he backed away from the bed. The shine in her eyes made her look like she might be about to lose her grip on reality in a second.

"Big Justin? That's not very original."

"If the name fits . . ." Justin continued to back away, one step after the other, eager to hit the hall so he could put some distance between himself and a very flustered Em.

"Can we pretend the past twelve hours didn't happen?" she asked. Her forehead creased, and he wanted to smooth the furrow away. "Let's just agree to never, ever speak of it again."

"If that's how you want to handle it, I'm totally on board." As much he would have liked their awkward entanglement to evolve into something a lot less embarrassing and a lot more sexy, he wasn't ready to broach the topic.

But a man could only take so much. After seeing her in all her gorgeous naked glory on the patio last night, he'd had to jump in the shower and pump his frustration into his hand. She hadn't even touched him then. Now that she had, it was like her touch had been branded on his skin.

"I'm going to go, uh, sweep up the glass in the kitchen." Justin backed into the hallway, his gaze still held by Em.

"Thank you." She bit her bottom lip, opened her mouth like she wanted to say something, and then decided against it.

"You want to take the golf cart into town and find a cup of coffee when I'm done?" The sooner they got back to normal, the faster this would be behind them. And he needed coffee to function. Em had ensured they wouldn't be able to make any at the house, so it only made sense to go out.

"Yes, please. I need to find out when my luggage will be here, too. If it's going to be a while, I may as well pick up a few things so I don't have to wear the same clothes for days."

"You can always wear what you had on last night," Justin teased.

The throw pillow she tossed at him went wide and bounced off the wall behind him. "We said we'd never talk about it. That means never. What happens on the island stays on the island, you promise?"

"Yeah, I promise." He held up his pinkie and she did the same, though she kept the same distance between them.

Ten minutes later, he'd swept up the glass with a broom and dustpan he found in a closet, then went over it again with the vacuum just to be sure there weren't any pieces left.

"You ready, Em?" It wasn't even nine yet, but if he'd been at home, he would have already been up for hours. Horses needed to be fed, stalls needed to be mucked out, and he would have already eaten a huge country breakfast. He'd checked the cabinets and except for a bottle of his favorite whiskey, they were bare.

Em had showered and had her wet hair tamed into a bun. The makeup she'd had on the day before had been scrubbed away. She was a beautiful woman, but he preferred her like this. Fresh. Natural. Genuine. She had a glow that came from the inside.

She grabbed her purse from where she'd left it on the kitchen counter the night before and pulled out her shades. "Let's see if we can find some coffee before I lose the ability to function."

It might have been wishful thinking, but the smile she gave him seemed a little brighter, a little sassier, a little more intimate than the ones she'd given him before.

Had something between them shifted? Or was she putting up a front, denying the possibility that there might be something there beyond friendship? He didn't know, but he sure as hell planned to find out.

17

Justin

"There's got to be coffee somewhere." Em tilted her head back and stuck her nose into the air. "I can smell it."

Justin breathed in the salty ocean air. They'd decided to walk and had just covered the mile and a half back to the end of the island where the ferry had dropped them off the day before. None of the souvenir and gift shops lining the road offered coffee. But same as Em, he caught a whiff of someone brewing a fresh pot, and his stomach gurgled.

"We could try the place we ate at last night," he suggested. It was off the road, set back along the beach. His nose had led him there the night before, and he was in desperate need this morning. Hoping he could count on his nose, he inhaled deeply.

"What do you think you are, a bloodhound?" Em joked.

"I'm a coffee hound." He turned, taking in another deep breath. "And I think our best bet of finding coffee is right over there."

She followed as he found the same trail they'd taken last night through the tall scrubby bushes and short palms.

It opened onto the beach, the teal-and-grass hut a few yards ahead.

"It doesn't look open, does it?" Em paused behind him.

He followed her gaze. Three sides of the hut had been open last night, but now thick pieces of wood covered the openings. Except for one.

"It might be open, let me go look." He walked toward the opening, the smell of coffee growing stronger. A song he hadn't heard in years drifted through the doorway, the soft notes reminding him of the last time he'd heard it. Right before his granny passed, he remembered her singing along while she whipped up a batch of her chicken-fried steak.

Em's hand on his back made him startle. "Are they open?"

"I can't tell. Doesn't look like it." While he leaned farther in, something nudged him from behind. "Cut it out, Em. I'm looking."

"Um, that wasn't me." Her voice came from several feet away.

Justin turned, putting him eye to eye with a giant, domed head. "What the fuck?"

"Tripod, get in here, you nosy bastard," a man called from inside the bar. "Sorry, folks, he doesn't mean any harm."

The huge tortoise ambled past him and walked straight through the opening and into the bar. Justin turned to Em, hoping for some sort of confirmation that she'd seen the same thing. "What was that?"

"Giant tortoise." The man stepped out from the dim interior and held out a hand. "Tripod's been with me now for about fifteen years. Lost his leg when he was just a tiny little thing. Gets along without it just fine, though, don't you think?"

Justin glanced after the tortoise, who hobbled over to the bar and nudged its nose along the top.

"Excuse my manners, y'all. I'm Chick. We start serving lunch at eleven if you want to come back then." He tipped the brim of a straw cowboy hat that had seen better days in Em's direction.

Justin squinted. The man standing in front of him didn't look anything like the only cowboy in history to earn two perfect rides. Justin did the math in his head. If his memory was accurate, Chick retired back in . . . hell . . . about thirty years ago.

Say he moved somewhere south where he spent a lot of time in the sun, and . . . damn . . . the older man in front of him did bear some resemblance to the bull rider whose picture he had hanging on his bedroom wall when he was a kid. But no one had heard about Chick in years. Not since he walked away from the sport at the height of his career. He had everything going for him, was in position to take home a second world championship, and poof . . . he disappeared.

"Mr. Darville?" Justin asked.

"Yes, son?" The man turned his steely blue gaze on Justin.

It was him. Justin would have recognized the eyes anywhere. There were stories hiding behind them. Hell, if his dad knew who was standing in front of him right now . . .

"You're Chick Darville, who rode Blue Bee Sting for a perfect ride in Denver."

The older man's eyes twinkled. "That's right, son."

Justin's voice took on an edge of excitement. "Then you rode Tailspin Torpedo a year later in Sioux Falls for another perfect ride."

"You seem to know your bull-riding history." Chick cocked his head. "Want to join me for a cup of coffee?"

Justin glanced from Chick to Em. She slid her sunglasses up to rest on top of her head.

"Any chance I can get a cup of that coffee to go? I need to track down my suitcase so I can change out of these clothes."

"I'll help you with that. Maybe I can take a rain check on that talk, sir."

"Don't be silly." Em moved past him and entered the bar. "Mr. Darville can keep you out of trouble while I find my suitcase. I'm a grown woman. I can take care of myself."

Chick clucked his tongue. "I don't know about you, son, but I think I'd give her the benefit of any doubt you might be harboring. Coffee's right this way. I usually don't come down here this early, but today seems like a good day to enjoy a cup or two on the beach."

Justin followed Chick inside, his eyes adjusting to the dim interior. The scent of coffee welcomed him. Em made herself comfortable on a stool at the bar while she waited.

The commercial brewer gurgled and spit out a burst of steam before going silent. Chick reached for two ceramic mugs and one paper cup.

"Take anything in it?" he asked. "Sugar's on the bar, but let me know if you need any milk."

"Just sugar, thanks." Em pulled two packets from a container at the edge of the bar. Her need for coffee pulsed through the air, like something tangible Justin could feel.

Chick slid the paper cup across the bar to her. "There you go. I'll keep an eye on your friend if you want to go look for that suitcase."

"Thank you." She reached out and patted the older man's hand.

Justin didn't recognize the look that passed between them. It was like they already knew each other, but that would be impossible. Unless . . . no . . . Chick had retired years before Em's dad rose to the top of the field.

Em wrapped her hands around her cup and slid off her stool. "Try to stay out of trouble for an hour or so, will you?"

"You sure you don't want me to help you track down your bag?" He was torn between tagging along with Em and having the chance to shoot the shit with a man he'd idolized as a kid.

"Nope. I'm sure y'all have plenty to talk about and if you go with me now, that means I'd have to sit around and listen to you later." She slid her shades back over her eyes as she neared the door. "I'm going to call the baggage office at the airport and if I need to, I'll take the ferry over to get my bag."

"Call me if you need me?" Justin put a hand on her shoulder. "I mean it, Em."

"I'll be fine. Seems like I've been getting into more trouble with you around than I have without you."

His cheeks prickled at the barb. That was all about to change.

Emmeline

Em took a seat at one of the tables close to the water, almost the same spot where she and Justin sat the night before. She lifted the cup to her nose and inhaled the scent of strong dark roast. Hopefully, it tasted as good as it smelled. While she waited for it to cool, she pulled up the number for the baggage office and dialed.

After a brief conversation and a long time spent on hold, Em was assured by the clerk that they'd deliver her bag to the house that afternoon. Seeing would be believing, but Em didn't have any other options. With that out of the way, she took her first sip of the dark brew and closed her eyes.

The warm breeze kissed her skin. It would be hot as hell later, but the temperature hovered in the low eighties now. With her eyes closed, her other senses heightened. Seagulls squawked overhead. Waves crashed along the shore. The salty breeze mingled with the scent of her coffee. Despite the number of awkward run-ins she'd had with Justin over the past twenty-four hours, she was glad they'd come.

She needed the break. Not nearly as much as Justin did, but still, spending all day every day with the under-six crowd took its toll. She loved working with kids and couldn't wait for Georgie to make her an auntie. She'd been trying to figure out what it was that had her in a bit of a funk.

Keisha said it was her biological clock, but Em didn't agree. Sure, she wanted to get married someday and have a house full of kids. But twenty-nine was still young, wasn't it?

Besides the couple of blind dates she'd been on lately, there hadn't been any prospects and she was way too smart to settle. If she was going to spend the rest of her life with someone, it had to be the right someone. None of her guy friends got ribbed for being almost thirty and single. Though Decker seemed to be on track with his latest. Out of the four of them, he was the most likely to tie the knot first.

Thinking about Decker made her wonder about Justin. His dad and brother had married young, though both of them ended up getting hitched to their high school sweethearts. Justin hadn't dated anyone seriously in high school.

He was way too focused on following in his dad's footsteps. But what about when he retired from bull riding?

A surge of heat radiated out from her belly as she thought about their interactions the night before. They'd never explored anything beyond the confines of friendship but based on her body's reaction to being so close to him, having her hands on him, there was definitely chemistry between them.

With the prospect of spending the next nine days with him, she needed someone to help her clear her head. She opened her eyes and picked up her phone.

Georgie answered on the second ring. "Thanks for letting me know you made it. I was worried about you last night."

"I was too busy getting caught naked in the hot tub by Justin to send a text."

"What?" Georgie shrieked. "Where is he now?"

"I left him talking to the retired bull rider while I tried to track down my suitcase." She glanced toward the bar area, where Justin and Chick faced each other across a high-top table. They appeared to be deep in conversation, so she relaxed and gave Georgie her full attention.

"The airline lost your bag? Sounds like the trip from hell so far."

"There's more. This morning I ended up with my bare hands on Justin's bare junk." Heat seeped back into her cheeks at the admission.

"What in the world's going on down there? You've got ten minutes to fill me in before I'm going to have to pee again. Your nephew seems to be straddling my bladder and I can't go more than a half hour in between trips to the bathroom."

"So, it's a boy?" Em's heart leapt. Georgie and her husband didn't want to find out the sex of the baby before he or she was born, but Em figured one of them knew. She kept waiting for her sister to drop hints.

"No. I'm just tired of referring to him or her as 'it,' so I decided to swap between pronouns. Please tell me all this misery will be worth it in the end?"

"Of course it will. You won't even remember any of this once you meet your beautiful baby girl."

"I guess that means you're still team pink?" Georgie laughed.

Em took a sip of coffee and leaned back in her chair. It was so good to hear her sister's voice. Since Georgie had moved down to San Antonio, they didn't get to see each other as often as they'd like, though they still checked in several times a week.

"Girls are easier to figure out. Boys are complicated."

"Most people would disagree with that statement. Now tell me what's going on down there and how you ended up with Justin's junk in your hands this morning."

Em replayed the events of the past twenty-four hours, skimming over the specifics of exactly how it had felt when Justin jerked his pants down.

"Where do you go from here?" Georgie asked. "I've always thought the two of you would be good together. No, not just good, but great. He's perfect for you, Em."

Her heart squeezed and her chest tightened. "That's ridiculous. Me and Justin?"

"What's so crazy about that?" Georgie pressed. "You're both loyal and wear your heart on your sleeve. Family always comes first, or at least that's the way it seems with him."

"Yeah, I think that's the main reason it would never work out between us." The spark that had ignited when Georgie mentioned Justin's name fizzled out.

"What do you mean?"

How could she explain to her sister what she hadn't ever figured out how to put into words? "Justin does put family first. That's why he could never be mine. He's willing to do whatever it takes, push himself past the breaking point, just to make his dad happy. I think you're wrong about us being the same. It would never work out between us."

18

❧

Justin

Justin eyed the old-timer across the table from him with a mixture of awe and respect. Chick Darville was a legend in his own time, and the years he'd been away from the ring had only multiplied the cloud of intrigue surrounding his legacy.

"I thought you retired to a ranch in west Texas." Justin looped a finger through his "Cowboy in Paradise" mug.

Chick shook his head. "That lasted a few years. Then the money started to run out and wife number four left me. I came down here for some soul searching about fifteen years ago and loved it so much I decided to stay."

"This place is great." He and Em hadn't ventured inside last night except to grab a menu. Now, in the bright light of day, he could appreciate the memorabilia that decorated the walls. Pictures of Chick and some of the other bull riders from his day hung over the bar. Tags from several of his rides were tied to a piece of twine and strung from the ceiling like banners.

"It's not a whole hell of a lot, but it's mine." Chick

rubbed a hand over the scruff on his chin. "What brings you all the way down here during rodeo season? I figured you'd be hitting the gym every day and training for a mid-season return."

"Yeah." The coffee was strong, just the way Justin liked it. He gulped it down, hoping the jolt of caffeine would clear the brain fog his head had been steeping in since last night. "My friend Emmeline won a trip down here, and I decided to take some time off and join her."

"She seems like a sweet girl."

"She is. I think she had an ulterior motive in getting me to come with her, though." It was the first time Justin had said the words out loud. Admitting it to Chick felt like a betrayal to Em. He set the mug back on the table and looked toward the water where Em sat, her phone held to her ear.

"You want to talk about it?" Chick asked.

Justin shook his head. "No, that's okay. I'd rather hear how you managed two perfect rides. It's been almost thirty years and no one's come close to matching that."

"Yeah, I suppose that's my legacy." Chick's eyes took on a distance that made Justin think the man was lost in some memories from a long time ago.

"It's an incredible legacy to leave behind." Hell, his dad would go ballistic if one of his riders pulled off a perfect ride. He could count the number of riders who'd managed that feat on one hand. And Chick had done it twice.

"I used to think so, too." Chick's mouth lifted up on one side.

"I'm not sure I understand."

Chick set his mug down on the table with a thud. "No, I suppose you wouldn't. From where you're sitting right now, I bet you think I held the whole world in the palm of my calloused hand."

Justin squinted as Chick held out his palm. Lines bisected the surface.

"It's all a matter of perspective. You're young, hungry for a title. I bet your shoulder isn't anywhere close to healing up right, and I'd bet my bar that you're planning on going back to competing, anyway."

Justin opened his mouth to deny it, but Chick put up a hand.

"It's okay. That's exactly what I would have done when I was your age. Time gives you the gift and the curse of perspective, though."

"I don't get it. What kind of perspective? What would you have changed?"

Chick inhaled and raised his brows. "Well, that's not a question I get very often. Most folks who come down here want to know what you asked at first . . . how did I manage two perfect rides. They want me to divulge some big secret they can take back to Kansas City or Phoenix or Calgary and put into practice so they can match my record."

Justin waited for him to continue. An uneasiness crept into his chest, squeezing his lungs tight, like his body already knew he wasn't going to like what Chick had to say.

"I'm going to tell you something that I haven't ever told another person." Chick leaned forward.

Justin shifted as well, moving closer so he wouldn't miss a word of advice.

"I should have quit way before I scored my first perfect ride." Chick slumped against the back of his barstool like the admission had sucked the life right out of him.

Justin's head pounded with the information. "But if you'd quit, you never would have—"

"Never would have gotten my fifth concussion. That turned me into a mean son of a bitch for eighteen months, and I lost my first wife over it."

"I'm sorry. We know that's one of the risks we take when we—"

"Never would have gotten stomped on by the bull that took me out of the running for another world title and put ten screws and a metal plate in my left leg. I don't mean to discount anything you're saying, but if I had it to do all over again . . ." Chick's jaw tightened, and he glanced out toward the ocean.

Justin waited for him to say something, anything, to put an end to the heavy silence that descended between them. Chick had been at the top of his career when he retired. Some rodeo announcers still brought his name up from time to time and talked about him in awestruck voices. How could he even imply that he might not have made the same choices if given the chance?

"There are some things in life more important than a belt buckle or a trophy with your name on it. I'll just leave it at that." Chick slid off his stool and headed behind the bar. "Get you another cup of coffee?"

"Sure." Justin took his mug over and set it down on the counter. "Can I ask you a question about what you just said?"

"You can ask, but I'm not saying I'll answer."

"Fair enough." Justin watched while Chick dumped the bit of coffee left at the bottom of his mug, then filled it to the brim. "You're part of rodeo history. A lot of folks would say your contribution to the sport has been instrumental to where it is today. What could possibly be more important than that?"

Chick rested his forearms on the bar and leaned toward Justin. His dark brown eyes were filled with sincerity, and Justin fidgeted with the handle of his mug while he waited for a response.

"That's the million-dollar question, isn't it, son? The answer is, every man has to figure that out for himself."

Emmeline

By the time Em hung up with her sister, the sun sat almost directly overhead. Justin and Chick sure were having a long conversation. Hopefully, the older man was knocking some sense into her friend. That was the whole reason she'd brought him all the way down here in the first place.

She looked over her shoulder to where Justin sat alone at one of the bar-height tables. He appeared to be deep in thought. She took the opportunity to study his profile. Could Georgie be right? Were the two of them meant for each other?

He'd always been good-looking. He had the kind of eyes that could make a woman's knees turn to jelly. She'd seen it happen herself. All he had to do was turn on the charm. The deep dimple in his left cheek pretty much guaranteed he'd get whatever he asked for. Add a gorgeous smile and a deep baritone, and women flocked to get their programs signed after a ride. Sometimes they wanted him to sign a whole lot more. Justin had called her with stories of women tossing their bras at him and begging for him to sign their boobs with a permanent marker. He handled it with the same self-deprecating attitude he carried with him wherever he went. He'd never been cocky like Decker or hidden in his shell like Knox.

He'd always just been Justin. She hadn't considered there being more than friendship between them until . . . well, until very recently. Since he'd canceled his appearances and moved home, she'd seen a lot more of him. While he'd been traveling most of the time, their connection was primarily over the phone or through texts. But since he'd been back, she spent a lot more time around him.

He still looked like himself. Same hair, same smile,

same tendency to tease her to the point of madness. But there was something else to him that she hadn't picked up by watching interviews on TV. He was calmer now, more steady. More grown-up maybe. Whatever it was, it damn sure was attractive.

No, not going to let herself go there. She shook her head, refusing to give any more thought to the idea that there could be anything more than friendship between them. The reason Justin was looking so good was that she hadn't been out with anyone she liked for way too long.

She'd pulled her profile from the dating app Keisha had convinced her to sign up for. Maybe over the next two weeks she'd rework it. Justin could give her some advice on what a guy might find attractive. That would definitely keep them in the friend zone. She couldn't afford to fall for her best friend. Would never even consider it if there was even the slightest chance he'd go back to bull riding.

"Hey, find your suitcase?" Justin had started heading her direction, the giant tortoise ambling along right behind him.

She shielded her eyes from the sun with her hand and glanced up at him. "They said they'll have it delivered to the house late this afternoon."

"Good. I picked up a brochure of things to do around here. You want to take a look and find something to do today?" He set a bright-colored brochure on the table.

Em reached for it, but before she could pick it up, the tortoise nudged his nose under her hand. "What do you need, Tripod?"

"I think he wants you to pet him." Justin rubbed a hand over the top of the giant animal's shell. "Chick told me he's used to getting a ton of attention around here."

"I bet." Em ran her fingers over Tripod's head. "It feels bumpy."

The tortoise stretched his neck out and shifted his back to the right. "He seems to like it."

"Maybe there's a boat tour or something that would help us get acclimated to the island. Did Chick give you any ideas?" She wanted to ask about what they'd discussed for over an hour, but didn't want to rush him. Justin would bring it up when he was ready.

"He said there's a turtle sanctuary down on Padre Island if you want to rent a car and take a day trip. There's not much to do here, since this island is mainly about vacation rentals and family homes. But we could take the ferry back to the mainland and wander around if you want."

"The turtle sanctuary sounds like fun. I'll see if I can find us a car to rent over the next couple of days. They also have horseback riding along the beach."

He snickered. "I didn't come all the way down here to pay someone to ride when I can ride as much as I want at home."

"You don't have a beach at home," she challenged.

"Maybe not, but I'm pretty particular about my horses."

"Oh, I get it." Em couldn't pass up the chance to give him crap, even about something so simple as a horse.

"Get what?" He shifted his palm to the other side of Tripod's shell.

"You're a snob." Em shrugged. He was easygoing about most things, but there were certain areas of his life where Justin could be as stubborn as the jackass her dad had bought for her mom for their tenth wedding anniversary. That animal wouldn't do anything he didn't want to, no matter what kind of incentive they used.

Justin laughed. "I'm not a snob. There are just certain things I'm particular about. I like 'em the way I like 'em and that's all there is to it."

She held up her pointer finger. "So, horses for one. Name something else you have to have your way."

He rubbed his palm over his belly. "Steak. It's got to be cooked just right, or it's no good. Medium-rare, with the right shade of pink in the middle. Mmm, maybe we can find a steak place where we can grab a bite while we're here."

Em added her middle finger. "That's two things. Is that it?"

He bit down on his lip and clucked his tongue. "Let me think for a second."

Tripod must have tired of the attention. He backed away from the table, then slowly turned and meandered down the beach.

"Um, there's only one other thing I can think of, but I don't feel particularly inclined to share." Justin picked up the brochure and studied the inside flap. "It says here we can join a snorkeling charter. Want to try that tomorrow?"

"Not so fast. What's the one other thing you're hell-bent on having your way?"

He crinkled his nose and cracked a grin. "You sure you want to know, Em?"

"Yes. How bad can it be?"

"Just remember, you asked for it."

Her stomach dipped and rolled while she waited for him to reveal what he didn't think she could handle.

"The first time I kiss a woman . . ." He tucked his chin against his chest and waited a beat.

The tips of Em's ears tingled. He was right—she didn't want to know. Before she could tell him to drop it, he glanced up at her, his eyes as clear as the topaz her mom had worn as a wedding ring for over thirty years.

"The first time I kiss a woman, I've got to do it my way."

19

❦

Justin

Em's cheeks flushed, the color going from light pink to a deep shade of red. He'd warned her not to ask. He wanted to point out that she was just as stubborn as him since she wouldn't drop it, but it seemed like a moot point now.

She twirled her empty cup around with her fingers. "Do I even want to know what you mean by that?"

"I don't know, do you?" He could have offered to show her. Even the idea of brushing his lips against hers made his pulse pound. He wasn't joking, though. A first kiss, especially with someone he really liked, had to be perfect. It set the tone for what was to come.

If the stars ever aligned and he got the chance to tell Em how he felt, he'd find a way to make sure their first kiss was the most perfect first kiss of all.

Em leaned against the back of her chair and crossed her arms over her chest. The color on her cheeks had faded like she'd gotten over the initial shock. "Try me."

His mouth went bone dry. "What?"

"Tell me how you create the perfect first kiss. I'm curious now."

He tried to swallow, but a lump lodged in his throat. Forcing it down, he pulled the chair from the table and dropped down onto the seat. He didn't have anything to lose . . . may as well see where this line of conversation would take them.

"Well, I like to be in control the first time I kiss a woman." He shrugged, wishing she didn't have those dark shades covering her eyes so he could get a clue about what she might be thinking.

"No surprise there. You like to be in control of every situation." Her lips pursed, drawing his attention to her mouth.

He shouldn't focus his gaze on her lips; that would only add to the unsettled turmoil in his gut. "Not always."

Em let out a soft laugh. "Don't try to distract me by making me give examples of twenty-some years of you having to be in charge. Do the scores of women you've shared first kisses with mind letting you be in control?"

She was teasing. He could tell by the underlying sass in her tone. It wasn't exactly a flirty vibe between them, but it had potential. "I think they appreciate it."

Em wasn't willing to leave it there. "And what makes you think that?"

"Well, they seem to like it."

"Kissing you?"

"Yeah."

"And how can you tell?"

He didn't want to get into details about kissing other women, not with the one woman in the world he'd always wanted to kiss and hadn't had the chance. "Do you want to talk about something else? Or grab a burger before we head back to the house to wait for your bag?"

"Are you avoiding the line of questioning?" Her eyebrows lifted above the frames of her shades.

Challenge accepted. If Em wanted to go there, he wasn't going to be the first to back down. "Not at all. What do you want to know?"

She leaned forward, resting her elbows on the table. "I want to know what makes you think these women love it when you take charge of all the kissing."

"I didn't say all the kissing. Just the first kiss."

"Oh, thanks for clarifying. I was under the impression the women you've dated in the past just stood around waiting for you to lay one on them."

Now she had him thinking about it. He had been the one to initiate intimacy in his past relationships. Was it because he liked to be in charge, or was it the type of women he tended to date? "That's not how it goes, Em."

"How does it go, Romeo?"

Maybe it was the way she kept pushing it, maybe it was the fresh ocean air, maybe it was the fact he'd been dying to kiss her for ten years and was afraid he'd never get the chance. He leaned forward, closing the distance between them.

It was probably better he couldn't see her eyes. If he had, he might have been too nervous to reach up and cup her cheek with his palm. He might have been too chickenshit to slide his thumb along her jawbone. He might not have had the balls to get to his feet, lean his whole body over the table, and lightly press his lips to hers.

Fireworks exploded behind his eyelids at the contact. His entire body came to life like he'd been operating on a low battery and someone had just plugged him in.

She didn't respond, just sat there, her hands at her sides, her lips soft and yielding under his.

The weight of what he'd done pressed down on him, squeezing his lungs, making it impossible to breathe. He pulled back, hovered over the table, trying to see past the black lenses.

Say something, Em. He silently willed her to make a joke and blow off what just happened. He'd done it this time. Way to fuck up a lifelong friendship. He closed his eyes while the pressure in his chest built. Any second, his heart would explode due to intense dumbassery.

"Justin." Em whispered his name, her voice quiet and laced with a tone he hadn't heard before.

He forced his eyes open, cracking them just enough to face her. He wasn't sure what to expect, but it wasn't the look she currently wore. Her lips parted, and she slid her sunglasses off her eyes to rest them on top of her head. He wasn't sure what level of idiocy he'd sunk to yet.

Em launched herself across the table. He barely caught her in his arms. Her lips smashed against his while her arms wrapped around the back of his neck. He pulled her onto his lap.

Her tongue demanded entrance, pressing against the seam of his lips. They parted and her tongue swept into his mouth. The taste of coffee lingered in her mouth, layered with peppermint. He'd barely had time to register that before his senses went on overload.

His skin tingled from the touch of her fingers at the nape of his neck. Her scent—a mix of something flowery and sweet—mingled with the salty breeze. Her heart hammered, a rhythmic *boom-boom-boom* he felt against his own chest. It matched the pounding of his own pulse that hammered through his ears.

Too soon, she broke away.

"Em." He smoothed his palm along her upper arm, not sure whether to apologize.

She opened her eyes, gazing up at him with a kind of heat he'd never seen before. "You want to do that again?"

Emmeline

What the heck just happened? Em's entire world flipped upside down and inside out. One moment she was looking at Justin like her very best friend. Then he touched his lips to hers, and everything changed.

"Maybe we should talk about things first?" He pulled his hand away from her cheek. She immediately missed his touch.

Talk . . . yes, they should talk. "Do you want to start us off?"

He reached up to rub his palm along the back of his neck. "How about a walk down the beach?"

A walk and talk. Under the circumstances, that seemed like a good idea. If they were walking next to each other, they wouldn't have to make eye contact. She already felt like her insides were on fire. Taking some time to let that heat cool off would be a good idea.

"Yeah, let's go for a walk." She pushed her chair back and got up. Her knees threatened to buckle, so she grabbed hold of the edge of the table.

"You okay, Em?" He reached out to steady her.

"Of course. The sand just shifted under my feet, that's all." The little white lie rolled off of her tongue way too easily, but she didn't want him to know how unsettled she was. If one kiss from Justin could turn her legs into wet noodles, there was no telling what kind of mind-blowing experience might be in store if they decided to take things to the next level.

"Should we head back toward the house or do you

want to walk a little farther in the other direction?" Justin shielded his eyes from the sun with his hand as he glanced down the beach the opposite way from where they'd come.

"Either." She didn't trust herself to make any decisions in the moment, no matter how small or insignificant they might seem. Less than a minute ago she'd been willing to climb into his lap and blow past the boundaries of friendship. She needed to compose herself, lock down whatever hormones had been released, and pull herself together.

"Let's go that way." Justin pointed toward a pier far off in the distance. "I think we've got enough time to go all the way down there and get back to the house before your luggage might arrive."

"Sounds good." Em tossed her empty paper cup into a trash can nearby.

Justin kicked off his flip-flops and left them by a lounge chair. "You want to leave your shoes here and we can pick them up on the way back?"

"Sure." She lined up her sandals next to his. Keeping the conversation to talk of walks and shoes was safe, smart even.

She fell into step next to him as he moved toward the wet sand at the shoreline. Seagulls squawked overhead, hoping for a snack. A light breeze blew at their backs, making the rising temperature bearable. Em kept her gaze on her toes, watching her feet sink into the wet sand as they moved away from the bar.

"I had a good talk with Chick." Justin finally broke the silence.

"Oh yeah?"

"He's given me a lot to think about."

Em hoped that meant Chick had talked some sense into her friend, though their conversation had lasted only about an hour. "Like what?"

Justin cleared his throat. "Like what I want my priorities to be."

"Mmm-hmm." She didn't want to sway the conversation one way or the other. Whatever decision Justin came to about returning to the tour had to be his alone.

"I've been riding bulls for so long, I don't know how to do anything else."

She stopped, the truth of his words smacking her like a two-by-four across the forehead. "Is that what you're worried about? There are a million things you can do."

"Like what?" Justin squinted down at her, his forehead creased.

"Like anything you want. You can go to college and get a degree . . ."

He shook his head. "I was doing good just to get through high school. There's no way I want to go sit in a classroom again almost twelve years later."

"What about taking Decker up on his offer and going to work for his dad's company?" She couldn't imagine Justin putting up with Decker every day, but at least if he went to work for Wayne Holdings he'd have job security and someone looking out for him.

"Not my scene." He turned to face the wide expanse of the ocean. "My dad assumes I'll help out with the bull-riding school once I earn that title."

Em's heart shriveled a little. "If you want to work with your dad and Jake, can't you do that without the title?"

Justin let out a soft laugh. "Well, sure, but what does that look like? Who's going to want to be trained by a man who couldn't get his own son all the way to the championship?"

"You've been to the championship round before." She brushed her finger against his arm, not knowing if she could trust herself to touch him without wanting to snuggle up against him. "Even if you never win a world championship title, you've already earned a spot in that elite group of bull riders who are the best of the best."

He wrapped his fingers around hers and gave them a squeeze. "You and I both know that doesn't count for shit without the title to prove it, at least not to my dad or Jake."

"So you're going to go back to the tour?" She wanted to comfort him but didn't know how. Feeling helpless, she squeezed his fingers.

"I don't know yet, Em." The uncertainty in his eyes let her know he was telling her the truth. "You'll never date a bull rider."

She bit down on her bottom lip and nodded. "I don't think I can. Not after what happened to my dad."

"I won't let that happen to me." He tugged her close enough to wrap his arms around her.

She pressed her cheek against his chest, inhaling his scent. "You can't know that."

"I'll tell you one thing I do know." His arms tightened around her. "That kiss wasn't just a kiss. Not to me."

It wasn't just a kiss to her, either. How could it be when they had so much history between them?

"I want you, Em. You're already my best friend, and I want more."

Her breath bobbled. "Before we let anything else happen, I think we need to decide what we want . . . what we can handle."

"I can respect that." His palm smoothed over her hair while he looked down to hold her gaze.

She wanted to tell him to forget what she'd said about not dating a bull rider. The moment their lips touched, her future clicked into place and he was at the center of it. How could she hold on to a stupid rule when she knew deep down in her heart that he was the only one for her?

Then an image of her dad struggling to hold his fork invaded her thoughts. He wasn't the same man now that her mama had married. Did she want to risk putting herself through that? Wasn't it better to nip whatever attraction she and Justin had between them right in the bud before it had a chance to grow out of hand?

There were too many risks, too many unknowns. Em closed her eyes for a long beat and doused all the heat she'd been feeling for Justin with a bucket of ice-cold reality. Unless he planned to retire, she couldn't open up her heart to him.

Not now.

Maybe not ever.

20

❧

Justin

The next morning, Justin woke up feeling irritable and cranky. Resolved not to mention the kiss again, he tried to put it out of his mind. The task proved impossible.

Em was everywhere. Every time he turned around she was next to him, returning his smiles, laughing at his silly jokes, or walking around in a hot-pink bikini that left little to his imagination. Not that he needed the use of his imagination to conjure up images of what she looked like in her birthday suit. Like he'd ever be able to erase that vision from his mind. It had been burned into his memory—a cruel reminder of what would never be.

They'd been taking it easy while they acclimated to vacation mode. This afternoon Em wanted to head to the beach on the north end of the island to see some sandcastle contest. She thought it would be a good opportunity to get some pictures of Rocky.

"What do you think about that one?" Em nodded toward a huge sculpture of a dragon.

"Impressive." Justin followed the design from the tip of

the dragon's tail, over each scale that had been delicately carved out of the sand.

"I think the kids would like this one." She set Rocky down in the sand near the flames coming from the dragon's mouth. Then she knelt to snap a few pictures. She had on her bikini top with a gauzy cover-up knotted like a skirt around her waist.

He tried to swallow but his throat was so damn dry. It didn't have anything to do with the way the sun beat down on his shoulders and everything to do with being exposed to so much of Em being exposed. What wouldn't he give for the opportunity to slide his hands over her hips and know her heart belonged to him?

"Oh, this one's good, too." She walked ahead to where someone had sculpted a mermaid rising out of the sand. The mermaid's hair flowed over her shoulders, covering her breasts, and her waist gave way to an intricately sculpted tail. "She's beautiful."

Justin wanted to tell Em that the sandy mermaid had nothing on the way she looked, but he wouldn't. First because it sounded cheesy, and second because the less he thought about and talked about how gorgeous she was, the better.

"Look, Justin, it's Tripod!" Em pointed to the next sculpture, a scaled-to-size replica of Chick's three-legged tortoise friend. "Says here this one was done by employees of A Cowboy in Paradise," Em read.

"It looks just like him." Justin held out his phone. "How about a selfie with the sand version of Tripod?"

Em stepped into his side and smiled at his phone. He snapped the photo, hoping he got both of them in the frame. It was hard to tell with the sun shining so brightly.

While he fiddled with the camera, trying to pull up the picture to check, he followed behind Em.

"Hey, watch out!" The warning came about a second too late.

Justin stepped forward and his foot slipped. Before he had a chance to even look up, he landed on his hip against some sort of sand structure.

"Oh no." Em turned around to head back to him.

Justin put out a hand to push himself up, causing more sand to tumble down.

"That was my sandcastle." A little boy standing nearby wiped sandy hands over his eyes. "It's ruined."

The kid couldn't be more than five or six. He seemed to be about the same size as the kids in Em's class.

"Hey, I'm sorry." Justin stepped away from the ruined structure. "I didn't mean to knock over your castle, bud. Looks like I should keep track of where I'm walking."

"He's okay." A woman holding a baby in her arms put her hand on the kid's shoulder. "I'll help you fix it once I get your brother fed."

Justin aimed for an apologetic grin, but the kid frowned up at him. "Hey, how about I help you fix it?"

The kid's eyes narrowed.

"We have time, right, Em?" Justin looked to Em, hoping she'd sense his need for assistance.

"We sure do. Would it be okay with you if we helped you do a little demo and reconstruction?"

The boy glanced at his mom, who gave a nod of approval. "Okay."

Justin grinned. This would be fun. He couldn't remember the last time he'd spent an afternoon playing in the sand. "Great. Should we talk about design first, or—"

The kid thrust a shovel at Justin's chest. "You dig the moat."

Em stifled a laugh as she set her beach bag down on the sand. "What can I do to help?"

"You carry the water." He held out a bright red bucket.

"All right. Let's get to building." Em took off toward the water's edge, her hips swishing back and forth, her tiny bikini bottoms visible through the sheer fabric.

Justin knelt down, shovel in hand, and began to dig. First, he had to empty the sand he'd sent crashing down out of the current moat. When that was done, he started digging deeper. The kid piled buckets full of wet sand in the center. His design lacked a plan and any kind of detail, but he seemed to be enjoying himself, so that was all that mattered.

A couple of hours after they started, Justin sat back on his heels to admire their efforts. The lopsided castle stretched about three feet tall, its spires reaching for the sky. Justin had dug out a river all the way to the shoreline so that every time a wave rolled in, the water filled the moat.

"What do you think?" Em asked.

"I like it." The boy, whose name they'd learned was Aiden, jumped up and down while he clapped his hands. "Mom, will you take a picture?"

Aiden's mom picked up the baby and walked over with her phone in her hand. "That looks amazing, honey, even better than before."

Aiden posed, a smile devoid of front teeth lighting up his face as he moved around the edge of the castle.

"Thanks so much for keeping him entertained this afternoon. My husband is supposed to be enjoying our vacation but had to call in for a work meeting this morning." Aiden's mom shifted the baby in her arms.

"It was our pleasure," Em said.

Justin nodded. "Yeah, I'm sorry I ruined it in the first place."

"Oh, don't be." The woman smiled and pressed a kiss

to the baby's cheek. "I wouldn't be surprised if he wants to stomp all over it before we head back to the house."

"Stomp all over it?" Justin turned just in time to see Aiden lift a foot. "What are you doing?"

"Now we get to tear it down," Aiden said. Then he stepped on the bridge Justin had spent fifteen minutes perfecting to stretch over the moat.

Em laughed. "I wondered how long it would take before he did that."

Justin sat back on his heels while Aiden pretended to be a dinosaur and then a robot who crashed into the castle from outer space. Em's laughter rang through his ears, making him wonder what it would be like if the two of them ever had kids. Would they have a sweet baby girl who looked like Em? Or a belligerent boy who'd take after him?

"All right, Aiden. Time to head back to the house so I can put your baby brother down for a nap." Aiden grumbled but headed back toward his mom. "What do you say to the nice people who helped you build the castle?"

Aiden turned around and ran back toward the remains of the castle. He lifted his hand in a high five and slapped it against Justin's and then Em's. "Thanks a bunch. See ya later, alligators."

"After a while, crocodile," Em responded.

"Well that was fun." Justin let his gaze drift over the ruins that remained of their hard work.

Em brushed the sand off her legs and reached for her bag. "You were really good with him."

Justin basked under the warmth of her compliment. God, he wanted it. Wanted a future where the two of them could take their kids to the beach for a family vacation. Where they could grow old together, sipping on sweet tea on their front porch in matching rocking chairs. The kind of life they could have together flashed before his eyes.

"Hey, Em." His voice was soft, low enough that only she could hear him.

"Yeah?"

"Want to head back to the house and cool off in the air conditioning?" He held out his hand.

She took it, sliding her palm against his. The contact sent a rush of need straight to his cock. He was tired of holding back, tired of depriving himself of the one thing in life he knew would make him happy.

But was he willing to give up his dad's dream to follow his own?

Emmeline

Justin swung their hands back and forth between them almost the whole way back to the house. He'd been so good with the kid on the beach. Em couldn't help but think about what kind of a dad he'd be. He might try to come off as a tough guy, but he had a soft, squishy center. The past couple of days had made her question everything. Was she really going to deny herself a chance at happiness if he decided to return to the tour?

They hadn't talked about the kiss since it happened. Both of them had been avoiding the conversation that sooner or later needed to take place. Em was tired of pretending she didn't like him as more than a friend. Now that she'd smashed through the chains that held that particular Pandora's box closed, there was no going back.

They'd barely stepped into the house when she rose onto her tiptoes and pressed her lips against his. "Thanks for a fun afternoon."

She meant it as a friendly peck, but the overwhelming magnitude of her attraction to him caught her by surprise.

She'd never felt such primal need before. Something deep inside urged her on.

"Thank you." Justin leaned into her, kissing her back.

Tired of fighting it, she gave in to the desire, pressing him against the back of the door, desperate to taste him again. The need to feel his skin on hers sent her fingers to the hem of his shirt.

Before she could slide it up, he reached one hand behind his neck and yanked the shirt up and over his head. He had the kind of muscles earned by a strict workout regimen and hard work. She'd seen him shirtless before and had admired the definition of his chest and abs like she would a pro athlete on any page of a sports magazine. Never had she dreamed of touching his bare skin. Now she couldn't get enough.

Her palms splayed over his chest, his muscles firm and solid underneath her fingers. His hands cupped her ass, pulling her even tighter against him. She couldn't think, couldn't suck in enough air to fill her lungs. Her nails dug into his biceps and she hoped she'd leave a mark. She needed proof that this wasn't just a dream. He turned them around so her back was pressed up against the door and the ridge of his erection aligned against the sweet spot of her core.

This was Justin, her best friend in the whole wide world. She should stop this madness before they did something that would change their friendship forever . . . something they both might regret. The thought tugged at the edges of her mind, yet her hand slid down, working on the button at his waistband as he slipped the hem of her shirt up her stomach.

His body was perfect, the broad shoulders, abs chiseled from marble, a cock that looked like it could break her. She licked her lips, impatient to taste him, to feel him, to let him devour her however he wanted.

It was too much.

She needed to feel him, all of him.

Gripping him tighter, she pushed her abs against him. Bare skin touched bare skin. Heat rocketed through her. He took control of the kiss, one hand cradling the back of her head as he ran a finger along the waistband of her shorts. Her hips bucked against him and an unexpected moan ripped from her throat.

She was wet, literally drenched with desire.

She wasn't going to drop her shorts and let him take her in the entryway, so she pushed off the door and maneuvered them toward the hall. He must have understood her intention. Cupping her ass in his hands, he lifted her up and carried her toward her bedroom. He tried to lay her on the bed, but she wouldn't loosen her grip, so they fell together.

"You sure about this?" Justin muttered against the shell of her ear.

"Yes." Her voice came out as a whisper. She was sure. Sure she'd never been so turned on, never hummed with desire, or felt her blood scorching her from the inside out.

With her sprawled across the bed underneath him, he had access to all of her. He slid her shirt up, his lips tracing the path over her navel. Her shirt passed her bikini top, then he pulled it over her head before he tossed it aside.

She propped herself up on her elbows, and his gaze fell to her breasts.

"You're so fucking beautiful."

Heat rushed over her cheeks. She'd never been 100 percent comfortable in her own skin. She'd rather have bigger boobs and smaller hips. Maybe longer legs, too. But the tone of his voice said he was sincere.

Her arms went over his shoulders, and she tugged him down to her. She'd rather have his mouth on hers than

have him tossing out compliments he probably felt obligated to share.

While his tongue tangled with hers, his fingers ran
along the trim of her bikini top. A shiver ran through her
at his touch, pebbling her skin. Justin cupped one breast
and slipped her top down, then ran the pad of his thumb
over her nipple. Sweet agony pooled at her core. She
wanted him. Wanted him more than she'd ever wanted anything in her life.

Her leg hooked around his waist and she drew his hips
to hers. He shifted and pressed down, providing pressure
exactly where she wanted it most. Then she bridged, lifting her pelvis to grind against his. The friction was almost
too much to take.

Eager for more, she untied the string on his swim shorts,
then tugged at the zipper. He slid them down before kicking them off the end of the bed. Her back arched as she
reached down and wrapped her hand around his penis.

He was hard as a rock, yet his skin was so soft it felt
like velvet in her hands. She brushed her thumb over the
tip, then rubbed the bead of moisture down his length.

"Em . . ." He hissed in a breath.

Her chest rose and fell while she gulped a lungful of
air. "Don't stop now."

The look in his eyes told her the last thing he wanted to
do was stop. His fingers hooked around the straps of her
bikini bottoms, and he jerked them down. Naked in front
of him for the second time in less than a week, she expected the same blaze of embarrassment from the other
night.

But all she felt was a deep ache. A throbbing need that
pulsed inside her, pushing her past her comfort zone.

21

❦

Justin

If Justin had it his way, she'd never be clothed again. The body underneath his hands was too beautiful to be covered up. If she belonged to him, he'd insist she walk around the house naked all the time so he could reach out and touch her whenever he wanted. Yeah, that didn't sound as Neanderthal as fuck. But he didn't care. He'd been waiting half a lifetime to have her in his arms.

Now that she was there, he wanted to draw things out, make their first time last as long as possible. Deep in his soul, he knew that he and Em belonged together. This was only the beginning. They'd have the rest of their lives to enjoy each other.

But there could only be one first.

He wanted it to be as perfect as possible.

The feel of her hand sliding up and down his cock provided a preview of what it would be like to sink deep inside her. Kneeling over her, he couldn't bring himself to touch her. She was too perfect. Too good for him. What they shared went beyond just a physical attraction. He didn't know how to explain it, but he had to have her.

But not just for one night.

This was the start of something that would last forever. He wanted to savor it, commit each inch of her skin to his memory. His gaze burned a trail from her face to her breasts and down the entire length of her body. There was so much skin to explore . . . so many things he wanted to learn about her. Did she like things hot and fast or would she prefer to be seduced with a slow touch?

What would she taste like? He couldn't wait to find out.

Did she like to be on top or underneath? He'd have her every which way known to man if she'd let him . . . from the front, from behind, and in any other way he could to claim her as his.

He wanted her.

No, *want* wasn't a strong enough word. Of course, he wanted her, but it went so much deeper than that. He didn't just need her; he was desperate for her. She was his other half. It was like he'd been living only half a life until their lips touched.

Fuck, he sounded like a lunatic in his own head.

They'd passed the point of no return when she took his cock in her hand. All he needed to do was see it through.

She glanced up at him through hooded eyelids, a punch-drunk look on her face. He couldn't wait to see what she looked like when he made her come.

He traced a finger down her side. She shivered and captured her bottom lip with her teeth.

"I'm going to make you feel so good, Em." Thoughts of how he wanted to do just that flooded his brain. Like a kid at an all-you-can-eat candy factory, he didn't know what to sample first. Pert, rosy nipples begged for attention from his tongue. His fingers itched to slide through her slick heat and find out how drenched she was. Her lips needed to be kissed again.

"Do it," she begged. "Make me feel good, Justin. I want you to." His name drifted from her lips on a raspy exhale, exactly like the sexy tone he'd conjured in his head. Being with her in real life was so much better than the times he'd pictured her face, imagining her lying underneath him while he jerked off into his own hand.

His finger teased a trail across her belly, then lower. He ran along the curve of her hip, then skimmed his palm over her thigh. She angled her head to catch his lips, lazily sweeping her tongue into his mouth while she cupped his balls in her hands.

His cock hardened even more, and his balls drew tight. Her touch was gentle, but eager. She slipped a finger behind his balls, easing it along the sensitive strip of skin. Pressure built. He wouldn't be able to hold back much longer, not with her teasing and taunting his cock with her hand.

"I wanted to take this slow, I swear." He whispered words against her ear as he put on the condom he'd grabbed from his wallet. "But I can't wait. I need you. Now."

Em must have felt the same way. Spreading her legs, she gripped his shoulders and pulled him onto her.

His lips didn't leave hers as he traced a finger around her clit. Her chest heaved. He slid a finger inside, gently exploring. She arched her back.

"You're so fucking wet." Her breath was warm against his mouth.

"Because of you." She spread her legs farther apart, encouraging him.

His cock nudged against her thigh. She adjusted her hips, angling to give him better access. He eased the tip of his cock into her, a promise of what was to come.

Thrusting her hips up, she wrapped her legs around his waist and clung to his shoulders as he seated himself deep inside.

"You feel so good, baby. So fucking good." He pulled back and pumped into her again. Her body responded to his, tightening around him. Every one of his nerves tingled in anticipation, building, stretching, waiting for release.

Emmeline

He set the rhythm, the agonizing in and out taking her to the brink of madness. Her hands tightened on his shoulders as she hovered on the edge, unable to do anything but wait for him to send her tumbling over.

"Look at me, Em. I want to watch you come undone."

It was the tone of his voice that did it, sent her hurtling into the unknown. The weight of his hips pressing down on hers was the only thing that kept her from spinning into an abyss of pleasure.

His mouth fit against her ear, murmuring all the deliciously naughty things he wanted to do to her all night long. As he strained, his entire body tense and on the edge of his release, the aftershocks of her orgasm crackled through her.

She clung to him, her heels digging into the curve above his sculpted ass, her arms locked around his neck, the walls of her sex clenched around him. Right when she thought she could catch her breath, another wave started. Relentlessly, he filled her, giving her no choice but to follow his lead.

Justin shifted her hips higher, adjusting the angle so he could go deeper. Somehow, her body stretched around him. He pulled back and thrust forward, his hips pistoning back and forth, his cock sinking deeper and deeper until it rubbed against that elusive spot that had never been breached.

The force of a second release tumbled over her. She didn't know up from down, front from back, or left from right. The only thing she knew, she knew with 100 percent certainty, deep down in her core.

This was right.

Whatever this was between them, whatever invisible line they'd crossed, it was meant to be.

The feeling stayed with her while Justin gently lowered her back to the bed. While he pressed soft kisses against her temple and brushed her hair away from her sweaty cheeks. While he disappeared into the bathroom and even when he returned and wrapped her in his arms.

She snuggled into him, burrowing into the crook of his arm to rest her cheek on his chest. "What the hell was that?"

His soft laugh made his chest rise and fall. "I don't know, but I liked it."

Warmth spread through her limbs. "Me, too."

"Can I tell you something, Em?" His finger made slow, lazy circles on her shoulder.

She shifted, resting her chin on her hand so she could see his face. "Of course."

"I've wanted to do that with you for a hell of a long time now." His breath blew against the sweat beading her brow.

Thinking of him as more than a friend had caught her by surprise. Had he considered it before? "How long?"

"I'm not sure I want to admit how long I've fantasized about us." His eyes met hers, a hint of vulnerability darkening the deep blue depths.

Her heart skipped a beat. "How long?"

He glanced at the ceiling. "About ten years, give or take a few months."

"Justin!" She pushed his side and propped herself up on her elbow so she could see if he was joking. "Ten years?"

"Yeah." He bit down on his lip, drawing her attention to his mouth.

She wanted to chase away his insecurity, so she leaned forward, slanting her lips over his. "Sounds like we have a lot of lost time to make up for then."

His palm smoothed over her hair as their lips met. Ten years. So much had happened in the past ten years. Why hadn't he said something before? Why hadn't he made a move?

She pulled back and studied him in the dim light. "Why didn't you ever say anything?"

He held her gaze. "Because I knew you'd never go for a guy who wanted to make a career out of riding bulls. Not after what happened with your dad."

Em nodded. She never doubted that he knew her better than almost anyone else, but his admission confirmed it. "You're right. I wouldn't have."

She wanted to ask him what happened next. Where did they go from here? But she didn't want to jinx anything. It was so new. She needed to step back and think about things.

A motor sounded outside the front window, and then the doorbell rang.

"Are you expecting someone?" Justin asked.

Em slapped her palm against her forehead. "Oh shoot. I bought a couple of things when I walked into town yesterday and they said they'd deliver for me so I wouldn't have to carry them."

"I got it." Justin got up and stepped into his shorts. "Don't go anywhere, okay?"

She sat up in the bed, the sheet clenched around her. "Where would I go like this?"

"I don't know. The other night you were wandering around on the patio without anything on." A chunk of hair fell over his eye. He blew a breath toward it while he pulled up his trunks.

"I was stressed and couldn't sleep. Everything was fine until that spider decided to interrupt." She stuck her lower lip out in an exaggerated pout.

"I'll try to figure out a way to make sure you're worn out enough to sleep tonight." Before heading through the doorway, he gave her the sassy grin he usually saved for when he, Knox, and Decker were planning on causing some trouble.

The front door opened, and she heard him say something to whoever stood on the porch. A few minutes later, he carried a couple of bags into the bedroom.

"Good." She sighed. "Now I'll have something new to wear when you take me out for my birthday dinner."

Justin crawled on the bed and resumed his spot next to her. He gently tugged at the sheet she'd pulled up to her chin. It slid down to rest under her chest. He held her eye contact as he leaned over, then pressed featherlight kisses on the sensitive skin between her breasts. "I don't think you need a new dress."

"No?" She reached for his waistband, wanting to feel the warmth of his skin against hers.

"Damn, Em. I think you look your best wearing nothing at all."

22

❤

Justin

Justin nuzzled his nose into Em's hair and breathed in her scent. She'd fallen asleep about an hour ago and he'd wrapped himself around her, loving the feel of her back pressed against his front. His arm rested at an awkward angle and had been tingling for the past several minutes. He didn't want to move and risk waking her.

Why had he been so worried about telling her how he felt? The way things happened between them this afternoon was so natural. True, they hadn't really talked about where things would lead, but it was clear they belonged together.

Even now, snuggled against each other, they just fit. There wasn't any awkwardness. He knew all of her secrets and she knew all of his. Unlike so many of the women who chased him down at rodeo events, Em wasn't after him because she wanted to sleep with a bull rider. He didn't have to pretend with her. Didn't have to try so hard to be someone he wasn't.

It was freeing to finally come clean. Though he hadn't sprung the L-word on her yet, it was only a matter of time.

Now that they'd moved beyond friendship, he was eager to hit all the milestones . . . first real date, first "I love you," first holiday as a couple. Damn, would they spend their first Thanksgiving together at her mom and dad's place or with his family at Jake's?

His lips spread into a smile as he thought about everything they had to look forward to. If Knox and Decker were there—and thankfully they weren't—they'd tell him to slow the fuck down. But Em wasn't some chick he'd just met. They had history together. They didn't have to go through all the getting-to-know-each-other months. They could jump ahead to the important topics of conversation, such as where did they want to live when they got married and how many horses did they want to have.

She stretched in her sleep and her eyelids fluttered open. He wondered what might be running through her head. She rolled over to face him and tucked her hands underneath her cheek.

With his arm free, he gave it a shake and tried to get some blood circulating again. "Did you have a good rest?"

"Mmm-hmm." She blinked, her long lashes fluttering against her cheeks.

He was so whupped, he even loved her eyelashes. They were long and black and framed her emerald-green eyes. There wasn't a single inch of her he wasn't madly in love with, though he definitely preferred some of her body parts to others. Like her mouth. He'd finally kissed the plump, perfect lips and it was everything he'd dreamed it would be and more. And her breasts. Not too big, not too small. Perfection, just like Em.

"Did you sleep at all?" Her voice still tinged with sleepiness, she studied him.

He shook his head, the scruff on his cheeks sounding

like sandpaper on the pillow. "Nah. I figured I'd rather lie here and watch you sleep."

"That sounds boring." She covered her yawn with her hand. "Sorry, I'm used to my eight hours a night at home."

"Yeah, well, you're on vacation and there's lots to do." He walked his fingers up her arm and brushed her hair away from her shoulder. "Sleep's overrated, anyway."

"Says the man who's been known to take three-hour naps in the middle of the afternoon." She let out a breathy laugh. "My kindergartners can get by on less sleep than you."

"Yeah, well, I'm not sleeping now." He bent forward to kiss her forehead.

"No, you're definitely not asleep. In fact, parts of you appear to be very much awake." Her gaze traveled down his chest and past his stomach, coming to rest on his hard-on. "Doesn't that thing ever get tired?"

"That thing?" He faked being offended. "I don't think that part of my anatomy has ever been referenced in such a crude way."

"Oh, I'm sorry." She batted her eyelids at him. "Does it prefer to be addressed by a different name?"

He could think of a few names he wouldn't mind, but he didn't want to say them out loud.

"Come on, I can tell you've thought about it." She ran a finger along his length.

"I don't want you to laugh," he volunteered. Plenty of guys had a special name for their dick. One of Decker's old girlfriends called his the Flesh Stallion. Justin had always thought of his cock as just that . . . a cock or a dick.

"I won't laugh. Promise." Em traced a cross over her left breast.

He lifted his hand and followed her finger with his. Her nipple hardened. Seeing an outward sign that she was turned on made his dick even harder.

"Tell me one of them." Her finger moved up to her mouth, and she kissed it, then transferred the kiss to his dick.

"Well"—he rubbed her nipple between his finger and his thumb—"Love Rocket has a nice ring to it."

"Love Rocket? Oooh, I like that. Can I take a ride on your Love Rocket, Justin?" Her brow arched, and she appeared to be waiting for a reaction.

"Not if you're going to mock it." Flirting with Em took their banter to a whole new level. She'd always been wickedly smart and had a sharp tongue to match.

"I'd never mock your rod of steel."

"Rod of steel isn't super original. The Man of Steel's probably claimed that nickname already."

"So, Love Rocket it is." She slid her other hand down and surrounded his cock with her palms. With the perfect amount of pressure, she rubbed his dick between them.

"You want to take a ride on my Love Rocket, is that it?" He rolled her onto her back and nestled his hips between her thighs.

She giggled and moved her hands out of the way before they got trapped between them. "Yes, Captain Justin. Should I buy a round-trip ticket or are you better at a one-way trip?"

"I'll get you a frequent rider card if you want."

"Are you going to punch it every time I climb on board?" Other than a subtle twinkle in her eye, she managed to keep a straight face.

He couldn't keep up the banter. Not with the way she'd slid her hands up and down his cock and the way his dick notched at her entrance.

"I'll punch it now if you'll handle the protection." He'd only had the one condom. Hadn't even planned on using that one, but thankfully he hadn't taken it out of his in-case-of-emergency supply.

She gazed up at him, her eyes losing their sparkle and

taking on a serious look. "I'm on the pill. Haven't been with anyone else in over a year. How about you?"

The thought of feeling her wrapped around him with nothing between them made his heart skip a beat. "I'm clean. Doc gave me a green light last time he ran labs. Are you sure about this?"

She put her hands on his cheeks and stared straight into his eyes. "If you're committed to being together, I don't want there to be anything between us."

"That's all I've ever wanted, Em. You're it for me." He would have kept going. Would have told her how he wanted her to be his last first kiss, his last lover. But he didn't want to freak her out if she wasn't ready to hear promises of forever. Especially not with his dick resting on her inner thigh.

She nodded. "Okay then. I've got one more thing to ask."

He braced himself, hoping she wasn't going to ask him for something he couldn't give her.

Emmeline

"That's it? You want to be on top?" The corners of his eyes crinkled like she'd just told him a bad joke.

"What's so funny?" Immediately, she went on the defensive. He could joke about nicknames for his penis all night long, but as soon as she made a request—

He flipped her over in one smooth move. "Is that better?"

"Yeah, as a matter of fact, it is." She slid up his body, straddling his hips with her thighs. "I'm not crushing you, am I?"

"Not at all. But even if you were, it would be worth it for this view."

She put her palms on his chest and leaned forward until

she could touch her lips to his. "What's so good about this view?"

"You've got amazing tits, Em." As if to prove his point, he pushed himself up far enough to suck a nipple into his mouth.

The moan started in the back of her throat and she let her head fall back. Justin wrapped an arm around her back to hold her in place. Each flick of his tongue against her nipple sent a wave of heat pulsing through her veins. Just when she didn't think she could take any more, he switched to her other breast.

She shifted on his lap until he sat up and faced her.

"You want to do it like this?" His voice was low. He wasn't in any rush this time. She could tell by the way he smoothed his palms over her skin. Like he had all the time in the world for her.

"Yeah, I do." She rested her arms on his shoulders and lined up her hips, ready to slide onto his cock. "Is this okay with you?"

Justin groaned as he pushed into her. "For the record, anything you want to do to me is okay with me. Got it?"

"Got it." She sucked in a breath as he filled her. Her breasts pushed against his chest and she folded her legs underneath her and lifted up onto her knees for better leverage.

He lay back, giving her full control. She set the rhythm, starting off by slowly sliding down onto him, taking his entire cock in, then clenching around him before sliding off, just as slowly.

Justin grabbed hold of her hips with his big hands but let her stay in control. He watched her through half-closed eyes, a satisfied grin on his mouth.

She continued, something inside her urging her to keep it slow and deep. This wasn't like the first time. That had

been a rush to climax. Like her body knew it needed release but was afraid she might shut it down when she came
to her senses. This was different. She was pouring every
bit of herself into the act. Giving every piece of herself
over to him. Like she'd been saving herself for this moment, for this man.

Now that they were here, she didn't want to hold anything back.

Justin must have been able to sense the intensity of her
feelings. His brow furrowed. The grin he'd worn earlier
gave way to a measured concentration. It was like their
bodies were speaking some nonverbal language unique to
them. She'd never been so tuned in before. Never noticed
every exhale, the way each one of his muscles moved, the
tic of his pulse along his jawline.

Her orgasm started from a place deep inside. A quick
fluttering of nerve endings that grew in intensity. Grew
until the sensation had spread through her veins. Until she
lost track of where her body ended and his began. She
leaned forward, using his chest as leverage, continuing to
glide up and down until she couldn't move. Until her orgasm peaked and a warm, sated glow spread through her
limbs. She slumped against him, her limbs useless.

"It's okay, babe. I've got you." Justin cradled her in his
arms, pressing kisses onto her cheeks, her eyelids, her nose.
"You're amazing, you know that? Watching you come on
my cock is the sexiest thing I've ever seen in my life."

Em let out a soft laugh. "Good thing you're easily
entertained."

He twined his fingers with hers and pulled them to his
mouth. "I'm not easily entertained at all. You're just really
good at putting on a show."

"No show. That was . . ."

"Incredible? Hot? Life-altering?" he guessed.

"All of the above." She rested her chin on his chest. "It's Love Rocket's turn. I think maybe I'll start to call you LR for short. Think anyone would get it?"

"You can call me whatever you want if I get to keep watching you ride my cock."

She nudged him, signaling him to roll over. Her muscles couldn't handle supporting her own weight. Justin would have to do the work if he wanted to chase after his own release. Flat on her back, she gazed up at him.

His hair fell forward and she wondered how long it had been since his last haircut. Her gaze drifted over his features . . . so familiar and yet so different in this particular setting. She knew him. Knew the map of his face, knew the contents of his heart. But they were getting to know each other in a whole new way. In that moment, she realized that was what she wanted.

Justin.

All of him.

As he nestled his cock between her thighs, she wrapped her arms around him and swore she'd do what she needed to do to keep him. Then she shook her head, ridding it of any thoughts that didn't have to do with him sinking into her, filling her.

He nibbled at her bottom lip before sucking it into his mouth. His hips swiveled around in a slow circle and she closed her eyes. She skimmed her nails up his sides while he took his time driving all the way into her before pulling out in slow motion. Then he did it again.

And again.

And again.

She didn't think she was capable of feeling anything after her last orgasm left her drained. But there it was, the tiny spark lighting up deep in her core. As Justin took his time, loving on her body with his, the spark grew.

He kept his pace, slowly sliding in, slowly pulling back out again until her entire body burned for him. Only when her fingers dug into his sides, when her teeth sank into his good shoulder, when her eyes had almost rolled into the back of her head . . . only then did he speed up.

She moaned, a long-drawn-out primal noise that didn't sound human. Justin joined her, straining, every muscle in his body taut. Together, they tumbled into it, holding tight to each other.

23

❤

Justin

"Are you hungry?" Justin smoothed her hair away from her face. He'd never get tired of looking at her. Never get tired of seeing her head on his chest, her thigh tossed over his hips.

"Maybe." Her stomach gurgled on cue.

"Maybe? Sounds like you're running on empty. Should we get cleaned up and see if we can find a grocery store nearby?" They had six more days stretching ahead of them, and he planned to spend the vast majority of them just like this, wrapped around Em and taking advantage of the king-sized bed. By his estimation, they'd burned about five thousand calories during their intense workout. If he wanted to make sure they had fuel to get them through the next several days, they'd need food. And plenty of it.

"Do you ever think about anything but food?" She put her hand on his chest and pushed herself up.

"Yeah." He kissed his finger before pressing it to her lips. "I've been thinking a lot about you for the past several hours."

Em sucked his finger into her mouth, then used her tongue to push it back out. "What are you hungry for?"

"You keep that up and we'll never get out of bed." He wouldn't let himself imagine what she'd look like with her lips wrapped around his cock. If he let his thoughts head down that path, he'd never want to get dressed. That wouldn't necessarily be a bad thing, but at some point, they'd have to take a break to eat.

"Give me ten minutes to take a quick shower and put on some clean clothes."

"I'm only going to get you out of them later." At least he hoped that's what would happen. He'd spent the past ten years dreaming about the two of them like this, but for Em, it might be happening too fast. He didn't want to push too hard.

"I'm counting on it." She got up and headed toward the bathroom, giving him a smile over her shoulder. "Hey, remember a while ago when you asked me about the last time I had a night I could rate a ten?"

"Yeah."

"Last night is my new ten night." She kissed her fingers, then blew the kiss his way as she disappeared into the bathroom.

His chest warmed, and he rolled over onto his stomach. Snuggling her pillow close to his chest, he took in a deep breath. This was what he wanted. What he'd never dared to hope for. A life with Em might actually be a possibility. The idea filled him with hope for the future.

While he lay there, trying to convince himself not to give in to the temptation to join her in the shower, his phone vibrated on the nightstand. He'd told everyone he'd be taking some time off for the next two weeks. The only person who might be looking for him would be his dad. Tightness spread through his gut.

The number on the phone confirmed it. Dammit. He didn't want to ruin the good mood spending the last few hours with Em had created. For once, he hadn't thought about sponsors or drawing bulls or how many points he needed to move up in the rankings. His phone buzzed again.

He flicked a finger against the red button, declining the call. There would be time to deal with his dad later. Right now, he wanted to give Em all of his attention. She deserved that, and a hell of a lot more.

A half hour later, they strolled between stalls at a farmers' market they'd come across on their way to the grocery store. Em had changed into a sundress and looked calm and relaxed with her hair pulled back and a floppy straw head perched on her head.

He held her hand in his, twining their fingers together and swinging their hands between them. For some reason, he felt like he needed to constantly be touching her. Like if he let go of her hand, she'd disappear. Or the bridge they'd built between them would fade and he'd find himself in the friend zone. It was still so fresh, so new, he wasn't sure he believed it.

"Do you want to go out tonight or stay in and cook something at the house?" Em stopped in front of a table selling fresh produce.

"I saw a grill on the patio. We could do chicken breasts and some veggies." He didn't care what they did, as long as they were together.

She picked up a bright red tomato and held it in her hand. "You eat vegetables now? Last time I checked your favorite vegetable was french fries. By the way, totally not a vegetable."

Justin reached for a zucchini. "I'm a lot more open to trying new things than I used to be. See this?"

Em eyed the green summer squash in his hand. "Aren't you sick of zucchini yet?"

"Not at all." He suggestively stroked his fingers over the zucchini, drawing a laugh from Em.

"How would you prefer that, Chef Forza?"

"I'd slice it up, then drizzle a little olive oil over the top. Then I'd sprinkle it with salt and pepper and either sauté it in a cast-iron skillet or drop it into a basket and stick it on the grill." He set the zucchini back down on the table.

"I'm impressed. When did you learn how to cook?" She crossed her arms over her stomach and cocked her head.

"I've learned a lot of things on the road. I got tired of eating beanie weenies out of a can and when I upgraded to the RV, I started experimenting and fixing some of my own meals." He matched her stance. "You think I'm all talk?"

"Not necessarily. I'd love to see your cooking skills in action."

He flipped his wrist over to check his watch. "Unless you want to eat around ten, I don't think I have time to cook tonight."

"Mmm. Of course." Em nodded and took a few steps down the row of stalls.

She didn't believe him. He could tell by the way she'd brushed him off and given him that almost invisible roll of her shoulder.

"Hey, tonight doesn't work, but how about tomorrow?" He caught up to her in front of a stand selling organic chicken out of the back of a refrigerated truck.

"You're going to cook for me tomorrow night?" Her mouth twitched like she was fighting back a smile.

"Yeah, I'll cook for you. You're going to love it, too."

"And if I don't?" She rocked back and forth on her heels.

"I see where you're going with this. I'll make it easy for you. If I cook for you and it's not the most delicious, romantic dinner you've ever had in your life, I'll . . ." He scratched his chin, trying to figure out what kind of stakes he was comfortable offering.

"Record a video reading a bedtime story to Rocky?" Em challenged.

"Sure. If that's what you want, you got it."

"Won't your bull-riding buddies give you grief if they see you reading a kid's book online? Especially to a rock like Rocky?"

"You're forgetting something, Em."

"What's that, Chef?"

He did something then that he'd never done before in his life—he winked at her. "I don't intend to lose."

Emmeline

With Justin committed to making dinner tomorrow, Em took it upon herself to make plans for an evening out. She'd only told Justin to wear his jeans and boots and pack a bag with his swim shorts.

"Are we close yet?" he asked. For the past ten minutes, they'd been riding a couple of bikes Chick loaned them. It was easier to get around the island on bicycles than trying to find a golf cart cab to go the short distance.

"Just up ahead." Em pedaled faster, eager to reach their destination. Timing was everything for their outing, and she didn't want them to miss out on what promised to be a romantic evening for two.

"You're kidding me." Justin slowed as they approached the stables. "Please tell me we're not doing a horseback ride on the beach."

She knew he'd be less than thrilled at the prospect of riding someone else's horses, but hopefully his lack of enthusiasm would change once they got where they were going.

"Suck it up. You're supposed to be going with the flow, remember?" Em climbed off her bike and leaned it up against a fencepost.

"But horses? Seriously?" Justin had traded his cowboy hat for a baseball cap and tugged on the brim while he brought his bike to a stop.

"Just wait here." Em left him standing outside while she entered the office area. Within minutes, the owner of the stables had them seated in the saddles of a shy mare for her and a spirited red Appaloosa for him. She checked to make sure the picnic dinner she'd ordered had been tucked into one of the saddlebags before they started on their ride. Satisfied they had everything they needed, Em clucked her tongue and signaled her horse to start moving with a gentle nudge of her heels.

"Where exactly are we headed?" Justin steered his mount to walk next to hers.

"You'll see." She could tell him but it would ruin the surprise. She'd much rather listen to him gripe and complain and have to eat his own words later.

The horses fell into a slow, lazy gait along the wet stretch of sand. Em relaxed into the saddle. It had been too long since she'd been on the back of a horse. Unlike Justin, she didn't have a stable full of mounts to pick from when she felt like going for a ride.

Justin let her take the side closest to where the waves rolled into the shore. He held the reins loosely in his hands and glanced out over the water. They were on the east side of the island so an unencumbered view of the ocean spread out before them.

They rode past mansions and smaller beach houses that looked like they'd been around for decades, before reaching the trail that would lead them to their destination. When Em had asked Chick about a suggestion on what they could do while they were in town, he'd mentioned the secluded spot that could only be reached by horseback or ATV.

She turned her horse away from the beach. The sand gave way to a trail covered with a thick tangle of palms and trees.

"Where the hell are you taking me?" Justin joked from behind her. The narrow path ahead didn't allow for them to ride next to each other so he'd fallen behind her as they wound through the overgrown vegetation.

"Patience is a virtue, you know." Em glanced back to catch his smirk.

"When have you ever known me to be a patient man?"

"It's never too late to start, right?"

Justin grumbled something in response but she couldn't hear him over the sound of rushing water that seemed to grow louder by the moment. The path opened up into a large clearing that faced the rocky wall of a cliff. Water rushed from the top, pouring down into a clear pool at the base.

Em sucked in a breath at the sight of the gorgeous waterfall. It was even more beautiful than Chick described.

"What the hell is this?" Justin stopped next to her.

"It's called Lovers' Falls. Chick told me about it." Em flung a leg over the saddle and hopped to the uneven ground.

"That's quite a name." Justin joined her. "Here, let's tie up the horses here and move closer for a better look."

Em handed over the reins of her horse, then pulled the picnic dinner out of the saddlebag before Justin led the horses to a spot under one of the trees. Spray from the falls created a light mist that landed in her hair and provided a bit of relief from the heat of the early evening.

"Now what?" Justin asked as he reappeared at her side. "Do you want to see how close we can get to the falls?"

"Absolutely." Em held out her hand. "Chick said you can climb behind them. Supposedly there's a path in the rocks that leads up to a spot where you can view the sunset."

Justin grabbed the handle of the bag holding their dinner and slid it over his shoulder. Then he gripped her hand in his. "Well, what are we waiting for?"

Em watched her step as she worked her way around the slick rocks to the side of the falls. The roar of water was deafening as it thundered over the top of the cliff and plunged seventy-five feet into the pool below. With the sun slipping in the sky, they needed to hurry if they wanted to catch the sunset.

They reached the falls, and she tried to find a spot to duck underneath. "Chick didn't give me details. Do you think we just walk through the water to find the trail?"

Justin shrugged. "Only one way to find out."

He tugged her into the water cascading down the side of the cliff. Unprepared for the cold shower, Em sputtered.

"That was easy." Justin let go of her hand to run his fingers through his hair. They stood in a damp, dimly lit area behind the falls.

She shook her head, sending droplets of water everywhere. "You could have looked for a way around instead of pulling me right through a waterfall."

"Where's the fun in that?" His voice bounced off the rocks.

"Let's find the path before the sun sets." Em explored the edges of the rock wall. "Hey, I think it's over here."

"Do you want to lead the way?" Justin gestured for her to go ahead of him.

"Are you being chivalrous or do you just want to look at my ass?"

"Will you hold it against me if I admit to both?" Justin joked.

Heat washed over her cheeks at the idea of him checking out her backside as she climbed the rocky path in front of him. Things between them were still so new. As much as she enjoyed the direction their relationship was headed, she was still processing their leap from friends to lovers.

Still, Em might have put a little extra swish in her hips as she continued up the path. Chick had promised gorgeous scenery and an unforgettable view of the island. She hoped the effort was worth it.

Just when she thought she might have misunderstood the directions, an opening in the rocks gave way to a small clearing at the top of the falls. She stepped through a curtain of vines and leaves. Her breath caught in her throat and she stopped.

Justin bumped into her from behind and wrapped his arm around her middle before she lost her balance. "You can't just stop like that right in front of me, Em."

She cupped his chin in her hand and turned his head to face the breathtaking view. "Look."

The west side of the island spread out underneath them. From this height the remaining sunbathers on the beach appeared the size of ants, and the boats on the open ocean looked like toys. The sun hung low on the horizon, a huge blazing ball of orange and yellow, while every shade of purple, red, and pink bled across the sky.

"It's gorgeous," Em finally whispered.

Justin pulled her back into his arms and brushed his cheek against hers. "Almost as pretty as you."

"Oh, stop." She leaned back, nestling against the hard planes of his chest, a smile stretched across her lips. "I'm pretty sure you're already going to get laid tonight. You don't need to ply me with compliments."

"I mean it, Em." He turned her around to face him. "You're the most beautiful thing I've ever seen. I've always thought so, I just never had the balls to tell you."

She blushed under his attention. "Should we find a spot to sit down and dry off while we eat?"

"And then?" Justin asked.

"And then what?" She could guess by the look in his eyes what he had in mind.

"How private did Chick say this spot was?" His fingers brushed a chunk of wet hair off her shoulder.

"Pretty private."

"Private enough for a dip in the pool below?" His eyes darkened a smidge. "Swimsuits optional?"

"Are you trying to seduce me, Mr. Forza?"

His lips curved into a lazy smile. "Is it working?"

She wrapped her arms around his neck and pulled his head down to hers. "You still think a horseback ride on the beach was a dumb idea?"

He laughed. "If it means spending time with you, I'm always up for it."

"Good. Let's dig into our picnic and then maybe we can set our clothes out to dry while we take a dip."

Justin slanted his mouth over hers and kissed her. She tangled her fingers in the damp hair at the nape of his neck, surrendering to the wave of emotion rolling through her. Every day she spent on this island, every minute she had in Justin's arms, was bringing them closer and closer together. The fear she'd been trying to hold at bay faded as his tongue swept into her mouth.

Things between them would never be the same. How could they? But she wasn't going to lose Justin as a friend; she was gaining so much more by letting him in. Whatever came next, they'd face it together. Now that they'd committed to each other, there was nothing that could pull them apart.

24

⚬~♡~⚬

Emmeline

Em wandered into the kitchen in search of coffee. Justin had kept her up until all hours. They'd stayed out late at the waterfall, then ridden the horses back to the stable. Even though they took advantage of the privacy of the pool by the falls, by the time they got back to the house, he was ready for another round. They couldn't seem to get enough of each other. Muscles she didn't even know she had ached.

"Sleep well?" He smiled at her as she entered the kitchen.

"When you finally let me fall asleep. What are you doing up so early?"

"It's after ten. Just getting a good start on the best meal of your life." He turned around and grabbed the new carafe they'd bought in town a few days before. "I just made a fresh pot."

"Yes, please." Em pulled a mug out of the cupboard and set it down on the counter.

Justin filled it, leaving just enough room so she could

stir in her two spoonfuls of sugar without spilling. He leaned down and kissed her forehead as he slid the carafe back in place.

"What do you have on?" Sleep still hovered around the edges of her eyes, and she wiped the back of her hand across her eyelids in an attempt to rub it away.

"Nothing." Justin had on a pair of shorts and an apron. That was it. Unlike the neutral beach decor that covered the rest of the house, the apron was black with white polka dots and hot-pink ruffles along the edges. He reached up to undo the bow at the back of his neck.

"Wait a sec. I kind of like seeing your domestic side."

His fingers stilled. "Really?"

"Yeah. Turn around, let me see the back."

He did what she asked, even clasping his hands behind his head and flexing his muscles in a cheesy pose. "Like this?"

"Just like that." While he stood with his back toward her, she grabbed her phone and pulled up her camera app. "Oh, that's good. Love it."

"Hold on. Are you taking pictures of me?" He whirled around and covered the distance between them in a couple of long strides.

Em squealed and ran into the living room. "Come on, Knox and Decker are going to love these."

"You wouldn't dare." He reached up and undid the ties behind his neck, then yanked the apron over his head.

"Wouldn't I?" She stood on the other side of the living room. The only thing separating her from Justin was the large sectional couch between them. She'd never send an incriminating photo of him to anyone, not even Knox and Decker. But she wasn't ready to admit it quite yet. Seeing him all riled up was too much fun.

"Nope." Justin studied her. "You feel bad when you step on a bug. There's no way you'd ever do anything to intentionally hurt someone. Your heart won't let you. It's one of the things I love most about you, Em."

Her chest squeezed tight. "Did you just drop the L-word, Chef Forza?"

He climbed onto the couch cushion, then stepped over the back of the couch to reach her. "Maybe."

"I think I heard it in there." She tapped her palm against her ear. "Unless I have water in my ear from that dip in the waterfall or the hour-long shower last night."

Justin rubbed his palms up and down her arms. "Would that freak you out if I said it?"

"Would it freak you out if I said yes, it would freak me out?" They were charting new territory here. It had only been a few days since their first kiss and now they were batting the L-word back and forth between them? At this rate, they'd be married with a dog before they left the island.

"Is it too late for me to back up a little bit?" He held her gaze.

She shook her head the tiniest bit. "Of course not."

He took in a deep breath, and her gaze followed the rise and fall of his chest.

"I said it's one of the things I love most about you. There are lots of other things I love about you, too. Nothing to freak out over, right?" He held out his arms, and she stepped into his embrace.

In his arms, her cheek resting against his chest, the sound of his heart beating in her ears, she felt as if the whole world faded away. Maybe a part of her always knew they'd end up here. Not here, in Decker's dad's house on Paradise Island, but here in the sense that the universe had always planned for them to find their way to each other.

She put her palms against the smooth, soft skin on his

back and burrowed closer. "What other things do you love about me?"

"Oh, now you're curious, huh?" He laughed. "Let's see. Where to start. I love the way you value your family. Love the way you interact with the kids in your classroom. You're so patient with them. Some of the stories you've told me, hell, I don't know how you do it. You're going to be a fantastic mom."

A mom . . . if she and Justin stayed together . . . would they have a family someday? Little towheaded boys with pint-sized cowboy boots who wore holes in their jeans, just like their daddy used to? Or green-eyed little girls who loved to ride as much as she did?

The idea of having Justin's babies rolled over her, tumbling through her head like poor Rocky had tumbled in the surf the other night. She might not have thought through all the ramifications of what hooking up with Justin would entail, but deep down, she was ready for it. All of it.

There was no need to rush, though. They could enjoy themselves. With him stepping back from competing, they'd have all the time in the world to figure things out.

The scruff on his chin brushed her forehead as he shifted. "You okay, Em?"

"Yeah. More than okay. You?"

"Never been better." He pulled back enough to put a finger under her chin and nudge her head up to meet his gaze. "You know what else I love about you?"

"What's that?"

"Your willingness to go the extra mile for others. When someone needs something, you're always the first one to step in, the first one to volunteer to help. Whether it's running to the market to pick up an item someone forgot like a red onion, or . . ." Justin waited, giving her plenty of time to jump in.

"That's a surprisingly specific example. If you need me to run to the store for you, all you have to do is ask." She clucked her tongue. "Is it just the red onion or is there something else you need me to grab while I'm out?"

"Oh, hey, you're going out?" Justin grabbed her hands and spun her underneath his arm like he was getting ready to swing dance. "If you're going to be out anyway, do you think you could stop by the market and pick up a red onion for me?"

"You're so predictable." She tucked her phone into the back of her pajama bottoms and ducked out of his arms, intent on getting back to the coffee she hadn't had a chance to sip yet.

"I wouldn't have asked if you hadn't said you were going out today." He followed her into the kitchen, the grin on his face proving he knew exactly what he'd been up to.

Ten minutes later, Em slid her feet into the flip-flops she'd left by the front door. "I'm heading out."

"Hey, wait up." The sound of Justin's bare feet slapping on the ceramic tile came closer. "You can't leave without giving me a kiss."

"Says who?" She liked that he didn't want her to leave without saying goodbye. Liked it a lot.

"Says me."

He still hadn't put a shirt on, and she was tempted to say to hell with the red onion and tug him toward the bedroom.

"Well, come get your kiss then."

He stepped into her personal space and put his hands on her hips. His nose nudged hers and he rubbed against it. Butterfly kisses, her dad used to call them. Justin tilted his head and grazed her lips with his. Anticipation built like a pressure valve waiting to blow off steam. He was a man of contradictions. She'd seen it from the sidelines as his friend and now she had a front-row seat to seeing how it played out as his lover.

He was soft and gentle, the way he caressed her skin, the way he lazily trailed his gaze over her like they had all the time in the world. But he was also hard and fast and pushed her to the edge of the safety zone, where she'd spent her whole life. Being with Justin was like riding a roller coaster while wearing a blindfold. She never knew what to expect, and the experience thrilled her to her core.

His mouth slanted over hers, taking the kiss deeper. She took a step backward and bumped into the wall. Justin slipped his foot between hers and nudged her legs apart. He moved his hand above her head, resting his palm flat against the wall. He leaned in closer, his hips connecting with hers.

His kisses made fireworks explode behind her eyelids. Little sparks of heat ignited throughout her body. If he kept it up, she'd drop her underwear and beg him to take her against the wall.

Justin must have had the same thoughts running through his head. He bunched up the material at her waist and tugged it upward. The hem of her dress moved past her knee and up her thigh. Now that she knew how good it felt to have him inside her, she craved it. The slightest touch of his fingers on her skin made her ache for him.

He knew it, too. She could tell by the way he slipped his finger below the waistband of her panties, dipped down to find out if she was ready. She was always ready.

"You're wet again, Em."

She nodded, her nose bumping against his.

"You can't go out in these wet panties." He slid them past her hips.

Eager for his touch, she stepped out of them and kicked them to the side.

A loud blaring beep came from the kitchen.

"Dammit. That's the timer. Time to flip the chicken." Justin's finger hovered right above her clit. "I should have known better than to start something I couldn't finish."

Her chest heaved as she sucked in a breath. "Can't finish?"

"Yeah, I'm sorry, baby. I'll make it up to you later. I've been dying to find out what you taste like. I was thinking a little dessert after dinner would be the perfect way to start our evening."

"You're seriously not going to finish what you started?" She wasn't mad, she was just . . . surprised.

"I figure I'll hold on to these to make sure you'll come back." He reached down and hooked a finger through the leg hole of her hot-pink panties. "Have I told you how good you look in pink? You look even better out of it."

Em clamped her hands to her hips. "Give me my underwear. You can't expect me to walk all the way to the market without any panties on."

He wadded them up and stuffed them in the pocket of his shorts. "I don't expect you to do anything. But if you think what we did last night was hot, try walking to the store and back again without your underwear on."

"That's crazy." She bit the inside of her cheek, still so turned on that if he touched her anywhere below the waist, she'd probably come all over his hand.

"I dare you."

She'd played that game with him before and had never stepped away from a dare. "Fine. But if I get a ticket for indecent exposure, you're paying the fine."

She pulled the door open and stepped out into the late-morning heat. Justin had her so flustered she'd forgotten to grab her hat. She wouldn't give him the satisfaction of going back inside. He'd probably think she was so turned on she couldn't make it down the driveway. She'd show him. Maybe she'd do a little shopping while she was in town or stop by and say hi to Chick on her way back.

She owed Chick a huge thank-you. Whatever he'd said to Justin had swayed him. Tracking him down and coming here had been the right move. Was it only a few weeks ago she'd been racking her brain, trying to figure out a way to get through to Justin? Look at them now.

The breeze picked up when she turned the corner, blowing right through her skirt and across her skin. Her dress was long enough that she didn't worry about the wind catching hold of it and exposing her bare bottom. Still, it felt naughty to be walking down the sidewalk without underwear on. Naughty and a little bit sexy, if she were being totally honest with herself.

What else would she let him do to her? It might be good to slide a toe or two out of her comfort zone. She'd never been one to break the rules or not live up to someone else's expectations. Her mom said it was because she was the oldest. Evidently, firstborn children tended to be more responsible. That certainly held true when it came to Em.

Justin was in the middle. Sandwiched between his older brother who ticked off every box listing traits of the oldest kid, and his younger sister who was still "finding herself," he walked the line between his need for fun and his desire to live up to his dad's expectations.

Em had never thought about how that affected him until now. While he could be carefree and rash and didn't seem to think about the consequences of his actions, other times he yearned for his dad's approval and would push himself beyond what seemed reasonable to reach his goals.

Something had shifted in both of them since they came to the island. Now all she had to do was figure out what it was so things wouldn't go back to the way they were before.

The sign for A Cowboy in Paradise loomed ahead. Em checked her phone for the time. The walk to Chick's place had taken about fifteen minutes. She'd need to be gone for at least two hours if she really wanted to get Justin back for the stunt he pulled on her way out the door.

With a spring in her step, she turned toward the beach. She could stop by the grocery store after a nice, long chat with Chick.

25

❧

Justin

Justin was halfway through prepping the potatoes when his phone buzzed on the counter. He wasn't in the right headspace to talk to his dad. If he ignored the phone long enough, it would stop ringing. And if he ignored his dad's calls long enough, maybe he'd stop calling.

All he'd asked for was ten days to step away from everything and give his mind a break. Based on his dad's initial reaction, it was like he'd told him he was going off the grid for the next eighteen months and moving to some tiny country that didn't even show up on a map.

For the first time in his life, Justin hadn't backed down, and when his dad figured a break might accelerate Justin's recovery, he was all for it. Just look where that had gotten him . . . alone with Em. Thinking of her, the moments they'd shared by the front door before she'd stalked off without her panties, put a smile on his face. It always had, but now the smile was a bit different. Instead of thinking about what it might feel like to kiss her, to touch his lips to hers, now he couldn't stop thinking about the way it felt to have her thighs clamped around him, to be buried up to his balls inside her.

He picked the kitchen towel up off the counter and fanned himself. Thinking about Em made him hot as hell. He tossed the towel next to the sink and started to cut open another potato. His phone buzzed again.

The number on the screen proved it wasn't his dad. It was Jake. Justin reached for it. What if something happened to his nephew? What if something happened to Dad?

"Hello?"

"Hey, little bro. Did you give up answering your phone while you're playing hooky in paradise?" Jake's voice held a teasing tone.

Immediately, Justin's pulse slowed. This wasn't an emergency call. His brother probably wanted to shoot the shit. "What's going on? Is everything okay?"

"No, everything's not okay." His dad's voice came through the line. "I've been trying to reach you for the past twenty-four hours. Did you get my voice mail?"

A muscle along Justin's jaw twitched. "No, sir. I told you, I'm taking a break. We can talk business when I get back next week."

"You listen to me, son. Next week will be too late. I might be able to get you a spot on the ticket in Oklahoma City next weekend. This is what we've been waiting for. They had a rider pull out, and I'm trying to sweet-talk them into letting you in. I need you to come home. There's a flight tomorrow that leaves Brownsville at eight. I can pick you up at the airport and have you at the trainer's by two."

"Hold up a sec." Justin shook his head. This wasn't happening. "Doc said he didn't want to see me back until next month at the earliest."

"You wait until then and you'll be kissing any chance of getting back in the finals this year so long. We both know what it takes to compete at this level. You man up, you work through it, you keep your eye on the goddamn prize."

Justin could picture his dad's face as the words came through the phone. He'd be pacing the farmhouse kitchen of the home they'd built right before Mom left. His mouth would be twisted into the scowl he always seemed to wear, and his lower lip would be puffed out due to the wad of tobacco he always had resting between his gums.

"I've got the ticket on hold. Can you get to the airport by eight or should I book the ten o'clock flight?"

It was too soon to leave Em. Things between them were too new, too fragile. He couldn't blow out of town like this.

"Dad, I can't. I told you I needed some time to make a decision about riding again."

"The only decision you need to make is which pair of chaps you want to wear in Oklahoma City. Let me worry about the rest. I've talked it over with the doc and he can give you a shot of steroids when you get back. Ought to help with the pain and give you some increased mobility. Your shoulder's going to feel as good as new, ain't that right, Jake?"

Justin cursed his brother for tricking him into taking their dad's call, even though he knew Jake didn't have a choice. That's how their father operated. He always got what he wanted, one way or another. That's the way it had always been.

"Yeah, when I knocked up my knee, that helped. It's what got me through the next few rides to get me qualified for the finals." Jake would back their dad up, no questions asked.

"I'm not sure I'm ready to go back yet."

His dad let out a loud sigh. "Look, I get it. Happens to all of us at some point in our career. You're not as young

as you used to be, son. Hell, your brother had won his two
titles and retired by the time he was your age."

Justin's gut clenched at the snide comment. It was his
dad's way of digging in, twisting the knife of guilt in his
back until he'd give in.

"There's a whole new class of younger men champin'
at the bit to knock you out and take your spot. Have you
seen that new kid from Brazil? He's young, he's smart, he's
hungry for a title. It's not his time yet, though. It's your
time, Justin."

Justin put his palm down on the kitchen counter and
leaned forward. He'd heard it all before. His dad may as
well copyright the speech.

"I hear you. There's something I've got to take care of
first. I just need a couple more days." A couple more days
wouldn't come close, but at the moment it was the best he
could do. He knew how Em felt about the rodeo; she'd always been up front with him about that. Things were different now, though. They needed time to talk about it.

"You're not the only one who needs this win, Justin.
You think we're the only ones who make a living out of
prepping guys to ride? We haven't had a champion come
up through our ranks since your brother won." His dad
lowered his voice. "Our reputation depends on securing
another win."

"What are you doing down there, anyway?" Jake asked.
"I heard you went down there with Emmeline Porter."

"Is that what this is about?" his dad asked. "You're just
lookin' to wet your whistle?"

"No, that's not what this is. Em and I have been friends
for years. By the way, it's none of y'all's business who I get
involved with." Anger coiled in his gut. He'd never disre-
spected his dad, but if his old man made one more comment about Em, Justin wouldn't be able to bite his tongue.

His dad backed off. Even he could sense when he'd gone too far. "Look, son. This family needs you. Business hasn't been so good over the past couple of years and if we can't bring in some real money this year, we might have to make some hard decisions."

Justin had been too young to be involved when his dad decided to start up his training business, but he could make an educated guess about why they were losing riders to some of the new outfits popping up. It might have more to do with how his dad treated his clients than it did with whether or not Justin had a title to his name. But family was family. His dad might not have always done things right, but he always did them for the right reasons.

"I hear you. All I'm asking for is a couple more days. Give me through the weekend?"

His dad mumbled a few curse words, too muffled for Justin to make out clearly, but he caught the gist. "I need to hear back from you by Sunday. If you want any chance of getting back in the run this year, you've got to decide by then."

"Sunday," Justin repeated.

His dad disconnected without a goodbye. Everything he'd needed to say had been said.

Justin set his phone down on the counter and pressed the heels of his hands against his temples. What was he going to do? If he didn't head to Oklahoma City, his dad and brother would be pissed as hell at him. But if he did, would Em understand?

He wasn't foolish enough to think she'd totally changed her stance on getting involved with a bull rider. She may have eased up, but she'd never truly be his until he gave it up for good. But how could he give it up when his family needed him to come through?

The answers didn't come. If he didn't make a decision, one would be made for him. Either he decided to go to

Oklahoma City and compete, or he stayed here and would incur the wrath of his dad.

He couldn't handle thinking about the pros and cons right now. The most gorgeous woman in the world was counting on him to feed her dinner tonight. That needed to be top priority. He'd bought himself a few more days before his dad would start hounding him for a decision.

Knowing his time with Em was limited, he promised himself he'd take advantage of every single moment. Starting with getting those potatoes in the oven.

Emmeline

The lunch crowd was in full swing when Em entered the private beach area of A Cowboy in Paradise. As she headed straight for the bar, she waved to the server who'd helped her and Justin the other night.

"Hey, is Chick around this afternoon?" Em asked. "I was hoping to catch him and ask him a couple of questions."

"Yeah, I think he's in his office upstairs." Claudia pointed to a set of steps behind the bar. "Just take the steps up and knock on the door when you get to the top."

"Thanks." Em headed in the direction of the stairs, stopping to run her hand over Tripod's shell as she passed. The tortoise rubbed the top of his head against her stomach and Em could have sworn she heard a purring noise like the one their neighbor's cat used to make.

"He's sweet on you," Claudia called out from behind the bar. "Tripod's an excellent judge of character."

Em grinned. She'd never been the object of a tortoise's love. Growing up, she and her sister weren't allowed to have pets because they might trigger her dad. He was much more sensitive to sounds back then and couldn't handle barks or chirps or any loud noises. Now that she lived on her own and was gone so much of the time, she didn't feel like it would be fair to the animal to have a pet.

There was something about Tripod, though. Being around him made her wish she had a pet waiting for her at home. That would be something else to add to the list of questions she was coming up with for Justin. With the number of animals the Forzas had running around their ranch, she couldn't imagine he'd have an issue with taking on a pet or two.

She reached the top of the stairs and knocked on the wooden door.

"Just a second." The sound of footsteps approaching from the other side of the door made her step back.

Then the door swung open and Chick stood there. "Hey, Emmeline. What brings you to my humble dining establishment on a Thursday afternoon?"

"Mr. Darville, hi, I was wondering if I could bother you for a few minutes of your time. I have some questions about your visit with Justin." She entered the office at his invitation and sat down on the edge of an antique chair that faced his desk.

"I'm always happy to oblige the request of a beautiful woman. What can I do for you this afternoon?"

She scanned the walls of the small office. Newspaper clippings hung in frames around the room. Pictures of Chick with celebrities decorated the walls. She spotted Muhammad Ali on one wall and a young Johnny Cash on another. No wonder Justin was impressed.

"I wanted to thank you for taking the time to talk with my friend."

"Of course. Justin and I had a great conversation. I hope it helped."

"I think so." Em lowered herself into a chair across from the cluttered desk. "I'm not sure how to phrase this, but I'm wondering if there's anything I can do for him when we get home. His dad's a pretty vocal man—"

"That's one way to describe Monty Forza, I suppose."

Em's pulse ticked up. "You know him?"

"Know of him is more like it. Though I suppose we did run in some of the same circles back then." Chick's chair squeaked as he leaned back. "I'm sure he's got his own ideas on what kind of turns Justin's career ought to take."

That was putting it nicely. Em's mouth curved up in a knowing smile. "Assuming Mr. Forza doesn't agree with Justin's decision to walk away from competing, is there anything I can do to support him? I know you made the decision to retire and experienced quite a bit of backlash."

Chick nodded. "Folks couldn't understand how I could walk away during my prime. I'd just won my second world title and earned my second perfect score. Everyone thought I was crazy for announcing my retirement."

"Why did you?" She hadn't planned on being quite so forward, but she was curious. "I'm sorry, you don't have to answer that."

"I don't mind. I'll tell you what I told your friend." He leaned forward and clasped his hands together on the desk.

Em scooted to the edge of her seat, sensing that whatever he was about to reveal might be the key to helping Justin through the next few weeks.

"Being a professional bull rider was the high point in my life. Earning two world titles, becoming the only man to ever score two perfect rides . . . the highs were so high it felt like my boots would never touch the ground again."

Her heart squeezed tight in her chest. Her father had said something similar. She wanted that for Justin, wanted him to succeed at a sport he loved, wanted him to finally earn the respect of his dad, but at what cost?

"The sport gave me so much." Chick's eyes misted, and he blinked a few times. "But it cost me everything."

A hollow pit opened in her stomach and Em pressed her palm against her belly, trying to chase the feeling away.

Chick glanced up at her, a haunted look in his eyes. "Lost the love of my life, lost touch with my kids. Yeah, it was great while it lasted, but if I had it to do all over again . . ."

Em glanced down at her lap and waited for him to continue.

"Hell, I had quite the run. All I've got to show for it now is this bar and some ancient memorabilia that nobody gives a shit about anymore." His watery brown eyes flickered to her. "Excuse my language."

She took in a shaky breath, awed by his vulnerability. "Thank you for sharing that with me."

"It is what it is. With regard to Justin, if Monty's still as 'vocal' as he used to be, your friend's going to need your support if he decides to walk away. Things are different now from when I retired. I had fans reach out, beg me to come back. Sponsors who doubled, even tripled their offers if I'd return for one more season. Those kind of offers are hard to turn down."

Em could only imagine the kind of pressure Justin's dad would layer on him. She'd been young when her dad got injured, and hadn't paid much attention to the business side of his career. All she knew was that when their dad couldn't keep working the land, they had to move from the acreage in the country to a smaller house on a standard-sized lot within town limits.

"You asked what you could do to help him. I'd say be

there for him like you are right now. Remind him of the important things in life, like his family and his health. Those are the kind of things that you can't easily get back once you've frittered them away." He held her gaze for a few long beats.

"Thank you, Mr. Darville. I appreciate your time so much." She reached out and set her hand on top of his where they rested on the desk.

"Hey"—he slid his hand out from under hers and reached for a card—"take my number. Give me a call if you or Justin need some help or get yourselves into a pickle with Monty."

She slid the card into her bag. "I don't know how to thank you."

He stood and walked her to the door. "Tell your friends about A Cowboy in Paradise. And come visit once in a while. It's nice to see friendly faces, especially those with a tie to my past."

"We will." She could have offered him a handshake, but opted to offer a hug instead.

He wrapped his sinewy arms lightly around her. "Take care. Make sure you stop by to visit before you head home, will you?"

"Of course." Em let her arms drop to her sides and turned to go. Now that she had a better idea of what might be waiting for Justin at home, she was eager to get back to him. He was giving up so much for her, and her need to protect him swelled within her.

Tripod was waiting for her when she came down the stairs. She patted him on the head and scratched under his chin.

"Everything go okay?" Claudia asked.

"Yeah, it was great." Em rested her hand on the bar. "If

I wanted to send something to Chick to thank him, any suggestions on what I could do?"

Claudia grabbed a wedge of pineapple from a plastic bin and slid it onto the rim of a giant cocktail sitting on the bar. "I suppose you could make a donation to the tortoise rescue he supports. Tourists for Torties, I think."

"Thanks." Em made a mental note to look it up as soon as she got back to the house. She had a cowboy waiting for her. Her cowboy.

26

Justin

By the time Em got home, Justin had prepped as much as he could for dinner and was sipping on a cold glass of iced tea on the patio. He heard the sliding glass door open and swiveled in his chair. Knowing she'd been running errands all over the island without panties on had kept him in a semi-hard state all afternoon.

"Took you long enough." He got up and met her half-way across the patio.

She slipped her arms around his neck. "Does that mean you missed me?"

"Can you feel how much I missed you, or do you need visual proof?" He pressed his hips against her belly.

"Mmm. Is that a Love Rocket in your pocket or are you just happy to see me?" She batted her long lashes against her cheeks.

"Why don't you reach in and find out?" Justin had been worried that the heat between them might have cooled off once they spent some time apart, but now, with her back in his arms, it only seemed to burn hotter.

She slipped her hand into his pocket and slid her fingers

along the ridge of his erection. "Poor baby. Has this been bothering you all afternoon?"

"As a matter of fact, it has." While she toyed with his cock through the pocket of his shorts, he bunched up the fabric from her skirt in his hands.

Em got to her knees in front of him and wiggled out of her dress. She hadn't had on a bra to begin with, and since he'd deprived her of her panties before she left the house, there was nothing preventing him from running his gaze over her skin.

She was everything he'd imagined and a hell of a lot more. Her hair tumbled over her shoulder, the light filtering in through the vine-covered arbor setting off the reddish-brown highlights. A smattering of freckles scattered across her shoulders, and he rested his fingers there while she gazed up at him with lust in her eyes.

Her breasts rubbed against his legs as she moved closer. She reached up to tug on the waistband of his gym shorts. His cock sprang free as she pulled them down his thighs. He glanced around, thankful for the privacy the shrubs surrounding the patio afforded them. Though anyone walking by would still be able to get a free show if they glanced over.

"You want to take this inside, or . . . oh."

She slid her tongue along the underside of his dick. Hissing in a breath, he curled his hands into fists. The smug look she shot him proved she knew exactly what she was doing. He tried to hold still and fight the urge to fist his hands in her hair.

Em continued to lick along his shaft, suckling and teasing and twirling her tongue around his sensitive head until he thought he would come before she even took him into her mouth. He couldn't do that. He'd dreamed of sharing a moment like this with her far too often to let it rush by without savoring every second.

While he willed himself to hold back, she rose up and took the very tip of his cock into her mouth.

"For fuck's sake." He reached behind him, resting a palm on the edge of the hot tub to keep himself from falling over.

Em didn't say a word, just glanced up at him, batted her lashes, and cupped his balls with her hand. Where did she learn to do this? He didn't want to know. Didn't matter. Whatever came before this, none of it mattered anymore. They belonged to each other now.

She continued to take him into her throat, easing her lips over him, careful not to let her teeth get in the way. He sank deeper, the heat of her mouth pulling him in. Her other hand splayed over his bare ass, and she used her palm to pull him forward, taking him all the way into her mouth until the tip of his cock hit the back of her throat.

Every cell in his body begged him to pump into her.

But Em had started this.

He was going to let her do it her way.

Her nails dug into his butt cheeks, and she increased the pace, taking him to the back of her throat, then sliding him almost all the way out before sucking him back in again. His hand gripped the edge of the tub, the other tightened in her hair as his release built.

Fuck, her mouth was made for this. Her tits bounced against his thighs and she rolled his balls between her fingers. He was going to come so hard he might not be able to stay upright.

"Em, I'm close, baby." She deserved a bit of warning so she could get out of the way.

He expected a few more strokes of her tongue before she wrapped her hands around him and finished jerking him off. But Em just looked up at him through half-lidded eyes, the sexiest thing he'd ever seen in his entire fucking life. He tried to shift his hips back, to pull out before he shot his load straight down her throat. Her grip on his ass tightened, her way of letting him know she wasn't planning on going anywhere until she was good and ready.

"Last chance." He'd held back as long as he could.

The edges of her lips curved, and she smiled up at him. Then she slid her finger along the sensitive spot between his balls and his asshole. He lost it. Every muscle in his body strained, tense, tight, clenching in that split second before he came undone.

He forced himself to keep his eyes open, to watch the look on her face as she took what he had to offer. She held his gaze, not flinching as his release went on and on and on.

When she'd sucked him dry, she popped him out of her mouth, licked her lips, and kissed her way up his belly. "I'm going to go clean up real quick."

"The hell you are." Justin scooped her up in his arms and carried her inside the house, not stopping until he'd tossed her on her back onto the couch.

"Justin! What are you doing?"

"Proving I can give as well as I can receive." He put his hands under her ass and pulled her to the edge of the couch. Then he spread her legs and sat down on the floor, his naked ass making contact with the cool tile. "You'd better get comfy, Em. I'm going to be here a while."

Emmeline

Em tossed her head back on the couch cushion. She hadn't expected him to return the favor, but who was she to say no to a little afternoon delight? The whiskers on his cheeks scratched against her inner thighs as he kissed his way up from her knee. She rested one hand on her stomach and the other behind her head as she sprawled out naked underneath him.

She thought she'd be embarrassed to have him see her bare-assed, but the look he gave her when he trailed his blue-eyed gaze over her skin went a long way in boosting her confidence. Justin accepted her exactly as she was . . . from the cellulite covering her backside to the extra pounds she always carried around her middle. Not only did he accept her, he seemed to be totally turned on by her. She loved the power she felt when she could drive him wild with desire.

He flicked his tongue against her inner thigh. Goose bumps pebbled her skin. His hand went under her ass, and he tilted her hips up.

His gaze met hers, and her nipples hardened at the need in his eyes. Then he ran his tongue up her leg, not stopping until he reached her clit. It was like he'd sent a wave of electricity through her veins. Her whole body tensed, focused on the single spot where his tongue touched her.

Her hips rolled up, and he put a firm palm on her stomach to hold her in place.

"It's my turn, Em. Be a good girl and hold still."

She turned her head to the side and bit down on her lip as he twirled his tongue around the bundle of nerves. He was driving her out of her mind.

Something on the coffee table drew her attention. A pink rock sat on top of a black swatch of fabric. Rocky! That was where she'd set him down last night.

"Justin, hold on a sec." She shifted her hips, but he followed, sucking her into his mouth. Sensations she'd never experienced before blurred her vision. She couldn't come in front of her classroom's pet rock.

She stretched, reaching her arm out toward the table.

Her fingers grappled for the bag even while her hips lifted into the air. Her need to ride out the release that hovered just out of her reach warred with her need to grab hold of the damn rock.

As Justin increased the pressure, the walls of her sex clenched. He was good at this. Too good for her to keep up her resistance much longer. She stretched her arm out as far as she could but still couldn't reach. Rocky lay there on his side, the two eyes she'd drawn on the side the kids claimed was his face staring right at her. The permanent black marker smile she'd added mocking her.

This wasn't happening. Couldn't happen. With a final effort that basically turned her arm into elastic, she shifted to the side of the couch and hooked the tie on the bag with her pinkie finger. Success! But there wasn't time to gloat. As she jerked the piece of fabric toward her and closed her fingers around Rocky, her hips rolled.

Justin startled and glanced up. She wasn't lying underneath him anymore. In her quest to get her hands on Rocky, she'd rolled herself right off the edge of the couch.

"Ouch." That one was going to leave a bruise.

"You okay, Em?" Justin moved from the end of the couch to hover over her. "What happened?"

At least she hadn't banged her head on the floor when she'd landed, or even worse, on the corner of the coffee table.

"Rocky happened." She opened her hand, holding up her palm where Rocky lay facedown.

"Am I being cockblocked by a rock?" Justin asked, his brow furrowed in confusion.

"Not anymore." Em tossed Rocky under the couch. He clattered across the tile and for a moment she worried that she might have broken him in half.

But then Justin grinned, spread her legs, and resumed

his position between her thighs. He breached her entrance with his tongue. As she wrapped her legs around his shoulders, she forgot all about the pink rock and gave herself over to the unbelievable sensation rolling through her limbs.

After she'd visited O-town not once, but twice, thanks to Justin's tongue, he crawled up her body and pressed a soft kiss to her lips.

"You okay?"

"Mmm-hmm." She propped herself up on her elbows, suddenly feeling a little shy. She'd never been so brazen with a man before and had never come so completely unhinged.

"Come here." He helped her up to the couch and put his arm around her, drawing her tight against him. "You're amazing, Em."

"Me? You did all the work just now."

He lifted his chin and kissed the top of her head. "I don't mean just because you're sexy as hell when you come."

Her skin heated at the compliment.

"I wasn't sure how you'd feel after the first time . . . if you'd think it was a mistake." His thumb brushed back and forth over her shoulder like he was nervous about where the conversation was headed.

"Do you?" She knew how she felt, but did he feel the same?

He tipped his head back to study her. "Do I think us getting together was a mistake?"

She nodded, not sure she wanted the whole truth. He'd be giving up everything by being with her. Would he regret it? Would he someday look back on this moment and wish he'd made a different decision? That was her biggest fear.

"No." His forehead creased like he'd never considered that option. "I've been in love with you for almost half my life. Always worried you wouldn't want me. I've always known how you felt about the rodeo. I didn't want to tell you how head over heels I was for you, because I knew you'd never be able to love me back."

"Oh, Justin." She sat up and pulled his head down to her chest, cradling him against her.

They sat like that for what felt like hours, her nails trailing lightly over his shoulder, his cheek pressed against her chest. She might have dozed off for a bit because she startled when someone knocked at the front door.

Justin jumped, too.

"Who is it?" Em jumped off the couch and hunched down in front of it. Though the windows on each side of the front door held frosted glass, she didn't have on a stitch of clothing. What if someone could see the outline of her body and figure out she was naked?

"I'll get it." Justin got up and walked to the back patio, unashamed and unapologetic in nothing but his birthday suit. He came back a few seconds later with his shorts on inside out.

"Hey," Em called.

He was already standing in front of the door. "What?"

"Your shorts." She pointed. Not only did he have them on inside out, they were backward too.

Justin shrugged and motioned her to leave the living room as he turned the doorknob. The hall leading to his side of the house was closest, so she ran toward it, closing the bedroom door behind her as Justin greeted whoever stood on the other side of the door.

27

❧

Justin

Justin pulled open the heavy front door. A guy in a white polo shirt with a logo embroidered over his left pec held out a giant bouquet of red and yellow flowers.

"I have a delivery for Justin Forza and Emmeline Porter here."

"I'm Justin." He reached for the bouquet, his mind spinning with possibilities of who could have sent them. "Does it say who they're from?"

"There's a card tucked inside. Have a Flowerific day." Free of his floral burden, the guy turned and headed back to the pink minivan parked at the curb.

"Thanks." Justin studied the bouquet. Were they even flowers? They looked like red plastic hearts with a long, yellow-colored thing sticking up from the middle. If he were going to send someone flowers, he'd probably go with something with petals. Roses were always a good choice. Not these odd plasticky things.

"Who was it?" Em peeked around the corner of the hall. She must have dug around in his suitcase. One of his T-shirts hung from her shoulders and she'd folded the waistband over a few times on a pair of his shorts to keep them from falling off her hips.

"We got flowers." He held them out to her, eager to be rid of them.

She squinted at the bouquet. "Who would send us flowers? No one even knows we're here except for—" She clapped a hand over her mouth, interrupting herself.

"There's a card." Justin pulled the tiny rectangular envelope from where it nested into the stems.

Em took it, sliding a nail under the seal to loosen it. She glanced at him, her worry obvious by the way she bit down on her bottom lip.

"What's it say?"

Her eyes scanned the card and color rose on her cheeks. "I'm going to kill him."

"Who?"

Em held out the card.

Hope you're having fun in paradise. Looks like you're letting it all hang out and baring your souls (among other bits to each other).

    Just wanted to let you know there are security cameras around the perimeter of the property (including the hot tub).

    Enjoy!

                      Smooches,
                        Deck

"How does he even know where we are?" Justin asked. Cameras around the perimeter . . . did that mean someone had seen Em in the hot tub the other night? He rushed to the patio and slid open the door.

Em followed him. "What are you doing?"

"I'm looking for a damn camera." Justin scanned the exterior of the house. There, in the corner, a small device mounted on the wall pointed toward the walkway leading to the beach. It was painted the same color as the wall and blended in so well he hadn't noticed it before.

A quick search of the rest of the rear of the house turned up two more cameras, both on the corners and pointed toward the beach.

"What did they see?" Em's hair fell forward, and she bit her lip.

"I think they saw you on the patio when you ducked behind the bushes and were trying to hide from the spider." He cupped her cheek with his palm and leaned closer. "Em, is there something you want to tell me about this house? Like who it belongs to?"

He'd caught plenty of deer in his headlights when he was out driving around the back roads of Texas at night. Like most of them, Em froze.

"Em?" he pressed.

She blinked her eyes closed and took in a long breath through her nose, like she was trying to calm herself down before telling him what he already suspected. "The house belongs to Decker's dad."

He clenched his jaw. "So, you didn't win a vacation for some teacher thing?"

"No, but—"

"And Decker knows we're here because it was probably his idea to have us come stay here for free."

She reached up and held on to his wrists. "Yes, but I can explain."

"Great. I'm all ears." He pulled his hands away and gestured toward the door. "Maybe we should go back inside so we don't give the guys back home such a show?"

She moved toward the door, her shoulders sagging, the smile he loved so much gone from her lips.

Once inside, she turned to him. "I was—I mean, we were worried about you. You haven't been yourself lately and your dad's been pushing so hard. I thought if you had some time away, it might help get your mind off things. Decker offered his dad's place, and I knew you wouldn't come if I told you the real reason."

His heart softened at the tone in her voice. How could he be angry when coming to Paradise Island was the only reason they'd ended up together?

"I'm not mad, Em." He caught her hands in his. "I just wish you would have told me the truth."

"I wanted to." The honesty in her eyes proved she meant it.

"Can we make a promise to each other?" He squeezed her hands. "No more secrets?"

She nodded. "No more secrets."

"Not even when it's hard?" He lifted their hands up to his mouth and kissed each one of her knuckles.

"Not even when it's hard." Her breath left her lips on a strong exhale. "I'm sorry."

He shook his head. "Not as sorry as Decker's going to be when I get ahold of that video of my girlfriend running around naked in the dark."

"Please tell me you don't think he watched it." She tilted her head back and groaned.

"If he knows what's good for him, he stopped recording as soon as he figured out what was going on and has already deleted it." Justin let go of her hands and turned toward the kitchen. "In fact, let's call him now to make sure he knows exactly what I'm going to do to him if I ever hear about that video again."

His phone sat on the counter where he'd left it hours ago. The timer he'd set as a reminder to preheat the oven flashed on the screen. He'd silenced his phone after his brother called and never turned the volume back up. It was four now and the dish he'd planned would take six hours on low in the oven. Dammit.

Now he had two things to take care of: rip Decker a new one and figure out what he was going to make Em for dinner so he didn't lose the damn bet.

Emmeline

Em bit into one of the chocolate cupcakes Justin had ordered. It was good but wasn't what she'd consider the best meal of her life. Justin had lost their bet, fair and square. He knew it, too. That's why he'd insisted they eat dessert first. He was hoping he'd buy himself some points by plying her with chocolate before bringing out the pizza.

"I think I should get a second chance at cooking for you. It's your fault I missed out on preheating the oven."

"My fault?" Em wiped a napkin across her lips. "How could forgetting to preheat the oven possibly be my fault?"

Justin pinched a piece of ooey-gooey cheese as he lifted a slice of pizza out of the box. "You distracted me on the patio, then wore me out. If I hadn't been so tired from prepping food all morning, I would have been on my game."

"You're telling me you'd rather have spent the afternoon cooking than getting a killer BJ for your Love Rocket?" He tossed his head back and laughed so hard that she was afraid cupcake crumbs might fall out of his mouth.

"When you put it that way, yeah, I think I'd choose to lose the bet every single time."

Em reached for her wineglass. After Decker's stunt of sending the naughty-looking flowers, they decided it wouldn't be out of line to raid the wine collection. The Chianti Justin picked out would go well with the pizza.

"I think we should toast." Justin held his glass up.

"To what?" She hadn't seen him in this good a mood in years. Not since the night he'd ridden a ranker bull and scored ninety-four points, his personal best. He'd stopped by her apartment on his way home that night, his eyes bright with excitement. Even though she hated the sport, hated it with every ounce of her being, she loved seeing him so revved up.

"To wherever we go from here. I'm in this for the long haul, Em. I can't wait to find out what the future has in store for us."

"To the long haul." She clinked her glass against his and they each took a sip. She couldn't believe how easily he seemed to be ready to step away from competing. They hadn't talked about it in depth yet, and she didn't want to ruin his good mood tonight by bringing it up. There would be plenty of time to figure it out when they got home.

She sprinkled a little Parmesan on the slice of pizza she'd picked up from the box and wondered what kind of job Justin might take on now that it looked like he'd be retiring. His dad wouldn't be happy, but she was sure Justin would always have a place at the family business. He had the kind of drive and determination that meant he'd be successful at most anything he set his mind to.

Once he got settled into a new career and they figured out where they wanted to live, maybe they'd be ready to talk about settling down for good. She always assumed he'd want kids, but they'd never really discussed it.

"Hey, I've got a question for you," she started.

"Oh yeah? What's that?" He reached across the table and swiped his napkin across her chin. "You had a little sauce there."

"Thanks."

"What's your question? Lay it on me." His eyes sparkled with humor.

It seemed like a good time to broach the subject, so she went for it. "You ever thought about having kids?"

"I'm assuming you're referring to the human kind?" Justin shook some red pepper flakes onto a fresh slice. He'd always liked a little more spice when it came to his food. No surprise he seemed to like a little spice in other areas of his life, too, as she was finding out.

Thoughts like that would only lead back to the bedroom. Or the patio. Or the couch. "Yes, the human kind. If you're in it for the long haul, I think you ought to know that I want to have kids someday."

"Kids are great, and someday sounds fine. By 'someday,' do you have a particular date in mind?" He held her gaze, his look steady, and the teasing shine faded from his eyes. He was taking her seriously.

"Not really. Although, I'll be thirty soon. And I'd probably want to start a family right away so I can avoid a high-risk pregnancy when I get older."

"You're turning twenty-nine in a few days. Thirty's still over a year away."

"It's different for guys. Your sperm stays viable until you die. That means you could become a dad at age ninety-seven or something. Women have a limited amount of time."

"You really think there are guys out there who wait their entire life to finally spread their seed when they turn ninety-seven?" His eyes crinkled at the edges.

"Whatever. Ninety-seven, fifty-four, thirty-two . . . doesn't matter. Guys don't have to think about it. My point is, I want kids and I don't want to wait until I have to go through a high-risk pregnancy when I'm of advanced maternal age to do it." Her stomach clenched. This was a deal breaker for her.

"What's your ideal age to have your first kid?" Justin asked, his tone dead serious.

She took in a breath through her nose and considered the question. Her baby sister was only twenty-four and would be delivering her first baby in the next three months. It's not like Em could turn back time, but she'd love to have kids around the same age as her nieces and nephews. Visions of them growing up together danced through her head.

She'd already promised Justin no more lies. So she squared her shoulders and lifted her gaze to meet his eyes. "I'd really like to have my first kid before I turn thirty-one."

Justin sat there, his pizza in his hand, halfway to his mouth. "That means you'd want to get pregnant when you're thirty."

"Great math, Forza. Mr. Campbell would be so proud."

"If you're pregnant for forty weeks, that would mean you'd want to get knocked up around your thirtieth birthday. Jake and Sienna had a hard time with the first one. We might want to start trying a few months before that, just in case."

"We?" She'd heard the word come out of his mouth.

"Of course, we. When is it going to sink into your gorgeous brain that this is a done deal? You want babies? I'll give them to you. You want to live close to your sister so you can see each other every day? I'll build you a house right next door." He let his pizza fall back to the paper plate in front of him. "You want to get married tomorrow, sweetheart, I'm all in."

He couldn't fake the sincerity that shone through his voice or the honesty in his eyes. Em swallowed back the sob that threatened to rip from her throat. Her eyes welled with tears.

"What did I say? What did I do wrong?" He rubbed her tears away from her lashes. "Tell me so I can fix it, baby."

"Nothing." She got out of her chair and climbed into his lap. "You didn't do anything wrong at all. I'm crying because everything is so very right."

His kiss chased her tears away. This was happening, really and truly happening. Em could hardly believe it.

She wrapped her arms around his neck, the pizza, cupcakes, and wine forgotten.

"Hey, I've got an idea." Justin pulled back. "Want to change things up and sleep in the other bedroom tonight? After we're done making love, we can look up and try to find some shooting stars."

Em didn't answer. She just climbed off his lap, took his hand, and tugged him toward the bedroom.

28

❧

Justin

The time he'd been spending on Paradise Island had been the happiest of his life. Justin had thrown himself into vacation mode. They'd gone snorkeling off the shore of the Gulf, spent an entire day at the turtle sanctuary down the coast, and tonight they were taking the ferry to the mainland to ride the Ferris wheel and stroll along the boardwalk.

Em's hair blew in the breeze as the ferry carried them across the water. Either she'd gotten some sun earlier that day when they'd walked along the beach, or she was happier than he'd seen her in a long time. Probably a little bit of both.

Justin squeezed her hand as the ferry docked. He couldn't remember the last time he'd ridden a Ferris wheel. Maybe when he was a kid and he and Jake had visited the Texas state fair. They only had a few more days in paradise, and he planned to enjoy them to the fullest.

He and Em joined the other tourists heading down the boardwalk. The scent of funnel cakes and caramel corn drifted through the air. Even though they'd had a big lunch, his stomach growled. Spending so much time with

Em was burning up a lot of calories. Must have something to do with the long cardio sessions they engaged in multiple times a day.

Em slowed her pace as she checked out the carnival games lining the boardwalk. A guy yelled for them to come over so he could guess her birthday. She kept walking.

A woman with a tall hat on called out and tried to sway them to step over and win a goldfish. "How in the world would we ever get that back with us?" Em joked.

"We could carry it on the plane and pass it on to Decker, though with the stunt he pulled I'd rather send him a bouquet of dead fish than give him a live one." Justin still couldn't get over the flower delivery. At least Deck hadn't seen much of anything beyond a shadowy silhouette of Em's profile. Didn't stop Justin from cussing him out and threatening to toss him in the chutes with a bull if he ever thought of doing something like that again.

The one positive to come out of that experience was that Justin had made note of the florist's name. He'd been trying to figure out a way to celebrate Em's birthday tomorrow, and with the help of the owner of Flowerific, he was going to more than make up for his ruined attempt at making her a romantic dinner by having a cake delivered while they were on the boardwalk. He wanted to be the first one to wish her a happy birthday and figured he could entice her out to the patio right after midnight and they could feast on chocolate cake.

"Don't worry, we'll figure out a way to get even. We're a team now so it's two against one." Em grinned, showing off her devious side.

She'd always enjoyed playing pranks, but he had no idea how sly her mind could get until they'd stayed up talking into the early morning hours the past few nights. The four of them had pulled some pretty big stunts back in high school but when she left for college and he started traveling so much, they hadn't stayed in touch as much as he would have liked.

Over the past week he'd gotten to know her on such a deeper level. The more he learned about her, the more he fell in love.

"Ooh, have you tried this one before?" Em tugged him toward a booth where a crowd watched while the attendant demonstrated how easily he could stand a milk bottle up by using a pole with a large ring suspended from it on a string.

"They're rigged, Em." He'd tried plenty of games at some of the state fairs where he'd ridden, and had never managed to win.

"I can do this one." She wrapped her fingers around his arm and gave it a squeeze. "We had it at the school carnival a couple of years ago."

"All right then, let's see you do it." He pulled out his wallet and handed over a five-dollar bill.

"That'll buy you one chance." The attendant handed the pole to him.

"I'm not playing, this is for her." Justin passed the pole to Em.

She held out her purse and he tucked it under his arm.

Em stepped up to the railing, then leaned forward. She lined up the pole so the ring was level with the lip of the bottle.

"You want to put a little wager on this one?" Justin asked. He still hadn't paid up for losing the last bet they'd made. The idea of reading a bedtime story to Rocky wasn't sitting well with him, and he'd do just about anything to relieve himself of that particular obligation.

Em turned toward him and set a hand on her hip. "What do you have in mind?"

"Well"—he scrubbed his hand over the scruff on his chin—"if you don't get it, I don't have to record the bedtime story."

"You really hate owing me that one, don't you?"

He nodded. "I really do."

"So, what happens when I'm successful?" The look in her eyes smacked of sass. She was confident. That could work in his favor. He'd always found that cockiness got in the way of performance. Every single time.

"What do you want?"

"Hmm." She tapped her finger against her lip, pretending to be deep in thought. "When I prove I can do it, I want you to come into the classroom to read to Rocky. I've got a Pete the Cat book that I think the kids would really enjoy. Especially when you play the guitar and sing the button song, too."

Justin laughed. "Hell no, Em. I haven't played the guitar in years."

She put her hand over his. "Good thing school doesn't start for another couple of months. You'll have plenty of time to reacquaint yourself with your six string."

"You know what? Fine. You set that bottle upright and I'll come into your class, read the book, and figure out how to play your button song." He'd been keeping an eye on two teenagers who'd been trying to lift the bottle for the past few minutes. Neither one had been successful. Maybe the game Em played at the school carnival wasn't rigged, but this version sure was.

"All right then." Em turned back to face the game, squared her shoulders, and leaned forward, easing the ring close to the lip of the milk bottle.

"There you go. A little to the left," Justin coached.

The ring connected with the bottle and started spinning. Justin glanced from the bottle to Em's face. Her brow furrowed in concentration, her lips parted slightly. She was playing to win.

"There!" The ring floated over the lip of the bottle. She looked over at him, victory in her eyes.

"Anyone can slip the ring over the tip there, Em. But now you've got to get it up."

Her mouth tipped up in a wicked grin and she refocused her attention on her efforts. Damn, she looked sexy like that.

"Come on, baby," she mumbled, her tone low.

Justin leaned in, his mouth close to her ear. "Promise me you'll talk to me like that later?"

Her fingers slipped on the pole and the milk bottle fell, landing on the fabric padding surrounding the stand. "Hey, that's cheating. You can't talk to me like that while I'm concentrating."

He backed up and shrugged. "You didn't say there were rules."

"I want a do-over. No talking this time." Em pulled a crumpled bill out of her pocket and handed it to the attendant. "No talking, not a peep from you or I'll make you wear a costume when you come in to read to my kids."

Justin mimed zipping up his mouth. He'd done what he needed to do by setting her off her game. Now it was her game to lose.

Emmeline

The ring slipped over the edge of the bottle again. Em shot a warning glare at Justin. He'd better not interfere this time. She eased the tip of the pole up—no sudden movements—that's what it would take to win.

The bottle rolled around on the wooden platform. This

was the point where she might lose it. She didn't want to give Justin the satisfaction of winning their bet, especially when he cheated. A shiver rolled through her as she thought of his warm breath on her ear. She waited until it had spread through her system before she attempted to lift the bottle any higher.

Justin moved closer. She could see him in her peripheral vision, but more than that, she could sense him. The hair on the back of her neck stood up as the weight of his gaze rested on her. Being an object of his intense scrutiny like that almost felt like a gentle caress. If she let herself, she could imagine his hands tracing the path of his eyes.

There would be time for that later. Now she needed to focus all of her attention on the task in front of her. Knowing he didn't think she could do it would make her victory that much sweeter.

She eased the tip of the pole up a tiny bit higher. The bottle spun slowly. Just a little bit more. The bottle stood upright, listed to the left, and then steadied itself.

A rush of adrenaline swept through her. She bumped her shoulder into Justin's arm and jumped up and down.

"That's a win." The attendant took the pole from her hand. "Time to pick your prize."

Em turned to Justin. He swiped his hand over his forehead.

"What do you think about that?" She couldn't resist rubbing it in.

"I think you got lucky." He leaned forward to examine the platform. "Maybe that's the winning setup, you know, the one they use when they demo the game so that people think they have a fair shot at winning?"

"You're kidding, right?" She cocked a hip. Why was it so hard for him to admit defeat? Probably went back to when he was a kid. It seemed like all of their present-day issues had been planted sometime during childhood.

Justin rolled a shoulder. "You did it. I'm just saying, it must not be as hard as they make it look."

She bit down on her lip, a little amused at his doubt and a little pissed off. "You think you can do it, too?"

"I don't know." He lifted a finger and scratched at the mosquito bite he'd gotten on his neck the other night while they sat on the beach and searched for more shooting stars.

"Double or nothing?" She arched a brow.

"Meaning what?"

"If you can do it, you're off the hook for all of it . . . the reading, the singing, the guitar playing . . ."

He evaluated her through half-closed lids. "And if I don't?"

Hmm. It would have to be something good. Something that would teach him not to doubt her. She screwed her lips up while she tried to come up with an idea he couldn't refuse. "If you fail . . . scratch that . . . when you fail . . . you have to come into the classroom, read the book, sing the song, play the guitar, and dress up like Rocky."

He balked, shook his head, and waved his palms in front of his chest. "You want me to dress up like a penis to come into school and read to impressionable five-year-olds?"

She would have laughed at the sheer amount of fear in his eyes, but she didn't want to scare him off. "They're five. They're not going to think you look like a penis."

"What about the first through fifth graders? The other teachers? Mrs. Richmond? Are they all big Rocky fans, too, or are they going to think a grown man has lost his mind and report me to Child Protective Services?"

Em snort laughed. "I'll make sure you don't look like a penis. Do we have a deal?"

"I'm going to regret this, aren't I?" He thrust his hand toward her.

"One more try." He handed the cash over and took the pole. Then he rested his hips against the railing, copying what he'd watched Em do a few minutes earlier.

"Just slip the big O over the end of the shaft," Em advised.

Justin stepped back from the railing and rolled his eyes. "Same rules apply. No talking, all right?"

Em bit her lip and nodded. "Just trying to give you some proven advice."

"I've got this." He resumed the position, wiggling his hips like he needed to loosen up before fully exerting himself. He was cute as an underdog. There was one thing Justin hated more than anything in his life . . . losing.

She couldn't put words to the absolute joy she felt in besting him at something besides a round of dirty Scrabble. They'd found an old version of the game in one of the cabinets in the living room at Decker's dad's house and she'd kicked his ass by playing *jiz* and *jo* off a triple-letter tile.

"I've got this," he repeated, his voice deep and soft. He leaned farther in, sticking his ass out behind him.

The sight of his glorious glutes encased in a pair of well-worn jeans made her fingers itch to touch him. She'd agreed not to talk, but he hadn't said anything about no touching.

As Justin slipped the ring over the mouth of the milk jug, she took a step closer. His lips tipped up in a grin of satisfaction as he started to ease the bottle to an upright position.

Em stepped close enough to breathe in his scent: a mixture of coconut suntan lotion and sun-kissed skin. She inhaled deeply. She'd never be able to get enough of him. Of his scent. Of his taste. Of his touch.

"What are you doing? Give me some space, Em." His grip on the pole faltered, but a quick flick of his wrist saved the bottle from tumbling over.

Not even close to giving up, Em figured it was time to up the stakes. She dropped her purse right next to him. Committed to not breaking his rule of saying anything, and vowing to not violate his request to give him some space, she bent over in silence to pick it up.

It wasn't her fault the miniskirt she had on rode up her thighs a little bit. She could have squatted down instead of bending at the waist, but where was the fun in that?

Justin dropped the pole and stepped behind her, his palms gripping her hips, his pelvis bumping into her ass. "What are you doing?"

"I dropped my purse and didn't want to interrupt." Her fingers closed around her bag and she stood. "Sorry, didn't mean to distract you."

He glanced to where the milk jug had clattered to its side. "You sabotaged me."

"What is it you're always saying to me? Keep your eye on the prize? Isn't that it?" She lowered her voice to mimic him and tried to remember the words she'd heard him preach in dozens of interviews over the years. "I don't let anyone, or anything, distract me. Whether I win or lose, it's up to me. My biggest enemy in the ring isn't the bull, it's myself."

He let his head roll back and gazed up. "Thank god you never pulled a stunt like that while I was on the back of a bull."

"No hard feelings?" Em tucked her chin against her chest and tried to hide the victorious smile threatening to split her cheeks.

"You got me." He spun her around so they stood facing each other. "I'll just have to think of it as a chance to spend more time with you when I have to . . . I mean get to . . . come into the classroom."

"That's the spirit." She rose to her tiptoes and pressed her lips against his. They had only a couple more days together. Would he feel the same when reality descended around them?

29

❦

Justin

"Now here's a game I can beat." Justin needed to redeem himself, and the game in front of him might be his best chance at saving face.

"What in the world is that?" Em stopped next to him and cocked her head, studying the contraption. Then she held out a tuft of pink cotton candy.

He nipped it from her fingers and the sweet taste of pure sugar melted in his mouth. "What's it look like?"

"Want to win that lovely lady a stuffed turtle?" The game attendant noticed them and headed over. "All you need to do is stay on the back of Quicksilver for eight seconds and you can take your pick of one of our giant sea turtles."

Justin looked up to where cheap stuffed turtles of various sizes hung from the tentpoles above.

"It's just like those mechanical bulls you've probably seen at the bars." The attendant leaned forward and muttered toward Justin. "Good way to impress the fairer sex. The ladies think bull riding's pretty sexy."

"Is that so?" Justin furrowed his brows and shot a quick glance to Em.

She pushed a giant cloud of cotton candy into her mouth instead of voicing a response.

"You don't even have to stay on the whole time. Two seconds will win you a tiny turtle. If you can manage four, you'll walk away with the mighty medium size." He flicked a joystick and the mechanical turtle executed a slow spin. "I had a five-year-old on here a few minutes ago. Kid nearly cleaned me out, and I had to cut him off after three rides."

Justin still hadn't decided whether or not he was returning to competing, but surely he could manage eight seconds on a kiddie ride. "What do you think, Em? Do girls find bull riders sexy?"

"Certain girls find certain bull riders sexy." She sidled up to him, being careful not to touch him with her sticky, cotton candy–covered fingers, and lowered her voice. "What about your shoulder?"

"I'll use my left hand. How hard can it be?"

A cloud of doubt settled over her face. "I don't want you to get hurt."

"Em, it's a turtle."

One of her shoulders lifted in a slight shrug. "If you promise you won't get hurt."

Sensing a sucker, the guy held out a waiver. "Sign here. It's just a precaution."

Justin scrawled his signature across the dotted line and mounted the broad back of the turtle. It wasn't exactly like riding a bull. Where the back of a bull dipped in behind its shoulders, the perfect place for a cowboy to clench his thighs together and hold on tight, the shape of the turtle's back rendered his legs ineffective. This would be a battle of will and upper arm strength.

He wrapped his left hand around the rope that had been rigged for a grip, and nodded to the attendant. The turtle began to move. A slow turn to the right gave way to a forward dip before spinning to the left. Justin held his right arm up in the air, years of practice and instinct taking over.

The pace increased, and the turtle dipped forward, then back again. Easy peasy. Justin's internal countdown matched the large digital numbers on the display mounted above. With three seconds to go, the turtle spiraled to the left, stopped suddenly, and twisted to the right. Justin held on, shifting his center of gravity to handle the rapid change in direction.

A loud buzzer sounded. The turtle slowed, then came to a stop.

Em clapped, tucked her fingers into her mouth, and let out a loud whistle.

Justin let go of his grip and slid off the back of the beast. It might have been a silly carnival ride, but it reminded him a bit of being on the back of a bull. Reminded him of how it felt to anticipate the moves of the animal underneath him, the thrill of completing a ride.

A few folks had gathered to watch, and he heard his name being tossed around in whispers and low voices.

"Hey, you're Justin Forza, the bull rider, aren't you?" A man standing by the railing held up a camera and snapped a picture.

The attendant eyed Justin. "You're a pro?"

"Well, I used to be. I got injured earlier this year and have been taking some time off."

"He's retiring." Em wrapped an arm around him, then rose up on her toes to kiss him on the cheek.

He wasn't going to correct her, not in front of a crowd and especially not in front of someone holding up a camera. But hearing her say those words out loud made him wonder where she'd gotten the idea he'd decided to step down. He hadn't said that specifically. Had he?

"You oughta told me you were a pro." The attendant reached up and pulled a giant stuffed turtle from a hook. "I should be giving you a small one for not telling me, but this one got busted up when his leg got caught in the door of the truck. You can have it."

Em held out her arms, trying to reach around the stuffed animal. "It's just like Tripod. I love it."

"Thanks." Justin hefted it onto his left shoulder and laced his fingers with Em's.

"You're retiring? How come I haven't seen that in the news?" The man holding the camera pointed it directly at Justin. "You want to make an official statement I can share with your fans?"

"No comment." Justin nodded at the folks gathered. "I'm on vacation with my girlfriend right now. If y'all have questions, you can send them to my agent or reach out on social media. Have a good night."

He pulled Em toward the ferry. They needed to talk and soon. Things needed to be cleared up between them before she said the wrong thing to the wrong person and caused him a ton of grief.

"Hey, what's going on?" She stopped short. "Did I say something wrong?"

He turned, his fingers still laced with hers. "I don't want to do this here. Can we wait until we get back to the house to have this conversation?"

"What conversation? What did I do?" Her gazed traced over his face.

"We need to talk, but not here."

"Talk about what?" She pulled her fingers from his grip.

He didn't want to do this now. Didn't want to do it at all.

"I'm not taking another step until you tell me what's going on." She crossed her arms over her stomach.

Justin let the stuffed turtle slide down his back. Clearly, she wasn't going to make this easy for him. The last thing in the world he wanted to do was hurt her. "Em, when did I say I was retiring?"

"Aren't you?" Her eyes, his favorite shade of green, had taken on a glassy shine.

He shifted his gaze over her shoulder. Looking at her face right now hurt too damn much. "I haven't decided. We haven't talked about it. Hell, I don't know where you got the impression I'd made up my mind."

"I don't know, I guess I might have come to that conclusion when we were wrapped in each other's arms in bed the other night." She turned her face away from him, but not before he saw her lower lids swell with tears.

"Hey, come here." He couldn't stand to see her upset. Wanting to comfort her, he reached out.

She brushed him off, wiped her fingers under her eyes, and hit him with a head-on gaze. The pain in her eyes was sharp enough to slice him in half. He almost doubled over.

"So, you're not planning on retiring? You're going to go back to competing? Even though your shoulder's nowhere near healed?" The hurt turned toward anger. He could see the change in the way her shoulders straightened, and she held her head back.

"That's not what I said, either. There's a lot to think about. It's not an easy yes-or-no decision."

"I'll make it easy for you, Justin. I'm out. I won't put myself through the same kind of pain my mom suffered. She didn't have a choice, but I do. I'm not going to stand by while you push yourself to a breaking point just to make your dad's dreams come true."

His breath caught in his chest. Is that how she felt? "You think I'm just doing this for my dad?"

"Aren't you?" Her jaw clenched tight, and she dared him to say otherwise.

"That's part of it. But the real reason I'm doing this is for you, for us. I've got nothing to offer you. No high-paying job with benefits. No college degree. The only thing I've ever been good at is spending eight seconds on the back of a bull. It's all I know." He held his arms out, willing her to see things his way.

"Don't put this on me. You've always been enough for me just the way you are. If you know me half as well as you think you do, you'd know that the absolute last thing I'd ever want you to do is risk your life and risk your health. You can't see it from the corner your dad's been backing you into, but you've got choices. You can find something you love that doesn't involve putting your life on the line every day you go to work."

"It's not that easy." He reached a hand out to her, but she turned her shoulder to him. "Come on, Em. Let's go back to the house. We can figure this out together."

"I'll go back to the house." She tugged on the ribbon wrapped around the big turtle's neck and managed to drag it over her shoulder. "I suggest you find somewhere else to stay, though. Until you figure out who you want to put first in your life, I can't pretend to be okay with you thinking of going back to competing."

"Em . . ." He wanted to fall to his knees and beg her not to leave him. Now that he'd had her, caught a glimpse of heaven with her in his arms, he couldn't bear to let her go.

"You have to choose, Justin. Me or the bulls. It really is that simple, isn't it?"

She had no idea the amount of pressure he was under. All he'd ever wanted, all he'd ever dreamed about, was making a life for the two of them. He wanted to buy a tract of land where they could ranch and ride, and fill their home with kids and dogs and even penis-shaped rocks if she wanted. But he couldn't afford to do that, to give her the life she deserved, without putting himself at risk.

"One more season. I can come back, finish strong, get the title for my dad, and win that prize money so I can give you the kind of life you need."

She clenched her jaw. "The only kind of life I need is one with you in it, Justin. All of you. Not a shell of the man I fell in love with like my mama got when my dad didn't know when to quit."

He wanted to reach out, to make her the promises she wanted. Anything to keep her from walking away.

But he couldn't.

She might think all she needed was him, but he knew better. Love could get a man only so far. If he wanted all the trimmings to go with it, he'd have to earn it. Helplessly, he watched her go.

Emmeline

Em was too stubborn to look back and too hurt to stick around and listen to all the reasons Justin thought he needed to go back to competing. She dragged the damn turtle all the way to the ferry and stuffed it into the seat next to her while she stared out at the sparkling lights of the boardwalk. They grew smaller and smaller as they left the shore behind.

By the time she got back to the house, she'd cycled through every emotion she could think of and some she'd never considered. She was pissed. Madder than a wet hen and a hornet all rolled into one.

Justin knew she'd never get involved with a rodeo man, yet he let her believe he was done. She never would have let him into her bed, never would have let him into her heart if she thought for half a second he hadn't pretty much made up his mind.

Anger gave way to frustration. How could he be so blind to not see that his dad had been manipulating him his entire life? He'd done it to his brother, pushing him to keep going, even after he'd hurt his leg. Jake would never admit it, but it was his dad's fault he'd never be able to chase his kids around a playground or navigate a set of stairs again. Sure, he had a world championship under his belt, but at what cost?

She punched the code into the keypad and opened the door. They hadn't left any lights on, so she cleared her throat and asked the house to turn on the living room lights. It felt wrong to come back without Justin. Hopefully, he'd have time to think and would show up in the morning with a clear direction in mind and a smile on his face. Until then, she'd have to wait.

The turtle lodged in the door, too wide to fit straight through. Em turned it, trying to shove it through with force alone. The back leg that had lost its stuffing caught on the door hinge.

"Come on, can't I catch a break?" Em put her weight behind it and pushed. The turtle squeezed through the door, but not before the cloth caught on the hinge gave way. Tiny beads of stuffing spilled all over the porch and into the entryway.

Em stumbled over the ledge at the door and tumbled into the house, landing on top of the turtle. She'd stubbed her toe on the step and ripped her toenail.

Damn, that hurt. She kicked off her sandal and noticed the blood. She'd have to clean up the stuffing in a minute. Right now, she needed ice. Hobbling toward the kitchen, her gaze caught on something out on the patio. She squinted, trying to figure out what had drawn her attention.

Moving closer, she could make out a huge vase of flowers sitting on the patio table. If Decker had sent another obnoxious bouquet . . . She slid the glass door open and sucked in a breath.

A crystal vase full of gorgeous blooms sat in the center of the table. The fragrance reached her all the way at the door, a mixture of roses and lilies and so many other blossoms she didn't know the names of. Her gaze traveled down the vase to a tall, round cake covered in chocolate frosting with pink writing.

Swirly letters spelled out "Happy Birthday, Em!" She reached for the edge of the table as her knees gave way. He'd said he had a birthday surprise for her when they got back. She figured he'd picked up another cupcake or two while he was at the market, but she'd never expected something like this.

Sinking into a chair, she stifled a sob. How did they get to this point? The past several days had been the happiest time of her life. She and Justin fit together like two pieces of a puzzle. They were stronger together than either of them was alone. Couldn't he see that?

While she sat in the chair, taking deep breaths of the flower-scented air to calm her nerves, her phone rang. Hope that it was Justin faded when she saw her sister's number on the screen. She didn't want to talk to anyone. Didn't want to put on a cheery face so someone could wish her a happy birthday.

She'd always been the stoic one, always been the one everyone turned to in a time of crisis. Maybe she should let someone else try to cheer her up for once. Her finger swiped at the screen right before the call was sent to voice mail.

"Hello?"

"I know your birthday's not until tomorrow, but I

wanted to be one of the first ones to call. Happy birthday!"
Georgie blew a noisemaker into the phone. Even though
Em's heart had been shattered into a million pieces, hear-
ing her sister's voice dulled the pain.

"Thanks, hon."

"What's wrong?"

Em tried to steady her voice. "Nothing. What are you
up to tonight? Is the baby moving around much?"

"Something's wrong. What did Justin do?"

"What makes you think Justin did something?"

"Because tomorrow's your birthday and you should
be celebrating and instead you've been crying." Georgie
growled into the phone. She'd always been the feisty one.
"Let me talk to him."

Em swiped her finger along the beads of frosting at the
base of the cake. "He's not here."

"Why not? Where did he go?"

"He didn't go anywhere. I left him on the boardwalk."
Tears threatened, but she held them off with a deep breath.
"He said he might go back to riding."

"What?"

Em pictured her sister, all four foot ten of her, riled up
like a miniature pinscher and ready to pick a fight with
someone several times her size. "I thought he'd changed
his mind. Based on how he's been with me over the past
few days . . ."

"Oh, sweetie, I'm so sorry. Men can be such dicks, can't
they?"

Em laughed. "Careful. My niece or nephew is listening.
You can't go around using your grown-up words anymore."

"I can think of several grown-up words I'd like to call
him. So, where are you?"

"Sitting on the patio at Decker's dad's house. I guess

Justin made arrangements for someone to deliver a big bouquet of flowers and a birthday cake while we were at the boardwalk. What am I supposed to do now?" She tried to blink back the tears, but it didn't work.

"Didn't you say Decker told you to help yourself to the wine collection while you were there?"

Em sniffled. "Yeah." No need to tell Georgie that Decker only offered after Justin reamed him for catching their late-night interaction on the patio on video.

"Then I'll tell you what to do. Go pick out a good bottle of red wine. One of your favorites, like a cab or merlot."

"You want me to sit on the patio alone and drink?"

"No, sweetie. My older sister once told me that the key to surviving a broken heart is chocolate cake and red wine. I'm assuming Justin knows you well enough to have ordered the right kind of cake?"

Em summoned a smile. "Your older sister sounds like someone who wasn't counting calories back then."

"Pfft." Georgie made a raspberry sound with her lips. "Everyone knows calories don't count on birthdays. And since I can't drink wine right now, you'll have to enjoy enough for both of us. There's just one more thing you need."

"What's that?" Em asked, her mood already improving.

"A fork."

30

~❤~

Justin

Justin wandered through the boardwalk, his mind replaying the conversation between the two of them, over and over and over, until he literally couldn't see straight. He sat down on a bench by the waterfront, hoping a solution would come to him. He didn't know how much time Em needed, but he'd stay away and give her space tonight.

With his head in his hands, he tried to figure a way out of the mess he'd gotten himself into. Em or bull riding. She'd dumbed it down to a choice that seemed so simple.

But it wasn't.

If he chose Em, he'd be letting down his family. He may as well issue a death sentence to the family business, and he could kiss any chance of ever proving himself to his dad goodbye. But if he chose to keep riding, he'd lose Em. His heart cracked at the prospect. For ten years he'd told himself he was doing it all for her. For the chance to build a future for the two of them. Why couldn't she see that?

He could understand why she'd want him to quit, especially with what her mom went through. He'd seen men lose it all . . . their families, their fortunes, their lives. Bull riding got into their blood like an addiction they couldn't beat. It wasn't like that for him. He looked at it as a means to an end.

Riding bulls had given him a ticket out of Blewit. Let him see the world. Provided him a glimpse of what his future might look like and a way to make it happen. All he needed was the big win.

He got up from the bench, not sure where to go. Em had probably made it back to the house by now. Hopefully, she'd seen the cake and had cooled down enough to enjoy it. Chocolate cake with fudge frosting was her favorite, always had been.

It had been a couple of years since they'd had a chance to celebrate her birthday in person. He'd been looking forward to seeing the look on her face when they got back to the house. And he'd really been looking forward to licking the fudge frosting off certain parts of her body if she'd let him.

All that was gone now.

He turned toward the ferry, figuring he'd head back to the island and find a spot on the beach to spend the night. By morning, Em would cool off. They could have the conversation they needed to have and figure out a way to get through this.

The ferry crossing seemed to take forever. As the boat approached the shore, the sound of country-western music floated across the water. Probably live music at A Cowboy in Paradise tonight. With nowhere else to go, Justin stepped onto the pier and turned toward the bar. They'd set a stage up in the sand and a couple hundred people sat in beach chairs or on blankets, taking in the show.

Justin dropped down to claim a spot at the back of the crowd as the band wrapped up a loud, fast-paced tune and started playing a cover of one of Knox's songs. He remembered when Knox wrote that particular tune. It was right after a breakup with his first girlfriend out of high school. Man, he'd taken that one hard. They'd dated a couple of years, and Justin really thought they'd end up together.

Then Knox found her in bed with his old man. There wasn't really any way to recover from that. His parents split and he lost his dad and the woman he thought he'd spend the rest of his life with. At least Knox got the last word. That song had been the second single he'd ever released and got him a spot on the Billboard charts.

Justin and Decker had rallied around him. Em, too.

That's what Justin needed right now . . . the company of his buddies, or at least one of them. Someone who had his back and would take his side. Though, that was the problem with going all in with Em. His best friends were her best friends, too. He'd have to handle this one alone.

While he sat there, his heart squeezing even tighter in his chest thanks to Knox's sad-ass song, his phone buzzed in his pocket. There wasn't anyone he wanted to talk to tonight except for the woman who'd made it crystal clear she didn't want to talk to him.

He ignored it, directing all of his attention at the stage.

"I thought that might be you." Chick stopped in front of him, with Tripod at his side. "This is a new group from Brownsville. They said they'd play for free, so I figured I'd give them a chance. What do you think so far?"

"I think they need to play something that won't have people crying in their beer." Justin reached out to run his hand along Tripod's shell. He wondered if Em had managed to get the giant stuffed turtle back to the house with her or had abandoned it somewhere along the route.

Chick squatted, and lowered his voice. "Sounds like you've had a rough night. Where's Emmeline?"

"Good question." Justin picked up a handful of sand and let it slip through his fingers. "We had a miscommunication of sorts."

"Is that so?" His eyes went soft at the edges. "Anything I can help with?"

Justin shook his head. "Not unless you have a way of going back in time?"

"You're out of luck on that one." Chick clapped a hand to Justin's shoulder. "But I've got a bottle of Devil's Dance small batch that I brought back from Tennessee. I've been waiting for a reason to open it if you want to join me for a drink. In my experience, that's the next best thing."

"Sure." Justin got to his feet and followed Chick to the bar. He didn't have anywhere else to be tonight. Letting some good whiskey numb his bad feelings sounded like an ideal way to spend the rest of the evening.

The bartender lifted a hand to wave as they passed between tables and headed to the stairs. Justin hadn't been in Chick's office before. Stepping into the small room felt like stepping back in time. Memorabilia from Chick's years as a rodeo cowboy spread through the bar downstairs, but here, every wall and horizontal surface seemed to hold a piece of his past.

"Don't pay any attention to that." Chick gestured to the walls. "I probably ought to box it all up and put it in storage, but that sounds like it would take more effort than it's worth."

"Do you miss it?" Justin slid into the chair in front of the desk.

"What? Putting my life on the line every day?" Chick let out a laugh. "As crazy as it sounds, yeah, sometimes I do."

Chick pulled two glasses and a bottle of amber liquid from his bottom desk drawer. He poured a couple of fingers of whiskey into each and handed one to Justin.

"Thank you." Justin clinked his glass against Chick's and took a sip. The smooth liquid rolled over his tongue before burning a trail all the way to his belly.

"You want to tell me what happened with Emmeline?" Chick asked.

Justin lifted his glass, studying the way the light danced through the liquid. "She didn't think I was going to go back to riding."

"Are you?"

"I don't know." Justin shifted his gaze to the wizened man across from him. "It's complicated."

Chick nodded. "It always is, son."

A few long moments passed, but Justin found the silence comforting. If anyone could understand the tug-of-war going on in his chest, it would be someone who'd walked the same road and faced the same choices.

"How did you know when it was time to give it up?"

Chick didn't respond right away. Then he tilted his head and tapped a finger on his knee. "I knew it was time when the things I wanted most shifted from what was inside the ring to what was outside of it. Does that make sense?"

Justin leaned back in his chair, giving serious consideration to what Chick had said. "I think so."

"I could have kept riding until my body was so broken I couldn't hold on anymore. Bull riding's in my blood and it sure as hell's in yours, too. But at some point, something comes along that's more important. It's different for everyone. For some guys, it's their health. For others, it might be their family. Doesn't mean a man's lost his love for the sport, it just means that something else takes up a little bit more of his heart." Chick took in a breath and nodded. "That's how it was for me at least."

Justin sat with that thought for a few long beats. That's exactly how he felt. "I think my dad's never found something more important. He loves my brother, my sister, and me, and I know he loved my mom before they split up. But for him, bulls have always come first. It's like he'll do anything, say anything to hang on to that part of his life."

"It can be that way with some of us." Chick tipped his glass to his lips.

Justin's phone started buzzing again in his pocket. Em said she didn't want to talk, but maybe she'd had time to think about it. He slid it out far enough to check the screen. His dad. Again.

"You're going to have to make your choice soon, son." Chick got up and walked around the desk, heading for the door. "I need to check on things downstairs. You're welcome to stay as long as you want. Just let me know if you want to talk again."

"I will. Thank you."

The sound of glasses clinking and people chatting came through as Chick slipped through the door before pulling it closed.

Chick was right. The time to make his choice was now. Justin answered the call and held the phone up to his ear.

31

❧

Justin

"Have you lost your fucking mind?" His father bellowed through the phone. "Of all the shit-brained, fucking thoughtless things to do . . ."

Justin jerked it away from his ear and waited for a pause in the torrent of four-letter words so he could get a word in.

"Are you listening to me?"

"What are you talking about?" Used to his dad's outbursts, he wasn't sure what had set him off this time.

"You're on vacation with your girlfriend, who just announced your retirement to the whole goddamn world? When did you think would be a good time to tell your manager about that? How about the new sponsor who just signed on for six fucking figures for the rest of the year?"

Justin put a hand to his temple, trying to stave off the onset of a throbbing headache. "I didn't say I'm retiring."

"You want me to play the video for you? Some guy posted it online, and it's been picked up by the nightly news. I've been fielding calls from your sponsors for the past two hours. Blaster's ready to pull the plug. I need you to get your ass home. Now."

"Dad, it was a misunderstanding. Em thought—"

"I don't care what Em thought. We need to get on top of this. Now. I've been patient. I know you've been working through some stuff, son. I was all for you taking some time, getting your head on straight, and doing what you needed to do to come back stronger than ever. But this is our family we're talking about. Our business. Our future."

Justin had seen his dad upset before. He was the kind of man who didn't hold back and never had any trouble letting everyone know exactly how pissed off he was about things. He pushed his own agenda in the name of the family, but Justin was tired of feeling like the weight of the Forza future rested solely on his shoulders.

"I can't come home yet. There are a few things I need to do down here first. I need another day or two at least, and then I'll head home to fix this." He had to talk to Em first. Had to patch things up before he headed home, or he worried he'd never get the chance.

"I've tried to be understanding, but this is it. I've got a meeting with your agent set up for noon tomorrow. If your ass isn't sitting across from my desk at twelve o'clock sharp, I won't have a choice but to cut you out, son."

Justin's heart leapt into his throat at the threat. "Dad, come on. Rumors fly around the circuit all the time. That's all this is."

"Not this time. I didn't want it to come to this. Honest, I didn't. You haven't left me a choice." His dad's voice cracked. "Please come home, Justin. We need you."

"Dad, hold on. We can work through this." The line went dead. Justin held the phone away from his ear.

His dad had gotten emotional before, had made empty

threats and tried to bulldoze his way through barriers set in his path. This felt different.

Justin couldn't afford to lose his share of the business, not if he was seriously considering retiring from bull riding and trying to give Em the kind of life he wanted. Dammit. A quick glance at his watch showed him he had about fourteen hours to get back to Blewit or call his dad's bluff.

He didn't want to bother his brother this late at night, but Jake was the only one who might be able to shed some light on the situation. With his heart thumping so loud his pulse whooshed through his ears, Justin pulled up the number and dialed.

"I wondered how long it would take you to call." Jake answered on the first ring.

"I just got off the phone with Dad. He sounds pissed."

"He is pissed. You know better than to make any kind of statement without running it past the team first. You should have seen his face when he heard Emmeline Porter announce that you were retiring. I seriously thought I was going to have to give him CPR." Jake let out a loud sigh. "What the hell's going on?"

"I don't know. Em and I kind of got together while we've been down here. I know how she feels about bull riding and since we hooked up, she assumed that meant I was ready to call it quits."

"Are you?" Jake asked. It was the first time they'd talked about the possibility of retiring. Justin always assumed his brother would share their dad's views on the subject, but maybe he ought to ask.

"I don't know. That last ride really fucked with my head. I've been working toward a championship my whole life. I don't know anything else. But I love Em. I figured if I could get the title, make my dad happy, win that million-dollar purse so I'd have something to start a life with . . . I just don't know anymore."

"Break it down, little bro. What do you know? Start with that and see where it leads."

"What do you mean?" Justin hadn't heard his brother talk like that before.

"I mean, you love Em. Do you love her enough to walk away from everything else?"

Justin rested his elbow on his knee and swiped his palm over his brow. He couldn't remember a time when his heart didn't beat for Em. Her face was the first thing he pictured when he woke up in the mornings and the last thing he saw when he closed his eyes to go to sleep.

"Yeah. I think I do."

"I never figured you for the pussy-whupped kind." Jake let out a laugh. "I get it, though. When I met Sienna, my priorities shifted into place. Trust me, when you have a kid, they'll change again. My wife, my family, they're the most important things in the world to me."

"What about Dad? He pushed you to the championships the year you won. You never should have been competing."

"That's where you're wrong, bro. Dad pushed, hell yeah he did. That's the only way he knows, and he's good at what he does. I never would have been ready for a season like that without him guiding me the whole way." Jake clucked his tongue. "But he couldn't have pushed me if I hadn't made up my mind that's the direction I wanted to go. I knew the risk going in, and I was willing to take it. The cash I won that season has set me up for life."

"So, you think I should go back? Finish up the season and make a real run for the title?" Jake had done exactly what Justin had planned. All along, Justin thought his dad had been the one pushing. Did it make a difference to learn that Jake had been in charge all along?

"Only you can answer that. Dad's in a bad place now, though. He invested a lot of cash into that business he was trying to start in Brazil. So many bull riders from South America are killing it in the pros right now that a group of investors thought they could organize some sort of local circuit to identify the best prospects and bring them to the US."

"That's why he's so desperate for a win."

"Probably so. Another Forza championship would go a long way in securing more clients." Jake mumbled something Justin couldn't hear. "Sorry, I've got to go. Lucas is having trouble falling asleep, and Sienna is wiped. Have you figured out what you're going to do?"

"Not quite yet. Thanks for listening, though. I appreciate it."

"I'm always here for you. You know that, don't you?"

"Yeah." If he didn't know it before, he sure as hell did now. Justin hung up, a plan starting to take shape in his mind.

32

❦

Emmeline

Em scrubbed at the hardened fudge frosting with a sponge.
She was right smack-dab in the middle of a red wine and
chocolate hangover after overindulging in both the night
before. To hell with it. Slipping the plate into the sink full
of soapy water, she let out a sigh.

She hadn't slept well at all last night. Had tossed and
turned until the sun started to peek above the horizon,
then gave up and rolled out of bed.

Even though she hadn't seen Justin since she left him
standing on the boardwalk last night, she felt him everywhere around her. His presence filled the beach house. His
shoes sat by the door to the patio. His cowboy hat rested
on the coffee table. His clothes hung in the closet in the
bedroom they'd been sharing. She'd intentionally slept in
the other room last night, but even his scent lingered on
the pillow.

Everywhere she turned, she saw reminders of him. The
obnoxious apron hung on a hook by the pantry. The new
carafe sparkled on the burner of the coffeepot. The giant

turtle he'd won smiled at her from the couch. It was too much.

She rinsed the bubbles off her hands and reached for a dish towel. Decker had always said the best way to get over a hangover was to indulge in the hair of the dog that bit you. She walked over to the fridge, where she'd stored what remained of the chocolate cake, and carried it over to the counter. Nothing like coffee and cake for breakfast.

Fork in hand, she'd just slid a big bite into her mouth when the front door opened. Her heart squeezed. Eager to set eyes on Justin, she forced herself not to go to him. It would be so easy to wrap her arms around him, nestle her cheek against his chest, and pretend like last night didn't happen.

She swallowed the cake and washed it down with a sip of coffee. She couldn't pretend last night didn't happen, because it had. It wasn't even seven o'clock yet, but she was ready to find out what he'd decided. Taking in a deep breath, she squared her shoulders and turned to face him.

He looked like shit. His hair stuck out in all directions and the scruff on his cheeks that seemed sexy as hell last night now made him look like he hadn't had access to running water in days. He lifted a hand and scratched at his chin, still unaware that she stood a few feet away in the kitchen.

"You're back." She didn't mean for it to sound like an accusation, but his head snapped up and his eyes filled with guilt.

"Hey, I didn't think you'd be up yet." A crease bisected his forehead. His gaze swept to the cake sitting out on the counter. "I see you found the cake."

"Yeah"—feeling like she'd been caught with her hand in the cookie jar, she slid the cake across the counter to him—"you want some?"

"No, I'm good. I'm sorry I ruined your birthday, Em."
He took a small step in her direction, then stopped.

She wasn't sure if she wanted him to come closer or
turn in the opposite direction. "It wasn't your fault."

"Wasn't it?"

"Look, Justin, I . . ." Words failed her. She didn't know
what to say to make things better. He was the one with the
power. Either he'd tell her he was retiring, or they'd be over
for good.

"I'm sorry I gave you the wrong impression about retiring. I thought you understood that I was still on the fence.
If I'd have known you didn't want to be with me if I still
planned on competing, I wouldn't have—"

"You wouldn't have what? Kissed me? Wouldn't have
shared my bed?" She'd opened herself up to him in so
many ways.

"Maybe." Justin winced. "I never meant to hurt you.
You've got to know that."

"The only thing I know is that I can't be in love with a
bull rider, and you can't seem to give it up. Where does
that leave us?" It didn't matter who kissed who first or that
if he knew then what he knew now that he might have
made a different choice. What mattered now was where
they went from here. Looking at the pain on his face, Em's
lungs squeezed tight.

She could see the decision in his eyes before he found
the courage to put it into words.

"I've got to go back. That guy who recorded us last
night posted the video online, and Dad's been trying to put
out fires by pissing on them all night long. He set up a
meeting with my agent at noon today, and I have to be
there."

"So, you're going back to competing?" Her voice shook.
She was losing him.

"Not necessarily." He cautiously stepped into the kitchen, like she was a wild animal who might spook at his approach. "I have to figure out how to smooth things over right now, and then I need to decide if I'm going to rejoin the circuit and finish out the rest of the year."

"What about your shoulder?" She waited for the hurt to consume her, for the pain to slice through her. All she felt was numb.

He reached across his chest to cup his right shoulder with his hand. "I don't know yet."

"That's it then?" Cold prickles marched up her cheeks. The numbness spread through her whole body while she waited for him to respond.

"No, that's not it. It's what I have to do today. The media got ahold of that sound bite of you saying I'm retiring. My sponsors are wondering what the hell's going on. I have to go back and buy myself a little more time."

"How do you plan to do that?" Once Justin made it back to Blewit, once his dad got his meaty paws on him again, it would be over. Wouldn't matter what Justin wanted to do, his dad always got his way. She'd been so stupid to think things might have changed. Such an idiot to think that the idea of being with her would be enough to pull Justin away from what he'd been working toward his entire life.

"I don't know yet, Em." He covered the rest of the distance between them and wrapped his fingers around her arms. "But I know I love you. I know that the time we've spent together has been the best in my life. I know the thought of walking out of here right now and not knowing if you'll wait for me is the scariest thing I've ever had to do."

Her heart broke at the combination of fear and love in his eyes. *Then don't. Don't walk away. Choose us.* That's what she wanted to say. That's what she wanted to scream in his face while she grabbed him by the arms and tried to shake some sense into him, this bullheaded, bull-brained man she'd fallen in love with.

But she couldn't do that. If Justin wanted to walk away from competing, he had to make that decision on his own. She didn't want him to leave because she gave him an ultimatum. Sooner or later, it would catch up with her down the line. Maybe in five years, maybe in ten. But at some point, he'd look at her and realize she was the reason he didn't reach for his dreams. That she was the one who'd held him back.

She couldn't do that to him, couldn't do that to them, couldn't do that to herself.

"I can't make promises I don't know I can keep any more than you can." She and Justin had been best friends long before she'd ever considered being lovers. As the woman who loved him, who wanted to keep him safe and do everything she could to secure a future for the two of them, she couldn't let him go.

But as his friend . . . the best friend who'd cheered him on for decades, who'd always had his back, she had to be there for him. As his friend, she might not always agree with his decisions, but she owed him her unwavering support. That's what he'd always given to her and what he deserved in return.

"Go. Your family needs you and you have to do what's best for your career."

"Em." His forehead crinkled. "I don't understand. Does that mean you'll be there for me?"

She wrapped her arms around him, already missing his touch. "I'll always be here for you, you know that. Just maybe not in the way we both hoped."

"But, I can't—"

"Shh." She silenced his protests with a gentle kiss, the barest brush of her lips against his. "I might not always agree with your dad, but he's right about one thing. Forzas aren't quitters. You've got to see this through, one way or another. Go. Do what you need to do."

"I love you, Em." He smoothed a palm over her hair and pressed a kiss against her forehead.

"I love you, too." She held back her tears for the short amount of time it took him to pack up his things. Waited until the door clicked shut before she collapsed onto the tile floor and wrapped her arms around her knees, trying to keep herself from shattering into a million pieces.

She'd finally found love.

Too bad love wasn't enough.

33

❧

Justin

Justin stepped into his dad's office at five past twelve, his hair still damp from a quick shower. He'd busted his ass to catch the first flight out of Brownsville that morning, then rushed back to his place to get cleaned up for his meeting.

"Hey, son. Thanks for cutting your getaway short." The relief in his dad's eyes surprised him. "Frank and I have been fielding calls all morning. It'll be good to clear things up and get an official statement out to the press."

Frank stood and shook Justin's hand. "It's been a rough couple of months, hasn't it?"

"Yes, sir." Justin took a seat at the small conference table that filled one side of his dad's office.

Jake had picked him up at the airport and had run out to grab lunch while Justin got cleaned up. He carted in a couple of bags of takeout from the barbecue place up the street and closed the office door behind him.

"I hope everyone's in the mood for brisket," his dad said.

Frank set the container Jake handed him to the side and focused his attention on Justin. "I'm going to cut right to the chase and ask the question that needs to be answered before we figure out where to go from here."

Justin nodded. He hadn't eaten anything since dinner last night, but food was the last thing on his mind.

"Are you retiring from the pro bull-riding circuit?" Frank clasped his hands together in front of him.

His father and Jake had been sorting through the plastic bags holding their lunch, but paused. The weight of three pairs of eyes made it hard to take in a breath, but Justin faced them all, his eyes clear, his chin up, his decision made.

"I am."

No one said a word. The only sound came from the bull-shaped clock that had hung in his dad's office for years. *Ticktock. Ticktock.*

His dad sank into his chair and pressed his fingertips to his forehead. "I thought it might come to this."

"I'm sorry, Dad. I know you want me to keep going, but I can't. You remember Chick Darville?"

"The only man in the history of the sport to post two perfect scores?" he snorted. "What's your point?"

"He owns a country-western bar down on Paradise Island. I asked him when he knew it was time to quit. He stepped away at the top of his game."

"Everyone thought he'd lost his fucking mind." Jake took a seat, obviously not sure what Chick had to do with Justin's announcement.

"He told me he knew it was time to quit when other things became more important. I'm at that point now. I know you don't understand, and I don't expect you to, but I've got to do what I feel is right. I hope that even if you can't understand my decision, you'll still respect it." Justin risked a glance at his dad.

"I get it, and I wish it was that easy." His dad looked up,

regret in his eyes. "You don't know the whole situation, though. I'm up to my eyeballs in debt."

"The Brazil thing?" Jake asked.

He nodded. "I should have looked into it more. The guy we hired to go down and set things up took off with the seed money. I took money out of the house and opened up a line of credit for the business. If I don't start repaying the loans, we're going to lose it all."

Justin tilted his head back and stared at the ceiling. "How much?"

"Seven fifty." His dad's voice came out softer than Justin had ever heard it before.

"Seven fifty?" Jake exploded out of his seat. "Are you kidding me? I knew you put some money into it, but I didn't know you pulled it out of the business. You're not just messing with your future, you're jacking around with mine, too. I've got a baby on the way. How could you do that without talking to me first? Jesus, I thought we were partners."

A strange sense of calm wrapped around Justin. He glanced from his brother, who paced the office, his hands gesturing wildly around his head, to his dad, who sat at the head of the table, silent, his cheeks drawn, his shoulders slumped. He had to fix this. It wasn't his fault his dad had made a bad investment, but he couldn't stand by and do nothing. Maybe this was his way out.

"Dad, you mentioned something about an event that new sponsor was putting together in Oklahoma City. What's the purse on that?"

His dad looked over, shell-shocked. "They're giving out a total of a million that night. I don't know how it will go. Nobody's ever tried a one-night event like that outside of the regular circuit."

"Can you get me in?" Justin asked.

"A few days ago I had them holding a spot for you, but now I don't know. It's next weekend. You haven't been training like you'd need to if you wanted to take a serious crack at winning."

Justin gritted his teeth. "I didn't ask if you thought I was ready. Can you get me in?"

Frank nodded, his fingers steepled in front of him, already spinning the possibilities in his head. "One last ride."

"That's what I was thinking." Justin grabbed the legal pad from in front of his dad and began to scrawl some notes. "We tell all my sponsors I'm retiring. Next Saturday night in Oklahoma City will be my last event. I'll sip their bottled water on camera. I'll wear their hats, their shirts, and their boots in the days ahead. I'll tattoo their logos on my ass for all I care, but if they want a piece of me before I retire for good, next weekend is their last chance."

"We can do a press conference ahead of time and charge big bucks if they want their logo on the background when you go on camera." Frank slid his glasses on and pulled out his phone. "How about a private event for your fans? We can sell tickets for a meet and greet Friday night. Maybe even a few of them if your sponsors want to get in on it."

"Whatever you need to do. Just tell me where to go and I'll be there." The energy in the room shifted.

Jake sat down and scooted back to the table. "You need me to do anything, I'm in."

Justin reached out to clap his older brother on the back. "Thanks, man."

His father rested his head in his hands. His shoulders shook.

Not sure whether his dad was laughing, crying, or

about to puke on the middle of the conference table, Justin leaned closer. "Dad? You okay?"

"I'm sorry." His dad lifted his head. Tears streaked his cheeks. "I've always tried to do right by you boys and your sister. After your mother left, I think I lost my way. I didn't mean for any of this to happen."

Justin shared a worried look with his brother. "It's going to be okay, Dad. We're going to find a way out of this."

"Together," Jake added.

"We'll get the money paid back to the bank and then we'll figure out how to move forward. If you want to make this a family business, I'm in, but we have to have an equal say in things. You can't bulldoze ahead and expect us to follow." Justin had never considered a future working with his dad and brother without a world title. He'd always felt like an outsider, the failure, the one who hadn't been able to hold up his part of the family legacy. Now he had a chance to save everything his dad had been working for over the years. He couldn't wait to tell Em about the change of events.

A tight hand wrapped around his heart and squeezed.

Em.

He'd come in here today prepared to walk away, ready to give up everything for her. She'd understand his need to save his family, but she'd made it perfectly clear that what they had on Paradise Island couldn't continue if he went back to competing.

He might have a chance to save his family, but now his chance at a future with Em was gone for good.

34

Emmeline

Em heaved the giant turtle through the doorway of her apartment. She should have left it in Decker's dad's place. Should have dropped it off the ferry instead of lugging it all the way back to Blewit with her. After Justin left yesterday, she spent most of the day wallowing in the other half of her birthday cake. Then she cleaned herself up, canceled her flight, and rented a car so she could drag the giant stuffed animal home with her.

If nothing else, her kids would love adding another friend to the reading nook in her classroom. Though they were going to be heartbroken when they found out Rocky hadn't made the trip home. She'd turned the beach house upside down and hadn't been able to find him.

Losing Rocky had been like the universe rubbing salt in her wound after Justin left. She thought that by stepping back and taking her heart out of the equation, she'd be able to encourage him to do what he needed to do. What was that saying . . . something about if you love someone, set them free. If they come back to you, then you'll know it's meant to be? It seemed like a good thing to put on a greeting card, but when it came to real life, whoever came up with that line could go to hell.

She trekked back down the stairs to retrieve her suitcase from the rental car, then slammed the door behind her and tossed the keys on the kitchen table. It felt strange to be home. Everything was exactly how she'd left it a week ago, but yet everything had changed.

There would be plenty of time tomorrow to drop off the rental car, pick up her mail, and try to figure out what the new normal would be. Tonight, all she wanted was to take a relaxing shower and try to get some sleep. She hadn't been able to sleep at all after Justin left. Seemed so odd that she would have gotten so used to sharing a bed with him in such a short amount of time.

She shed her clothes in the bedroom, picked up a fresh towel from the linen closet, and had just turned on the water in the shower when her phone rang. Tempted to let it go to voice mail, she checked the screen. Her mom never called past nine unless there was an emergency.

Em answered, her heart already pounding. "Mom? What's wrong?"

"It's your dad. He tried fixing that leak under the sink after dinner tonight and bumped his head. I told him not to worry about it, but now he's spouting off about riding in Cheyenne this weekend and trying to pack up his things. I wasn't sure who to call, and you said you'd be back tonight. Is there any chance you can come over?"

"Of course." A shower would have to wait. "I'll be there as soon as I can."

"Thanks, honey."

Em pulled on the same clothes she'd been wearing before and grabbed her keys and purse. Dad just needed to be reoriented. It had happened quite a bit right after his injury. He'd be fine one day, then wake up the next and think he was late for a job he hadn't worked at in years.

Bumping his head must have triggered him.

When she pulled into the driveway, her mom met her on the stoop. "How is he?"

"Stirred up worse than a hive of angry bees." Mom gripped her arm. "He's been doing so well for so long. I don't want it to be too hard on you."

"I'll be fine, Mom." Em brushed past her mom and entered the house. The floor lamp in the living room leaned on the back of the couch. Her daddy's recliner sat on its side, another victim of the inexplicable rages that used to plague him.

"Where are my chaps, Marguerite? You know I can't ride without them." A loud crash came from the bedroom.

Em moved down the hall, her heart in her throat. "Daddy? It's Em. You okay?"

"I'll be right as rain when your mama tells me where she hid my chaps. You know she doesn't want me riding anymore, but how else am I supposed to keep food on the table?" He'd dumped everything out of the drawers from the dresser. Shirts and socks sprawled across the bed.

"Dad, come here. Look at me." Em took a step closer.

"Em? Is that you? What happened, sugar? You're all grown up." He squinted at her like he was looking at her for the very first time.

"I am all grown up. Turned twenty-nine yesterday. You bumped your head, Daddy. When that happens, sometimes you get confused." She sat on the edge of the bed and patted the space next to her. "You want to come sit down and I can tell you what happened?"

He put his fingers to his temples. "I bumped my head?"

"That's right. It's going to be okay, though." Em patted the spot next to her again.

He sat down, his face masked by a cloud of confusion. "I have to ride in Cheyenne tomorrow night."

Em put an arm around his shoulder. She hated when the confusion caught him in its tangled web. "There's no event in Cheyenne tomorrow." She reached for the remote to the small flat screen TV she'd given her parents for Christmas last year. "Let me see if I can find something for you on one of the sports channels."

Usually, if she turned on a bull-riding event, it would snap her dad out of his confused state. Seeing the younger riders competing and not recognizing the names of the competitors or the bulls typically did it. She flipped through the channels, hoping there would be something to clear up his brain fog.

She stopped when an image of Justin appeared on the screen. He was talking to one of the regular announcers, a man Em had been watching since she was a kid.

The announcer held an oversized mic and turned to Justin. "I'm here with Justin Forza, one of the riders we've been keeping a close eye on this season. Justin, you injured your shoulder on a ride back in February. Everyone's been waiting for you to come back to the tour. This was supposed to be your year, but now you've got a big announcement to make, is that right?"

"Yes, sir."

Em's heart clenched at the sight of him. He'd shaved off the scruff he'd grown on vacation, and she wanted to reach through the screen to run her palm over his smooth cheek.

"Is it true you're retiring?" The announcer shoved the mic in front of Justin's face.

He took in a deep breath and looked straight into the camera. "Yes, sir."

The remote fell out of Em's hand and clattered to the floor.

"I know him." Her dad pointed a shaky finger at the screen. "That's Monty's son."

"That's right, Daddy." Tears welled in the corners of her eyes. Justin was choosing her. She'd walked away, given him the freedom to do what he needed to do, and he was choosing her.

"I know your fans are going to be disappointed. I hear they've got one more chance to see you ride, is that right?"

Wait. One more ride? No, that's not how this was supposed to go. She leaned forward, his image on the TV screen blurred through the tears that had started out as tears of happiness.

"I'll be riding in the Blaster Bull Master event in Oklahoma City next weekend. If fans want to see my final ride, tickets are on sale now and there are even a couple of special events they can attend."

"The sport sure is going to miss you."

"Thanks." Justin tipped his hat at the camera. "It's been a wild ride, but it's time for me to focus on other things now."

The announcer turned back to face the camera, and it zoomed in on him, cutting Justin out of the picture. "You heard it here first, folks. Pro bull rider Justin Forza will be taking his final ride next weekend at the Blaster Bull Master event . . ."

Em tuned him out. Justin was retiring, but he thought he had one more ride in him. Despite his injured shoulder, despite the fact that he hadn't been training as much as he should, despite his knowing that she couldn't stand by and watch. Not with her heart on the line.

Her dad put his arm around her and pulled her into him. "It'll be okay, Em. That boy knows what he's doing. He learned from one of the best."

"Daddy? Are you feeling better?"

"Yeah, but I've got a hell of a headache. I think I'm going to lie down. What happened in here? Did your mama lose her wedding ring again?" Dad rolled onto his back and pushed the clothes into a pile on her mom's side of the bed.

"Something like that. I'll clean this up in just a few minutes." She leaned down to press a kiss to her dad's forehead while she made eye contact with her mom.

He closed his eyes.

Mom wrung her hands together while she waited for Em in the doorway. "Let me fix you a cup of tea before you go."

Em nodded and followed her mom to the kitchen. She didn't want to be alone right now. A cup of tea with her mom would delay having to return to her apartment with the knowledge that she and Justin were over for good.

"Has he been having many episodes like that recently?" Em sat at the kitchen table while her mom filled the kettle with water from the sink.

"Not often. I think when he bumped his head, it might have triggered it. Oh, and the neighbor boys were playing in the backyard. Your dad gave them one of his old practice barrels and a buzzer so they could pretend to be bull riders. Do you think the buzzer set him off?" Mom turned the knob to light the gas burner, then set the kettle on the stove.

"It's so hard to see him like this. I can't imagine what it feels like for you." Em got up from the table and offered her mom a hug.

Her mother wrapped her arms around her and squeezed. "All marriages have their ups and downs. It all evens out in the end."

"Does it?" Em pulled back, leaving a hand on her

mom's slim shoulder. "If you knew what you were getting in for, what the future would hold, would you still have done everything the same?"

"Done what the same?" A deep crease formed between her eyebrows.

"You know"—Em broke eye contact, glancing at the flames licking at the bottom of the kettle—"marrying dad."

"Of course, I would." Her conviction drew Em's attention. "Why would you ask such a thing?"

Em bit down on her lip. She didn't want to cause her mom any pain, but it seemed important to know. "What about Dad's injury? He's not the same person you married."

A low whistle came from the teakettle. Mom let her hands fall from Em's shoulders to turn off the burner. "I'm not the same person he married, either."

A hollowness grew in the pit of her stomach. "What do you mean by that?"

Mom slid her hand into an oven mitt and reached for the handle of the kettle. "We've been married for thirty-two years. Both of us have changed, and thank goodness for that."

"But—"

"You think our lives were ruined because of what happened to your dad." She poured the steaming water into the ceramic mugs she'd set on the counter.

"Weren't they? We had to move. You had to give up our house in the country with that big garden you loved. I was just a kid, but I can remember riding the mare your dad gave you when you got married. All of it went away."

Mom passed her a mug with a bag of chamomile tea steeping inside. "I loved that house, especially the garden. And I still miss my horse, though he passed away quite a few years ago. We never could have anticipated your dad's injuries, but those things were just that, Emmeline . . .

things. My love for your dad, for you and Georgie and the life we were building together, was so much bigger than my need for any of that."

Em followed her mom to the table and slipped into her spot, the one she used to sit at for family meals over the years. The tabletop had seen better days, but the scratches and grooves on the surface were reminders of the experiences they'd shared. She supposed that was true of people, too. The scars, both physical and emotional, marked the passage of the years, the passage of experiences.

"What's bothering you, sweetheart?" Mom took her spot at the table and set down her tea. "Is it Justin? Did something happen while you were away?"

Em hadn't planned on sharing her heartache. Her mother had enough to worry about. But her mom might be the only one who could empathize with what she was going through . . . the conflicting feelings waging war within her heart.

She took in a deep, steady breath and fiddled with the tab of the tea bag hanging over the edge of her mug. "I love him."

Mom nodded. "I know."

"You do?" Em turned her head, catching the hint of a smile that played across her mother's lips. "How could you know when I just figured it out myself a few days ago?"

"Because I know you." Mom reached across the table and rested her hand on top of Em's. "He's going back to competing, isn't he? I saw him say it on TV while you and your dad were in the bedroom."

Em was done putting on a brave face. She'd tried to convince herself that nothing bad would happen, that Justin knew what he was doing, that one more ride would truly be the end. The tears welled in the corners of her eyes, then spilled down her cheeks. She was tired of crying, tired of feeling helpless against the magnetic pull the tour had over him.

"He thinks he's invincible. I'm worried he's going to get hurt again." She wiped the heel of her hand across her cheeks. "What can I do? How can I stop him?"

Mom shook her head and squeezed Em's hand. "You can't stop him, honey. All you can do is to be there to pick him up if he falls. I tried to get your dad to stop riding. I reasoned with him, threatened him, issued ultimatums. All that did was make things harder. Especially for your dad, who was only doing what he felt he needed to do. I finally gave in and realized that when I said I loved him, I had to love all of him."

"But he got hurt."

"Yes, he did. But every time he went into that arena, every time he climbed onto a bull, he knew I'd be there for him. It made him a better man, made him a better rider. If you love Justin like I think you do and want to try to build a future together, he needs to know he can count on you." Mom moved her hand to cradle her mug and take a sip of tea.

Em stared into her mug. Her mom was right. Justin deserved to have her support. She'd always had his back as a friend. But was she willing to go all in? Was she willing to be there for him in the way he wanted—in the way he needed—no matter what?

The tea didn't spill any secrets or give her the answers she craved.

Justin had made his choice. Now it was her turn to make hers.

35

⟡

Justin

Justin liked to get to an event a couple of hours early. It gave him time to go behind the chutes and check out the bull he'd drawn for that night's ride. Since he hadn't been training as hard as he would have liked, he also wanted the chance to check in with medical and get stretched out.

After spending plenty of time under the strong and capable hands of one of the attending physical therapists, Justin wandered down to peek at Twinkle Toes, the bull he'd drawn for his last event. He and Twinkle Toes had a past and had taken turns besting each other over the years. Twinkle Toes was a ranker bull and had a tendency to head straight out of the chute and take a sharp turn to the left. After that, anything could happen, especially on a bull who liked the limelight even more than the cowboys he tried to buck off his back.

Justin chatted with a couple of the stock contractors and other folks who made things happen behind the scenes. He'd missed the camaraderie of being part of the tour since he'd been away. He'd probably miss it even more once he was done for good, but it was time.

His dad and Jake had offered to keep him company before everything started, but Justin had a pre-ride routine he'd practiced over the years and preferred to stick to it. He nodded a greeting to the other riders as he headed into the locker room and unpacked the bag he always carried with him. With a few minutes to spare before he needed to put in an appearance at the meet and greet Blaster Energy Drinks scheduled, he pulled out his bull rope and tied it on the gate next to all the others.

He'd wait until after the photo ops with fans to prep his rope and change into his boots and riding jeans. Caked with dirt from his ass hitting the ground too many times to count, his jeans were headed to the trash bin at the end of the night. At least he wouldn't be sorry to see those go.

"Last ride tonight, huh?" One of the rookies his dad had been training stopped in front of Justin.

Justin looked up, his glove in his hand. "Yeah."

The rookie had that look in his eyes—the same one Justin used to see when he glanced in the mirror—the one that told the world he was there to win.

"How can you walk away? I mean, I can't think of anything I'd rather do. They'll have to carry me out of the arena kicking and screaming someday."

Justin didn't want to burst the kid's bubble. He'd felt that way, too, way back then. Rather than dump an ice-cold dose of reality over him, Justin just nodded. "I hope that happens for you, I really do."

He jerked his T-shirt over his head and traded it for the starched white shirt with his sponsors' logos. He'd been through this routine so many times it was almost second nature. As he worked his way down his shirt, sliding the buttons through the tabs, his mind drifted toward Em.

He wondered what she was doing tonight. He'd tried to reach out after the meeting at his dad's office but ended up leaving her a voice mail to let her know what he'd decided.

One more ride.

He'd hoped she'd get in touch, but he understood why she couldn't. He had to do what he needed to do, and she had to do the same. They'd always be there for each other as friends, but that's as far as it would ever go. He'd let her down.

It didn't matter that everything he'd done—every ride he'd taken, every bull he'd bested up to this point—he'd done for her, for them. She said she didn't care that he didn't have much to offer beyond the trivial amount he'd stashed away in his savings. He was ready to call her on it and see if she meant it . . . walk away from the only thing he'd ever known to give her the peace of mind she needed.

He would have done it, too, if it hadn't been for his family. How could she fault him for wanting to come through for them?

It didn't matter now. The only thing that mattered—the only thing that he ought to be worried about now—was the eight-second date he had coming up with Twinkle Toes. The appearance fees and event sponsorships his agent had pulled together would help, but the only way to save the ranch that had been in his family for generations and the business his dad and brother had built was to win the event.

Justin slid on the boots he'd buffed earlier that day and shrugged on the bright orange vest Blaster Energy Drinks had supplied. Then he left the other guys in the locker room and headed to the concourse level where Blaster was holding its big event. No matter what went down between him and Em, he'd have to get himself in the right head-space to give the fans and his sponsors what they needed tonight.

Even if he was having a hard time getting his heart into it.

"There he is, the man of the hour." His dad motioned Justin over to where a professional photographer had set up his equipment.

"Hey, Dad." They did the half-handshake, half-hug thing while fans snapped photos.

Turner from Blaster Energy Drinks stepped up to the mic and said a few words about how thrilled they were to be involved in the event. Then he turned things over to Justin.

Justin took in a breath and eyed the long line of fans that stretched around the perimeter of the room as he stepped in front of the camera. A glimpse of caramel-colored hair at the side of the room caught his attention. His pulse quickened and his throat went bone-dry. It had to be Em.

"Hold up a sec?" he asked the photographer.

He didn't wait for a reply, just took off toward the spot where Em had disappeared. She'd changed her mind. That had to be it. He found her at a high-top table. She had her back to him, and he didn't recognize the two men and woman sharing her space. As he moved closer, disappointment squeezed his chest. The hair was right, but the rest of her was wrong, all wrong.

She turned around, confirming what he already knew. Not Em. "Oh, hey. Can I grab a photo real quick?"

"Sure." Justin forced a smile and posed next to the woman and her friends while someone from the table next to them snapped a few photos. "I hope y'all have a good time tonight."

"Good luck. We'll be rooting for you." She turned to her friends to check over the pictures.

"Thanks." Justin walked back toward the front of the room, shaking his head. He needed to get through the next hour, then head back to the locker room if he wanted to pull himself together before his ride. It wouldn't do any good to wish for something he couldn't have. That would just fuck with his head. The last thing he needed tonight was to sabotage himself with mind games.

The photographer snapped photos of him posing with fans. Then Justin signed programs, pictures, and even a body part or two. He squatted down to high-five the kids and stood tall for pictures with some of the folks who'd been following his career for years.

It was bittersweet, really. He'd finally decided to give up his drive for the world champion title so he could have the one thing he'd always wanted . . . a relationship with Em. Tonight he'd have his last ride and leave the arena without either.

Damn, thinking like that would end up getting him hurt. He needed to focus, to get his head back into the zone.

The line died down, and Justin found Turner in the crowd. "Y'all get what you need?"

"Sure did." Turner held out his hand. "Even though it's been way too short, it's been a pleasure working with you. Good luck tonight."

"Thanks." Justin shook the man's hand, grateful for the opportunity he'd been given. He turned to head back to the locker room, not sure how he was going to pull this off. It wasn't the pressure. He could handle that. It was the focus. He'd always been crystal clear on the reason behind his ride. His priorities had shifted, and he hadn't been able to reengage that fire that burned deep in his belly. Knowing his shot with Em was gone had extinguished the flame.

"Hey, Mr. Forza." The photographer jogged over, his camera in hand. "Can I get one more photo?"

"Yeah, sure." Justin dragged his gaze up from the floor.

Emmeline

Em stood in front of the photo backdrop, her teeth worrying her lower lip. She was wrong to come, wrong to surprise him at the last minute before the most important ride of his life.

Then his eyes met hers. He stood fifteen feet away, but the force of his gaze swept over her like a tidal wave. Her heart stopped beating; her lungs stopped taking in air while she waited for some sign from him. Was he happy to see her? Pissed at her for jacking with him at the eleventh hour?

He squinted. "Em?"

"Did you leave your glasses at home again, cowboy?" It wasn't the right time for a joke, but it wasn't the right time for anything, really.

Justin covered the distance between them in a few long strides, stopping short when he reached her. "What are you doing here?"

"Can we go somewhere to talk?" She glanced around the room. Most of the people were chatting and drinking and not paying them much attention, but a few stood close enough to hear what she needed to tell him.

"Sure, um, let's step into the hall." Justin threaded his fingers with hers and tugged her toward the door.

His hand felt so right in hers. How could she have been so stupid to think she'd be able to live without him? It hadn't even been a week since she'd seen him, and she'd barely been able to get by.

Justin pushed through the door to the hall and led her to a secluded spot between two pillars. The thunder of hundreds of footsteps above them echoed on the concrete. Why hadn't she come to her senses back at home where they could have had a conversation in the privacy of her apartment or on the patio of his dad's place?

"Are you okay?" Justin stopped and turned around to face her. His gaze ran over her and he held both of her hands in his. "Is something wrong?"

"No, I'm fine."

"Your dad? Did something happen? What is it, Em?" His eyes softened at the edges.

She wanted to reach up and run her palm over his cheek, wrap her hand around the back of his neck, and pull his mouth down to hers.

"Justin?" His dad's voice bounced off the cement walls. "You've got fifteen minutes before showtime."

Em's heart spun in circles, just like the bulls she was about to see perform.

"Got it," Justin called out. Then he tilted his head toward her. "I've gotta get ready. Are you sure you're okay?"

Now or never. They didn't have much time, and he needed to hear what she had to say just as much as she needed to say it.

"No. I'm not okay." The admission threatened to open the floodgates. She swallowed the raw emotion surging in her chest and forced it back down.

"What is it?" Justin let go of her hand to cup her cheek.

"I haven't been okay since you walked out the door on Paradise Island. What we had, I'm not ready to—"

"Hey, Justin." His agent stepped around the corner. "You really need to head back to the locker room to finish getting ready."

"Got it." Justin didn't look over, didn't break eye contact. He stared deep into her eyes, like he already knew what she was going to say. Like he could read her mind. Maybe even read her soul. "I've got to go. Can this wait?"

She shook her head. "No."

"I don't want to be an ass, but can you speed it up then? I'm supposed to be center stage when they play the national anthem." His mouth quirked up into that self-deprecating grin of his.

"I'm sorry." She gripped his hands tight. "I miss you. I know I said you had to choose, had to pick between me and bull riding, and I wanted to let you know I was wrong."

His forehead creased, and he squinted at her from under the brim of his straw Stetson. "I don't understand."

She took a deep breath. There wasn't enough time to tell him everything. "I love you. All of you. That means I can't pick and choose. I can't only love the parts of you I want to. Loving all of you means I have to love the things about you that scare me, too."

He put a finger under her chin, nudging her face up until she had to meet his gaze. "What are you saying, Em?"

"I'm saying I'm here for you. All of you. I want to be with you, even though you scare the crap out of me every time you get on the back of a bull. No matter what happens tonight, I'll be waiting for you after."

He stared at her, his gaze bouncing back and forth from her eyes to her mouth. "Are you sure?"

She nodded, not trusting herself to speak. Tears stung the back of her throat, threatening to spill from her lashes.

His hands moved to her cheeks, and he pulled her mouth to his. Her world tipped upside down as he captured her lips. How did she think she'd ever be able to live without him?

Too soon, he pulled away. "I've got to go, Em. I'm

sorry. Can we continue this"—he shook his finger between them—"whatever this is, after I ride?"

"Of course." She straightened his hat, which had been knocked crooked during their kiss. "Come back to me, Justin."

He grabbed her hands in his and held them to his lips. "I love you, Em."

"I love you, too."

His smile was so bright it could have lit up the whole state of Oklahoma. "I'll see you in a few."

Nodding through her tears, Em blew him kisses as he jogged backward down the hall and disappeared through a doorway. She'd made it this far. Now she just needed to see the rest of the evening through.

"You okay there, sweetie?" Her mom pushed off from the wall where Em had left her standing while she went after Justin.

"Yeah." She wiped a tissue across her cheeks.

"We don't have to go in there if you don't want to. They've got TVs set up in the lounge. We can even find a spot under the stands and wait until it's all over." Her mom took her hand. Strength flowed through her, infusing Em with a kind of courage she'd never known before.

"I want to be there for him. If he looks for me in the crowd, I want him to see me smiling and cheering him on."

"You got it, sweetheart." Mom pulled a pair of tickets out of her pocket. "He'll see you all right. We're right next to the chutes. You ready for this?"

"Thanks so much for coming with me tonight." Her mom had called in several favors to be able to leave her dad with someone they trusted overnight. For that, Em would always be grateful.

"You're welcome. Should we go find our seats?"

Em nodded. Her mom might be the only one in the

world who had any idea of the darkness that threatened to suck her under tonight. And when the man who held her heart climbed onto the back of a beast whose sole purpose in life was to destroy him, there was no one she'd rather have sitting next to her.

36

⌒～♡～⌒

Justin

Justin made it through the opening, his feet barely touching the ground. Em had come around. He didn't know what had changed her mind . . . hell, he didn't care . . . all that mattered was that she still wanted to be together. He'd gone from not being able to get his head on straight to having it floating in the clouds. If he wanted to stay on the back of his bull for the full eight seconds, he needed to focus.

Now.

He changed into his riding jeans and tied his boots tight around his ankles. Since Blaster Energy Drinks was playing up the fact tonight would be his final ride, he was the last rider on the schedule. With nothing to do but wait, he went to work on his bull rope. A lot of the other riders were superstitious about the way they prepped their ropes. Justin was the same.

He pulled out his special rosin and started the same routine he'd gone through hundreds of times before. As he prepped the rope, he slowed down his breathing and connected with that place deep down inside that he called "the zone."

He'd arrived in Oklahoma City hoping for a miracle. Em had delivered it.

Knowing she'd be waiting for him after his ride grounded him, centered him. His focus zeroed in on the task at hand. He visualized the ride, letting it play through his head half a dozen times . . . anticipating which direction Twinkle Toes would take out of the gate, imagining how the rope would feel in his hand.

He was ready.

"You're up, Forza."

Justin grabbed his rope and headed toward the chutes. It was time to dance.

The crowd went wild as they caught sight of him, but all he cared about was doing the job he came to do. Totally focused, he got up on the chute and dropped his rope over the side. It didn't take long to get settled on Twinkle Toes's back. Justin pulled his helmet on and glanced out at the crowd.

Em's smile caught him by surprise. She sat with her mom only a few yards away. He lifted his hand to wave. Em had never watched him ride in person before. Knowing she was there gave him the extra boost of confidence he needed. It was time to do this.

The announcer ran through the standings. Unlike a lot of the other events he participated in, this was a one-night deal. Usually he had three or four nights to work on his score, but tonight the winner would take all. The rookie his dad trained held the lead. Justin needed at least a ninety-one to top him. He shifted his shoulder back, ignoring the twinge. In less than a minute, it would all be over.

He nodded at the cowboy manning the gate.

The gate swung open and Twinkle Toes lurched to the left. Justin held on, one hand in the air, the other gripping the bull rope like his life depended on it. In many ways, it did.

Twinkle Toes landed on his front legs and kicked his back legs out behind him. Justin adjusted, anticipating the moves before the bull had a chance to make them. Time slowed. Justin felt every jarring movement. His jaw clenched on his mouth guard and he squeezed his thighs around the bull's broad back.

The buzzer sounded.

He'd done it. Joy bubbled up through his chest. Now all he needed to do was get off the bull and find Em. He waited until the bull turned, and then hopped off, his boots hitting the dirt with a thud.

The bullfighter stepped in front of Twinkle Toes, diverting his attention. Justin made a beeline for the railing, but he wasn't fast enough. Twinkle Toes caught him with a horn and tossed him up into the air like a rag doll.

Justin shot a glance toward Em. Her mouth hung open, her eyes wide.

That was the last thing he saw.

Then it all went black.

Emmeline

"Want to take a break?" Mr. Forza put a hand on Em's shoulder.

"No, thanks." She shook her head.

"Can I get you a cup of coffee? Something to eat?" he asked.

Em ripped her gaze away from watching the steady rise and fall of Justin's chest long enough to glance at his dad. "I'm fine, thanks."

Mr. Forza nodded and resumed pacing the perimeter of the hospital room. He was only trying to help. None of them knew what to do. Decker sat in the waiting room with Jake and Jenny. Em's mom and dad kept calling for updates. Even Knox had texted several times and was on the verge of canceling his show in Mobile the next night so he could fly back for a few hours.

Em couldn't unsee the beating Justin had taken. The eight-second reel played through her head on repeat. He'd almost had a perfect ride. She could see the smile on his face when the buzzer sounded. Then he hopped off the back of the bull. The bullfighter waved to get the animal's attention, and the bull seemed to be heading toward the chute.

Then the unthinkable happened. The bull turned toward Justin and charged. His horns connected with Justin's backside and sent him flying through the air.

The arena that had been buzzing with excitement a few seconds earlier went silent. Justin hung there, halfway over the railing, not moving.

She shuddered and pulled herself out of the memory.

The door to Justin's room opened, and the doctor came in. She'd been providing updates as often as possible, though there wasn't really anything anyone could do until Justin opened his eyes.

"How's he doing? Any change?" She glanced at Em, who'd been by his side since they admitted him two days ago.

Em couldn't bear to meet her gaze. Nothing had changed. He hadn't done so much as wiggle his pinkie toe and she'd been there the whole time. His dad had offered to take over sitting by Justin's side so she could go back to the trailer to get some sleep, but she didn't dare leave.

What if he woke up while she was gone? What if he needed her?

"No change." She forced the words out, wishing she could report something different.

"Don't worry." The doctor grabbed his chart and scanned his vitals. "It's still early. He's been through a lot, but he's young and strong."

Mr. Forza funneled a hand through his thinning hair. "Is he going to be okay? He's got to be."

The doctor set the chart down and gave a comforting smile. "His body needs to heal. We should know more in another day or two."

"Thank you." Em tried to offer a smile but couldn't quite bring herself to tilt her lips up. Her mom always said it took more muscles to frown than smile, but she didn't care. All she wanted was Justin. Justin teasing her about Rocky. Justin cradling her against his chest. Justin touching his lips to hers.

They hadn't had enough time together. It wasn't fair.

"He's got to be all right." Mr. Forza shook his head. "He's just got to be."

"I'll check back in a bit." The doctor gave them both a reassuring nod, then headed back out to the hall.

Em couldn't imagine what Justin's dad was going through. No doubt, he probably blamed himself for his son's current condition. If it weren't for him pushing so hard for all those years, for making a bad gamble on that business venture, maybe Justin wouldn't be here. Maybe he would have walked away when he had the chance.

It didn't matter now. Justin wouldn't want anyone else to take the blame.

"What am I going to do with him if he doesn't make it? If he needs around-the-clock care?" Mr. Forza mumbled more to himself than to her, but she wanted to answer him, anyway.

"He's got me." She turned to face him. "No matter what he needs, I'll be there for him. That's what it means to love someone. You've got to love all of them."

It had taken her a long time to learn that valuable lesson, but now that she had, she planned on living by it.

"He's lucky to have you in his life." Mr. Forza nodded, a combination of heartbreak and awe mingling together in his expression.

Em focused her attention back on Justin and tried to will him to open his eyes.

Justin's hand moved. His fingers tightened around hers.

"He's waking up. We should get the doctor back in here." Em made a move to get up, but Mr. Forza was already at the door.

"I'll go." He yanked the door open and pulled it almost closed behind him.

"Hey." Justin cracked his eyes open.

She'd never been so happy to see his baby blues. They looked even brighter against the bleached background of the hospital sheets.

"Hey, beautiful"—his hand tightened on hers—"did I win?"

Leave it to Justin to defy death, come out of a coma, and then ask whether he won before he even saw the doctor. "Yes. You got a ninety-two. You did it."

His smile widened. "How long have I been out?"

"Two days. We've been so worried." She lifted a hand to slide it next to his cheek. "How do you feel?"

"Like I got run over by a bull." He shifted his legs and winced. "I did, didn't I?"

Em nodded, her eyes brimming with tears. She hadn't

cried as much in the last five years as she had in the past five days. "Yeah, you did."

Mr. Forza entered the room, the doctor right behind him. "He's awake. Son, I was going out of my mind."

The doctor checked his vitals, peered into his eyes, and listened to his heart. "You gave us a bit of a scare, Mr. Forza."

Justin sighed. "That seems to be my style."

"We'll have to keep an eye on you for the next twenty-four hours, but things look good." She nodded toward Justin's dad. "If he's up for it, he can have visitors come back, but only family."

"I'll go get Jenny and Jake. They both want to come back and make sure you're all right."

"Okay." Justin nodded.

The doctor left, followed by his dad.

Justin motioned for her to move closer. "If only family's allowed in here, how did you sneak in?"

"Oh"—heat danced across her cheeks—"your dad told them I'm your fiancée. I didn't want to leave you. It would have killed me to sit out in the waiting room all this time."

"You surprise me, Em." He struggled to sit up. "I never figured you for much of a liar."

Her jaw dropped. Did he seriously just wake up from a coma and accuse her of not telling the truth?

"Can I make an honest woman out of you? Will you marry me?" His eyes sparkled, and he gave her the smile he saved for special occasions. The one he'd given her the day they met.

"Is that the only reason you're asking? To keep me from being a liar?" Her heart did a series of backflips in her chest. He hadn't lost his sense of humor. That was a good sign. A sign he would be okay.

He squeezed her hand. "I'm asking because I love you. Because I can't imagine spending another day on this earth without knowing you belong to me and I belong to you. What do you say?"

"I say yes." She leaned over and kissed him.

His arms went around her back and the change in his position, coupled with the enthusiastic way he kissed her, sent his heart rate monitor out of control.

The nurse burst into the room, his dad, brother, and sister on her heels. "What happened?"

Justin held up their hands. "We just got engaged."

Epilogue

❦

Emmeline

Em checked her watch. Justin was supposed to be bringing dinner home tonight. They had a lot to celebrate. The rookie he'd been working with had just earned enough points to qualify for the world title finals and would be competing next month in Vegas.

She poured herself a glass of wine and sat down in one of the chairs on the front patio to wait. What a difference a few months could make. So much had changed, though she'd never felt more settled and at peace.

"Hey there, watch your step." She leaned over to run her hand over their new addition's back. Ever since she and Justin returned from Paradise Island, she'd been volunteering at a local turtle and tortoise rescue. They'd both fallen in love with Tripod down on Paradise, so they'd decided to set up a habitat for one of the giant tortoises that came through the rescue. They'd named him Chick and he'd been living with them for the past two weeks on the tract of land Justin bought with the funds left over from his big win.

Chick nudged his head into her thigh, and she rubbed the top of his shell. He was almost as old as his namesake.

As she shielded her eyes against the sunset, Justin's truck pulled into the gravel drive. He hopped out and headed her way, a big brown paper bag of takeout and a small box in his hand.

"I was starting to get worried." She reached for him, always eager for his kiss, whether they'd been apart for a whole day or just a couple of hours.

"Sorry. I had to stop in town to pick up a package." He pulled the door of their double-wide trailer open and set the bag inside.

"What kind of package?" Em got up to follow him in but he stopped her.

"Come here. I've got something I want to show you." He led her back to her chair.

She perched on the edge, apprehensive about his big surprise. The last time he'd surprised her like this he'd shown her this tract of land. That ended with her agreeing to live in a trailer while he worked with a builder out of Tyler to make the custom home he had in mind a reality. They'd broken ground on the house a few days ago, but it would be a long time before they could move in.

"Your surprises make me nervous. You know that, don't you?" she asked.

"You're going to like this one, I promise." He pulled his pocketknife out and sliced through the tape sealing the box closed. "Here, open it."

Em set her glass down on the side table next to her chair and reached for the box. It was about the same size as a box of tissues and weighed just as much. If this was another one of his pranks . . .

"Better hurry, dinner's getting cold." Justin stood on the edge of the brick patio he and his brother had built so they'd have somewhere to sit and watch the sunsets.

Em eyed him with skepticism. "What is it?"

"Just open it."

She eased back the flaps and pulled out a bundle of tissue paper. It unrolled in her hands, revealing a familiar black velvet drawstring bag.

"What? Where did you find him?" Her fingers fumbled with the ties, and she finally pulled them free, releasing Rocky Von Poopster. Rocky grinned up at her, his hand-drawn eyes and mouth a welcome sight.

"I had Chick go back and scour the beach house. You'll never guess where he found him."

"On the patio?" Em guessed.

"Nope. Remember that night on the couch? When you freaked out because he was watching?"

Em's cheeks burned as she recalled exactly what they'd been doing at the time. "Um, yeah."

"You pulled him off the coffee table and he must have fallen under the couch. Chick found him right before Decker's dad gutted the place." Justin rocked back on his heels, evidently pretty proud of himself for orchestrating such a coup.

"How did you convince Chick to go on a treasure hunt for a rock?"

"It was an interesting conversation, that's for sure. I just told him that your class mascot somehow got left behind when we visited last summer. He didn't get a load of Rocky's unusual attributes until he found him. You sure you don't want me to chisel a little off the top, so he looks a little less like a dick and a little more like just a smiling rock?"

"The kids are going to be thrilled. We've been looking for weeks for a new mascot, but all they've come up with so far is a weird round rock with a hole in the middle."

Justin's brows shot up. "Maybe it's time for Rocky to have a little fun."

"You think he's that hard up that he needs a fling?"

"Nah. They'd have to become friends first." Justin sat down in the chair next to her and pulled her onto his lap. "Everyone knows that best friends make the best lovers."

"Is that so?" She wrapped her arm around his shoulder and nestled her cheek against his chest.

"Worked for us." He pressed a kiss to the top of her head.

Yeah, it had worked for them. Despite the road they'd traveled to get to this point, it had been worth it. "Hey, guess what."

"What's that?"

"Now that we've found Rocky again, you can make good on that bet you lost. What was it again, dress up like Rocky and come into my classroom to read a Pete the Cat book and play the button song on your guitar, right?"

"After all I went through to bring him back, you're still going to hold me to that silly bet?" Justin brushed her hair away from her cheek, his fingers lingering on her jaw.

She'd never get enough of him.

She'd also never get enough of teasing him. "Maybe I can make a brisket and we can invite everyone over for a trial run. Georgie's in town with the baby next weekend to visit Mom and Dad. And Knox is playing close enough that he could come by, too. What do you think?"

Justin shook his head. "Why not invite everyone? I'll call Decker and see if he and Miranda are free. Jake and Dad are out of town next week to check on that new property we're looking at in Montana, but hell, I'll see if Jenny's available."

"If you're up for it." Em grinned.

Justin tucked his chin against his chest. "I've got a better idea."

"Really?" She didn't doubt he'd find some way to avoid humiliating himself.

"How about we change it up?"

"What exactly do you have in mind?"

"Instead of me coming in to read to the kids, how about I dress up in a tux and we invite them to a wedding instead?"

Her heart stuttered. "A wedding? At school? Are you crazy? Mrs. Richmond would never agree to that."

He didn't say anything, just stared at her, his lips tipped up in a smug smile.

"No. You didn't." Em knew that look. It was the look he gave her when he asked for permission after he'd already done whatever he wanted to ask about. Like the time he took her to look at a new truck to see what she thought about it, then told her he'd already bought it for her.

"Maybe I did."

"When's this maybe wedding supposed to happen?"

"Whenever you want. I figure we'll have a wedding with friends and family, then hold a smaller party at school so the kids can celebrate with us. Give me a date and time and I'll be there. Can I take a pass on dressing up like our favorite rock and slide a ring on your finger instead?"

Em nodded. "I guess you'll go to any lengths necessary to avoid that Rocky suit."

"What do you say?" He leaned forward, his lips mere inches from hers.

"I say yes."

Yes to letting him off the hook. Yes to getting married and having a party at school. Yes to a future with her best friend who also happened to be the man who held her heart.

She'd always say yes to him.

Acknowledgments

Huge thanks to Andrew Giangola of the PBR for taking the time to chat with me about the ins and outs of professional bull riding. Any oversights or errors when it comes to writing about the sport are mine alone. Kristine Swartz, Mary Baker, and the entire team at Berkley deserve my most sincere thanks. Without their efforts, my words would never make it off my hard drive. To my fabulous agent, Jessica Watterson, here's to wrapping up lucky book number seven together! I'll always be grateful for having you in my corner.

Writing is a solitary endeavor but thanks to my author friends, I've never felt alone. Special thanks to the authors in my MM: Aidy Award, Bri Blackwood, Claudia Burgoa, M. L. Guida, and J. L. Madore. To the Romance Chicks, especially Christina Hovland and Renee Ann Miller, who have been there from the start, and the authors of the Must Love Cowboys group for giving me a place to talk about cowboy romance. Hugs to Serena Bell, Brenda St. John Brown, Jody Holford, and Megan Ryder for helping me stay on track. And to Dawn Luedecke, who's been roped into more than one of my big ideas and keeps smiling.

To my family and friends . . . my sister, who reads every word, my mom who won't stop telling all of her friends to buy my books, and my besties, who don't even read romance (believe me, I'm working on changing that one word at a time!) but who pick up my books when they see them in the wild just because they want to support me . . . thank you, thank you, thank you!

I can't let a book go out into the world without acknowledging the people I lockdown with . . . my hubby and our three children, who now tower over me and are old enough to fix their own chicken nuggets when mom needs to finish "just one more chapter" before calling it a day. I wouldn't be able to do what I love to do without their love and support.

And last but definitely not least, to you, dear reader . . . especially the members of my Crushin' It Crew and newsletter list. You're the reason I write. Thank you for picking up my books and trusting me to entertain you for a few hours. I'll never take you for granted, and I appreciate you more than you'll ever know! If you'd like to stay in touch, please sign up for my newsletter at dylanncrush.com. Thank you!

Keep reading for an excerpt from the first book in
Dylann Crush's Tying the Knot in Texas series . . .

THE COWBOY SAYS I DO

Available in paperback from Berkley!

"I do."

Lacey Cherish blinked multiple times, trying to see through the obnoxious fake eyelashes her assistant had talked her into wearing at the last minute. Her fingers fiddled with the microphone in front of her as she silently willed the reporter from the television station in Houston to give it a rest. Not even forty-eight hours into her term as the newly appointed mayor of the little town of Idont, Texas, and she already had a full-blown crisis on her hands.

The reporter didn't back down. Instead, she got up from the metal folding chair, causing the legs to scrape across the linoleum. Lacey squinted as she fought the urge to cover her ears. Her upper and lower eyelashes tangled together and she struggled to peer through the dark lines barring her vision.

"Let me rephrase that." The reporter cocked a hip while she consulted her notebook. "You expect us to believe you're going to find a way to put a positive spin on this?"

Lacey inhaled a deep breath through her nose in an attempt to buy some time and answer with what might sound like a well-thought-out response. The problem was, she was winging this. No one had been more shocked than she was to find out the biggest business in town, Phillips Stationery and Imports, had closed their doors. The company had made their headquarters in Idont for over a hundred years, starting as a printing press then moving into manufacturing, and importing all kinds of novelties from overseas.

"I'm sure Mayor Cherish will have more to say as the situation unfolds." Leave it to Deputy Sheriff Bodie Phillips to bully everyone back into line. He was part of the problem. Granted, he wasn't the ogre who decided to shut down the warehouse, but he did share DNA with the two men in charge.

"I'll have a statement to the press by the end of the week," Lacey promised.

Her assistant stepped to the microphone as Lacey moved away. "Thanks, everyone, for coming. As Mayor Cherish said, she'll be prepared to address the closing by the end of the day on Friday."

"You okay?" Bodie appeared at her side. He angled his broad chest like a wall, as if trying to protect her from the prying eyes of the people who'd turned out for the press conference at city hall. All six of them.

"Yes. No thanks to you." She summoned her best scowl, ready to chastise him for interfering in her business. It didn't matter that much when they were kids, but he needed to see her in a different light now. She was the mayor, after all, not the same scrawny, bucktoothed little girl who used to follow him everywhere.

"I'm just as surprised as you." The look in his eyes proved he was telling the truth. She'd never seen that particular mixture of anger and frustration, and she was pretty sure she'd been exposed to all of his moods. "Dad didn't say a word to me about this, and I spent the holidays over at their place, surrounded by the family."

"Well, you and your dad aren't exactly bosom buddies, now, are you?" She gathered her purse and shrugged on her jacket before heading down the hall to the back door of the building.

Bodie followed, taking one step to every three of hers. Damn heels. She would have been much more comfortable in a pair of Ropers, but her new assistant never would have let her step in front of a microphone without looking the part of mayor. Which was precisely what Lacey paid her to do.

"Hey, you can't punish me for something my dad and my pops decided to do." Bodie stopped in front of her, his muscular frame blocking the door, his head nearly touching the low ceiling.

Lacey clamped a hand to her hip, ready for a throwdown. "I'm not trying to punish you. I just don't understand how all of a sudden, after a century in business, they decided they can't make a go of it anymore. And breaking the news right after the holidays?"

Bodie shrugged. "I don't know, Sweets."

"Stop calling me that. I'm the mayor now." She pursed her lips. Why couldn't he take her seriously? She'd figured the childhood nickname would have disappeared, along with her aggravating attraction to the man who'd been her big brother's best friend all her life. But here she was, back in Idont where nothing had changed, especially the way her traitorous body reacted to Bodie Phillips.

"Aw, come on, Lacey. You'll always be 'Sweets' to me." He grinned, dazzling her with his million-dollar smile. Well, maybe not million-dollar, but she'd been there when he had to go through braces twice, so it had to be worth at least five or six grand.

She resisted the pull of his charm. He'd always been able to tease her back into a good mood when hers had gone sour. But this was different. The only reason she'd run for mayor was because her dad had been forced out of office after a particularly embarrassing public incident. In which he drove a golf cart into a pond. A stolen golf cart. While drunk.

His stunt earned him his third DWI and twenty-four months of house arrest. During her tenure as mayor, she hoped she could polish the tarnished family name and turn the tide of public opinion about the Cherish family. That, and she couldn't find a real job. Evidently a degree in communications wasn't worth much more than the paper her diploma was printed on.

"What am I going to do, Bodie?" She shook her head, her gaze drawn to a section of chipped linoleum on the floor. The whole town seemed to be falling apart.

"Maybe it's time to consider merging with Swynton."

Lacey jerked her head up, causing one of her fake eyelashes to flop up and down. "Please tell me you didn't just suggest we wave good-bye to our roots and hand our town over to that obnoxious man." She tried to reattach the line of lashes against her eyelid.

Bodie didn't bother to suppress his smile. "Come on, Lacey. You've got to admit, their economy could run circles around ours. I know you don't care for Buck, but he's doing something right over there."

She pressed her lips together. The only thing Mayor Buck Little was doing was turning the once-semicharming town of Swynton into a hot pocket of cheap housing and seedy businesses. "Have you seen how many building permits they've issued in the past three months? If he had it his way, we'd end up with empty strip malls and low-rent apartment buildings all over town."

"At least that would create jobs and give people some affordable housing options." Bodie leaned against the wall. "My family's business was our biggest employer."

"I know." Lacey gritted her teeth, wishing with all her heart she had someone to talk to about this. Someone who might be able to offer a realistic option, not just confirm everything she already knew about what a sorry situation they were in. "I need to think."

Bodie pushed open the door leading to the back parking lot and swept his arm forward, gesturing for her to go first. "You want to grab lunch over at the diner and talk?"

"I can't now. I'm late for my shift at the Burger Bonanza." She jammed her sunglasses on her face, crushing them against the stupid lashes as she brushed past him through the door into the sunny but chilly February day.

"When are you going to quit that job, Lacey Jane? The mayor shouldn't be flipping burgers and mixing milkshakes."

She turned, jabbing a finger into Bodie's chest. "I'll do what I have to do to pay the bills." She jabbed harder. "And I'll do what I have to do to keep this town afloat."

Despite her effort, the concrete plane of his pecs didn't budge. Damn him.

He grabbed her hand, twirling her around like they were doing a two-step instead of sparring about the future of their hometown. "That's one thing Idont has going for it that Swynton never will."

"What's that?" Lacey stumbled as he released her, not sure if she was dizzy from the spin or off-balance because of the way her hand had felt in his.

"You." Bodie tipped his cowboy hat at her as he walked away. "You're determined, I'll give you that, Mayor."

She adjusted her purse strap and tried to compose herself as he climbed into his pickup and drove away. Bodie wasn't one to dish out compliments, especially to a woman he'd considered a pesky nuisance most of his life. Either that was the nicest thing he'd ever said to her or he wanted something. Knowing him, it was the latter.

That would give her two things to think about while she worked her shift at the Burger Bonanza . . . how to save the town of Idont, and why in the world Bodie was trying to butter her up like a fresh-baked biscuit.

"You're late." Jojo stood at the counter, loading her arms with blue plate specials. "Watch out for Helmut, he's on a bender."

"Thanks." Lacey slipped off her heels and slid her feet into her flats before tying an apron around her waist. "Where do you need me today?"

"Why don't you start on the floor and take over the grill when Helmut leaves?" Jojo had been waiting tables at the Burger Bonanza since she and Lacey started high school. If Helmut had taken the time to name a manager, Jojo would be the natural choice. But instead he paid her the same as the rest of the waitstaff and expected her to keep everyone in line.

"Sounds good." Lacey grabbed her order pad and made her way to the front of the restaurant.

"Table twelve just got seated." Jojo nodded toward the corner booth.

"Got it." Lacey headed that way, her eyes on her notebook. "Hey, can I get y'all something to drink?"

"Well, look who it is." The voice that had squashed a thousand of Lacey's childhood dreams drifted across the table.

Lacey lifted her gaze to stare right into the eyes of her high school nemesis—Adeline Monroe. "Oh, hi, Adeline.

It's been a long time." And thank God for that. Adeline lived over in Swynton. It used to be the only reason she'd cross the river that divided the two towns was if she was on the hunt for some too-good-to-pass-up gossip. What was she after now?

"It sure has. And look at you. I heard you came back." Adeline leaned over the table, lowering her voice, that familiar glint in her eye. "Is it true you got yourself elected mayor?"

Lacey nodded. "Yep, sure did. Now, what will it be? A round of Burger Bonanza Banzai Shakes? Or can I start you off with a basket of buffalo bites?" She tried to pull a smile from deep down, but it seemed to stick on the way to her face. Half of her mouth lifted, the other half slid down, probably making her look like an undecided clown, especially with the damn lashes still glued to her eyelids.

Adeline turned to the man next to her. A quick glance at the giant rock on her left hand confirmed he was probably her fiancé. What happened to the curse Lacey had cast at graduation? Adeline was supposed to be hairless and withered by now, or at least well on her way. Instead she looked like she'd just stepped out of a salon. Every highlighted hair was in place. Her eyebrows were plucked to perfection and there was no sign of premature aging.

"Lacey, I'd like you to meet my fiancé, Roman." Adeline put her hand on Roman's arm, obviously staking her claim. As if Lacey were going to try to hump the man right there at table twelve.

"Congratulations. Nice to meet you, Roman." She managed to correct her awkward expression and forced a smile. "Are you ready to order?"

Adeline's smirk faded. She ran a manicured nail down the side of the menu. "We'll take two Burger Bonanza baskets with fries. Diet for me."

"Do you have iced tea?" Roman asked.

Lacey nodded. She'd been afraid the man couldn't speak. She wouldn't have put it past Adeline to marry a man incapable of talking back to her. He probably didn't get a word in edgewise most of the time. "I'll be back in a minute with your drinks."

She tucked her order pad into the front of her apron. First the news of the Phillips business closing, now an unexpected visit from Adeline. Bad news usually came in threes. What would happen next?

It took less than a minute to find out. As she approached the soda station to grab two cups, someone grabbed her arm.

Bodie.

"Mayor Cherish, you'll need to come with me." His voice was all business. The commanding tone sent a shiver straight through her. But his lips twitched. A hint of humor shone in those deep gray eyes. She'd spent way too much of her life thinking about what it would feel like to lose herself in those depths.

"What are you doing here? I've got a shift."

"I'm aware of that." His fingers closed around her elbow, eliminating any argument, propelling her toward the door. "But we've got a problem that needs your attention. Now."